FOSTERED H(E)ARTS

Nothing's fair in
Love
&
Basketball

Lena Knight

A note from the Author

Please note that this is a work of fiction, created by my imagination. Naturally, some scenes were inspired by personal events. The story may also entail some triggering subjects, so be advised.

Thank you in advance for giving my story a chance. Hope you like it… Happy reading.

Content warning: mention of loss, sexual harassment of a minor, abuse of a minor (of page)

Lena

Disclaimer: *The author acknowledges that all songs, lyrics, movie titles, book titles, trademarked statues, and brands mentioned in this book are the property of and belong to their respective owners. The use of these trademarks is not authorized, associated, or sponsored by the trademark owners.*

No part of this book may be reproduced in any form or by any electronic or mechanical means, including information storage and retrieval systems, without written permission from the author, except for the use of brief quotations in a book review.

No part of this book may be used or reproduced in any manner for the purpose of training artificial intelligence technologies or systems. The characters and events portrayed in this book are fictitious or are used fictitiously. Any similarity to real persons, living or dead, is purely coincidental and not intended by the author. All brand names and product names used in this book are trademarks, registered trademarks, or trade names of their respective holders. The author is not associated with any product or vendor in this book.

For all the broken souls… know you're perfect.
If you don't believe me… maybe you'll believe your future
book boyfriend.

PLAYLIST

The playlist is part of Chapter 49 and is available on SPOTIFY

Chapter 1

"Come on, dude, you've got 2 minutes to shower, and we need to sprint out!" Ben yells as he breezes by me to get the first empty cubicle.

"Where's the fire? The class is not for another…" I look at my watch: 35 minutes.

"Yeah, but theirs is still going on, so we have to hurry!" he shouts back. The room is filled with the whole team, each under a showerhead, scrubbing at full speed.

"Whose?" I remove my shirt and toss it on the bench by the wall.

"The girls, dumb-ass," someone screams from the showers.

Now it all makes sense.

"You guys are crazy." I shake my head, turning on the water, setting it to just the right of lukewarm.

"Trust me, Ty, you *want* to be there," Cole says, his brows dancing up and down.

"I am nothing if not a team player." I give in and join their fast pace.

"That's the spirit," Parker yells from across the room.

"I thought you were gay?" I quickly work, scrubbing my hair, loving the sensation on my scalp.

"True, but I am nothing if not a team player!"

"Touche!" I holler back.

All at once, as if an alarm has gone off, we turn the taps and start getting dressed. The next thing I know, we're power walking to the performing arts hall.

"Thank God it's still not over," Ben sighs with relief the second we get in the hall overlooking the large mirrored studio, filled with girls in the middle of a dance. The entire Basketball team is glued to the glass, focusing on said girls. Amused, I join them, allowing my eyes to be blessed by the view. Girls in short shorts, tights, tops, tight shirts... Girls with different body types, hair colors, all hot in their own ways... following Ms. Lynch at the front.

The team is well acquainted with Ms. Lynch, the woman assigned to carry out our punishment for the fight we caused during the first game of the season. The only thing the coach could think of to punish us was to embarrass us; his words were around *'If you can't act like men, then maybe I should indulge you'* right before he laid out his master plan.

Subjected to two and a half months of dance lessons, all so that we can perform a formation-type choreography in front of our friends and family at the Christmas benefit. For the last month, we've been practicing the cha-cha twice a week, and today is the day we're supposed to have our first practice with our forced-on dance partners.

Right now, I am looking at all the potentials focused on their reflections.

Well, all except one.

Love at first sight. I've heard of it, read about it, seen it on multiple screens, and witnessed it happen to my brother. On the other hand, I haven't had the pleasure of experiencing it. That is, until I laid my eyes on a blonde wonder.

Right there, overlooking a crowded room with bright lights and loud music, I get struck.

Experienced symptoms: all-around butterflies, shortness of breath, stopping of the heart, stiffness of the muscles, chest pains, temporary focused blindness (as in - not able to see anyone or anything else other than her), tightening of the throat, arousal, and spiking high temperature. To sum it all up - the whole nine yards.

A special kind of lighting strikes me, and my body goes into shock. It's that kind of thing that no doctor can fix, no remedy for the illness, no cure, no way of ever going back. In all honesty, I'm not planning on going back. I like the feeling, the moment it has its hand in consuming me, I am done for. The problem is that I want, need, and am determined to get more.

The entire room blurs out, making her the sole focus of my view. She is the only one not showing off her body, wearing a loose t-shirt with her sleeves pulled up over her shoulders and basketball shorts. Her blonde hair is tied in a ponytail, swinging from side to side. Her mouth opens to the lyrics, and she moves in sync with each beat. It's as if she's feeling the music, immersed in it with closed eyes, all the while nailing every step. I forget how to breathe, looking at her, transfixed, and I swear, time stands still for a moment. A bit of frustration comes over me due to her closed eyes, making me desperate to see them - the color, the shape, her soul.

Noticing the direction of my stare, Ben snaps me out of the trance. "Don't even think about it, man."

"What's the story there?"

Ben takes a deep breath, the warning kind, before he says, "That's Maddie, the volleyball captain, and you don't stand a chance. No offense."

"Some taken, but tell me more," I demand, intrigued.

"Look, Johnny, trust me when I tell you, don't go there."

I chuckle at the name drop from before either of us was born and fight the urge to sing out the timeless tune.

"Points for the reference, but if you don't mind, indulge me." I am practically begging, ready to go down on my knees even.

"Fine, your funeral," he gasps, then gives me what I need, placing his arm around my shoulder. "She's the all-around player of the year, number one in the state, and doesn't do basketball players. Trust me, we all tried and failed miserably."

Of course, she isn't going to make it easy, and we haven't even met.

"Minor setback," I deflect. "Keep going."

"You have a death wish, I see," Ben sighs, shaking his head. "She got here on a basketball scholarship."

"But I thought you said she plays volleyball?"

"Patience, brother, patience, I was about to get there." He rolls his eyes for emphasis.

"Did you ever read about a big-shot high school player that all the majors wanted to draft, and she turned them *all* down?"

"Yeah, from Chicago, Stevens something."

I stare at the beauty, her eyes still closed, entranced in her world. She looks breathtaking, and the info dump I was just overstimulated with makes her unreal. But there she is, flesh and bone, intimidating and inviting all at once.

Ben squeezes my shoulder and points at the person I'm developing an obsession with. "Meet Maddison Stevens."

"Damn," I mutter.

"Yeah, bro," Ben agrees, praising how she quit basketball and turned to volleyball to keep her scholarship. He didn't say anything about the reason she quit basketball, only how she spent the summer training for a whole new sport before trying out for the volleyball team and making the second string. By the following season, she was crowned captain.

Impressive is too small a word to describe her.

The music stops, and all the girls scatter to the corners, grabbing their towels and bottles. I check the time; it's probably just a break, since there are fifteen more minutes till our torture starts. Unable to look away, I soak her in, and the switch. Taking a place in the right corner, she grabs a blue bottle and chugs it right before she spits some of it out, bursting into laughter over something a tall redhead says. Her smile is even more captivating than I imagined.

The clapping of Ms. Lynch's hands gets all the girls to momentarily stiffen before they go back to their former places. The redhead and Maddie do a cute handshake with wiggling fingers and their tongues sticking out right before they take their positions. Her eyes close the moment the music starts, and her fingers start drumming to the beat, tapping the side of her thigh, and when she begins her steps, I can't look away.

Diverging from the dance before the break, she moves more sensually, swaying her hips, deep diving into the salsa rhythm, and it is the worst - slash - best thing any man could witness.

"Does she have a boyfriend?" I turn the question to Cole.

"Are you deaf or just need an ear cleanse?" It's Ben who drawls, "It doesn't matter; she does not do basketball players."

"Not what I asked, Ben."

"As far as I know, she's a free woman."

That she sure is!

Chapter 2

"You have an admirer," Emma's statement makes me spit out the water I've been gulping down into straight-out laughter.

"Dude, I really don't have the nerves for your crazy right now."

"That's just mean." She drags a neon pink towel across her sweaty forehead.

"You love my mean," I point out, and she smiles, tilting her head to the side.

"And you love my crazy."

"Yes, I do. All the way."

"Ok, I forgive you," she practically gushes.

"Would you care to explain what the hell you were talking about?"

"I know you were in your trance, but there are like a dozen guys up there checking us out, and *you* caught the eyes of the newest transfer." She motions over her shoulders with her eyes, and I follow the direction, shaking my head.

"Do we have to take you to the eye doctor? No one is checking me out."

"Oh, honey…" With a patronizing tone, she pats the top of

my head like the good girl I am. "They are all checking you out, trust me, but one in particular is *checking you out*." She plays with her eyebrows as she emphasizes the last words.

I turn my focus to where Ben is talking to Colt and one individual next to them. Something within me sparks. I have the pleasure of being hit on by Colt every time I run into him at the gym. Colt is hot, like drop-dead hot, with a dimpled chin and curly brown hair, broad shoulders, and a wall of muscles. But he's a basketball player, which is a big NO-NO for me. Regardless, he is not really my type. Now, the guy he's talking to, he, on the other hand, checks all the boxes. Truth be told, I have no such boxes to be checked. I don't have a specific type, per se; it's more of an internal feeling followed by a tingle in a particular southern area.

"That's Tyler, the new shooting guard."

And there it is, dang it.

"The one that got transferred from Tennessee?" I try my best to hide my disappointment.

"That's the one. And babe, trust me when I tell you, he's good in every single way possible."

I bet he is.

"Too bad… he is hot," I say matter-of-factly, subtly scanning his features. Even from way down here, I can tell he's tall and drop-dead gorgeous.

"Fuck MJ, you wouldn't break the rule, even for that perfect specimen of a man?"

"No, babe, not even for the perfection that is him."

For a split second, I even consider it, but let's keep that between us.

"Come on, ladies, back to formation," Ms. Lynch claps

out, and we all jolt to our assigned places. Emma gives me the wiggle, and I join in with my fingers. On cue, we both stick our tongues out, whisper-screaming, "Bitcheees!"

I can honestly say I am one lucky bitch to have Emma by my side and in my corner. I dreaded starting college, starting over, and doing it all alone. Emma was the only person who managed to keep my anger in check. Slowly but loudly, she got me out of my funk and, without much effort, became someone important. She calls me on my bullshit on the regular, forces me out of the room more than I would like her to, and loves me unconditionally. She is my best friend, roommate, and teammate, both on and off the court. Red, shoulder-length hair, perfectly rounded eyebrows, dark lashes, and captivating green eyes that command all the focus, making them the center of attention. A small nose surrounded by freckles and a set of envious, full lips, Emma is a walking dick magnet. Guys drool at the mere sight of her and shit their pants the moment she opens her mouth. One thing about her, that love or hate her kind of a thing, is the fact that she has no filter, like none. She speaks her mind, her truth, and gives her piece of it without hesitation. It's a quality I admire, even begged the master to teach me her ways. But unlike the outgoing Queen, I am more of a hybrid, as in, half introvert, half extrovert. Though I love spending time cuddled up in my bed with a book in my lap, I also have no trouble fitting into any crowd, but I am not as open to telling someone off unless it's called for. Emma is a force to be reckoned with, and I'm right there to witness it all as her number one fan.

Taking our stance, we give each other the wink right

before I close my eyes and start moving my fingers to the beat. One of my favorite songs from the class is beginning to play, and I am already gone. Emma signed me up for the dance class to lift my spirits, and it worked like a charm. For 90 minutes, I can lose myself and let go completely. Fuck the world and everything that comes with it. I enter a specific state of mind. Dancing is something I have always loved, but I had never done it choreographically. In all honesty, I was skeptical, but one step in, and I was hooked. I fell in love with the feeling, the way my brain turns off when the speakers turn on.

The hardwood squeaks as I move my left foot aside, sliding it behind. I lift my right hand and sway my hips as two men sing of pain in Spanish. I don't feel the pain, though... as long as I'm moving, there is no pain: just me, the music, and the smell of polish.

One thing I admire about Ms. Lynch is that she keeps the dances and the songs diverse. Every choreography is accompanied by a different language, from Turkish, Russian, all the way to some I couldn't even decipher.

"Ok, girls. Remember the Christmas benefit choreography?" Ms. Lynch performs her clapping routine to capture our undivided attention. "Well, today we will try it with the male partners," she finishes off just as the door swings open.

Emma's devilish smile finds me. There are no words to describe how excited she was for this. Unlike me, she has a thing for basketball players; she likes her victims tall and fit, and she is determined to find out which of the players knew how to dance. The drool fest starts, and all the girls gawk,

16

biting their lips, playing with their hair. Emma, on the other hand, has her signature prowl stance: hands on her chest, giving her breasts a bit of a push-up, back arched, and ass on display, rounded up with a deadly expression.

"This is the basketball team," Ms. Lynch says, pointing her hand in the direction of the eye candy, like she's presenting a PowerPoint slide. "I'm sure you all know each other."

Giggles and whispers fill the room, and I roll my eyes. Other girls have been excited for this part, while I've been dreading it for the past month, ever since I was informed about the whole ordeal.

"Ok, boys and girls, stand in your formation and meet your partners."

Chapter 3

When we step inside, all the girls are lined up while Ms. Lynch gives us instructions: "OK, boys and girls, stand in your formation and meet your partners."

I move to my spot slowly, wishing every force out there to be on my side, to grant me one wish and one wish only. My feet meet hers, and my heart jumps to my throat.

Thank you, Morgan Freeman!

"I'm Tyler, Ty for short." I extend my hand, and she takes it, bringing her eyes to mine. A tingle spreads from the tip of my fingers all the way to my toes at the soft touch of her hand.

"I'm MJ. Nice to meet you."

"What does the J stand for?"

"Hmm?" Her brows furrow, and fuck me if it isn't the cutest thing ever.

"The J, what does it stand for?"

If I blinked, I would've missed the barely recognizable side-lip twitch that escaped her.

"That's for me to know and you *not* to find out."

"Ok, Feisty!"

Ms. Lynch claps her hands, and everyone turns to face her.

"Ok, let's try it and see how it looks. Remember, except for the chorus part, you all dance not facing each other, with girls in front of the boys. Now, this is your only warning: I expect you to exhibit nice and clean behavior. You are not in high school, and this is a serious matter with possible consequences if you even dare to mess it up," Ms. Lynch threatens.

We all nod, trying to hide our smiles.

The second I take my stance behind MJ, instant realization hits me. By the looks on my teammates' faces, they all came to the same conclusion. We're in for two months of practicing with these girls, with our dicks pressed to their behinds. It's going to be a painful eight weeks, that's for sure.

The music starts, and I slowly pull my arm around her waist, placing it over her stomach. The action makes her flinch, and she goes rigid, so I move my thumb, grazing her slowly, which seems to relax her. She's about half a foot shorter than yours truly, giving me just enough of a vantage point. Our feet start moving, and our bodies collide, almost as if morphing into one. Every step we take is perfect; she leads, and I follow. Sliding forward with four steps to each side, we repeat the motion in reverse before turning to face each other. I open my palms for hers, and she fills them with her warm touch, eyes closed and head pointing down.

"Look at me, Feisty!"

She obliges, opening her eyes and lifting her beautiful head.

There you are.

Damn. I swallow, because how the hell is this girl real? Heart-shaped face, sandy blond hair, and pink, flushed, bow-shaped lips. Not a sight of makeup around her thick, dark lashes or on her dry lips. Fighting the urge to wet them, I turn my attention back to her eyes.

"I had a bet with myself and won," I quip.

Doing the cha-cha slide, her eyes never leave mine, and it does something to me.

"Do tell." There is playfulness in her tone, and I must say… I like it.

"There was a discussion in my head regarding your eyes."

She narrows them without saying a word.

"I said that they were blue. I was right!" I exclaim, "Damn, I knew they would be trouble."

"Is that so?"

"That's so," I conclude, careful not to step on her toes.

"What did you win?"

"That's for me to know and you to find out."

She smirks, and damn if it doesn't strike me right in the chest. My eyes slip down to her necklace, and I smile. A delicate golden chain holds two separate pendants, each featuring a little golden number. How comical is it that she has my jersey number around her neck? I wonder what they represent…

The chorus finishes, and I move behind her, placing my palm back on her stomach, making her flinch again.

Hmm. I sense a pattern here… But before I can get in my head about it, she slightly turns, as if to check who the hand belongs to, and a set of goosebumps appears on her neck. Waiting for the second chorus, I keep on with the steps, focusing my attention on this one girl in front of me. The moment she turns to face me again, my heart jumps to my throat, and in that moment, I know that I am a dead man. She offers me her hands, her eyes lock on mine, and I take it all in. Locked in a staring contest, we dance like no one's watching, in perfect sync. When the music stops, she immediately steps away from me, turning her attention to the front.

Ms. Lynch makes a long stride to the center, whispering with the TA before addressing us. "That was decent. I must admit, I am surprised to say the least. Now take a minute to refresh, and we will do it one more time before the ladies have to go."

Oh, thank you, MF.

"You are so screwed, man." Ben comes to my side, pushing me with his elbow.

"Don't I know it!" I shake my head and push him right back.

"So I guess we'll be seeing you at the game tomorrow?"

I raise one eyebrow, and he tsks, clicking his tongue.

"Oh, you are so fresh... The girls are opening their season tomorrow, home game."

"You guys watch volleyball?"

They never mentioned it before, but it makes sense if the season hasn't started yet.

"Noooo," me drags in a mocking tone. "We watch chicks play volleyball. Have you seen what they play in, tight shirts and short shorts, and I mean short." His eyebrows dance like they're making a statement of their own.

I can't tame my laugh.

"So, you'll be there?"

"You're damn right I'll be."

"Oh, Johnny, Johnny, Johnny, you're a goner."

"You have no idea," I say with a shrug.

On my way back to my mark, I lock eyes with MJ and stumble. She doesn't laugh at me, though; something I find endearing. She steps in front of me, and I can feel her closing her eyes the second the first note plays. It's weird to experience it up close. I not only see it but also feel it: the freedom that captivates her throughout a song. I can do this forever, get lost while watching her do the same.

"Where do you go?" I blurt out of nowhere.

"Sorry?" She turns sideways, speaking over her shoulder.

"Where do you go?" I repeat, and she bites the inside of her cheek. There's a beat of hesitation, but it quickly disappears.

"Anywhere but here," she says under her breath.

"Is it nice there?"

"It's perfect there."

"Is there a beach?"

"Why? You like the beach?"

"I love it," I admit. Some of my best memories are from the beach; even the ones I barely remember anymore, but wanted to keep.

"Sometimes there's a beach," she whispers, and I notice her skin flashing out another set of goosebumps.

"Other times?"

"The woods, a mountain, the back seat of a car."

At the tempo switch, we turn to face each other and do the side steps.

"Back seat of a car? Do tell," I muse, and she scrunches her nose in the cutest way.

"Nothing pervy; it is just another place I get lost in."

"Another place where the music takes you?"

"Exactly." Her soft smile fades. "But mostly I go back in time."

Something about it seems important, so I file it away.

"Miss Stevens, Mister Hart, do you mind?" our dance teacher scolds, interrupting the moment. "Others are trying to focus!"

"Sorry, Ms. Lynch," we both say in unison, getting back to our steps.

Chapter 4

"No way are you reading right now," Emma yells at me, leaning on the doorframe of my room, hands crossed over her chest.

Of course, I'm reading right now. I barely slept last night. The enemies turned to lovers at two AM, then broke up - the bastards. Not to mention, I need to distract my mind from a certain brown-eyed boy. Somehow, my dance partner managed to occupy my every thought.

"Dude, I got like fifty pages left I need to finish in order to finally sleep," I whine.

"Come on, I need to Netflix and chill. Pleeease." She takes out the big guns, her cute green puppy eyes, and it works, like always.

"Fine," I give in, "but horrors are vetoed."

I am not in the mood to be scared to death, not after the romance rollercoaster I endured.

"No worries, darling, the new Outer Banks season is ready to be streamed."

"Well, you should've led with that. I'll get the popcorn." I stand up from my bed and pass by her.

"And I'll get the Dew's!" she exclaims, her feet dragging

behind me.

A bowl and a pack of microwave popcorn in hand, I step into the common area, noticing Darla, one of the girls from my floor, crying on the couch.

Full disclosure, I am an empathetic person. If someone is crying, I instantly hug them, whether they want one or not. Seeing someone I know makes me feel worse, more intrusive.

One thing I hate is people asking me if I'm okay when it's apparent I'm not. So, that's one question I avoid asking at all costs.

"Darla, what can I do?"

I take a seat next to her and put my hand on her shoulder, letting her know I'm here for whatever she needs.

"Oh, hi, Maddie. I'm sorry, I had to get out of my room." I can see her feet nervously bouncing.

"Do you want to come to ours?" I offer, and she shakes her head. "Oh, no, that's ok, I just needed a minute!"

"If there is anything I can do, please let me know." I hope she can feel the sincerity in my voice. "If you want to talk about it, I am here, and I don't judge nor do I share."

"I think I may be overreacting, but I got a weird vibe from one of the DD drivers."

Every hair on my body stands on end.

"Did he do anything?" I pose that question way too quickly.

"No, but he kept looking at me in the mirror, and it just gave me the creeps."

Girl intuition is something I don't take lightly, so I go with my gut here with another inquiry. "Did you get his name? We could report it."

She stiffens, shaking her head.

"No, I gave him the wrong address, and walked the rest of the way. I didn't want him to know where I lived."

"Smart thinking," I revere. "If you want, I can check the database tomorrow; they have pictures of all the drivers. We can look over them together."

"I don't know," she hesitates, and I try to ease her. "We can just put him on the only men's list."

"Ok, that's a good idea. Thank you, Maddie," she gives me a shy smile, and I sense something still off, so I play on a hunch.

"Is there more?"

"It's just..." She takes a deep breath, "When I told Rebeka, my roommate, she made fun of me and told me I was crazy. I had to get out of the dorm, and I just started crying."

"Do you need me to kick Rebeka's ass?"

That relaxes her tense shoulders, and I get a glimpse of a genuine smile. Not that I wouldn't do it, because I dang straight would kick Rebeka's ass. She's had a thing against me since day one. Always hissing when I pass her by, sending specific comments my way, so it's not like she doesn't deserve an ass-whooping.

"Not necessary, I will give her a piece of my mind when I calm myself fully," she tells me, more assured and relaxed.

"If you ever want to talk, you know where to find me."

"Thanks, Maddie, I mean it." She stands up, turning toward the door.

"No problem," I say back as she leaves for the bathroom,

leaving me alone with the microwave.

Three minutes of popping later, I'm back in my dorm, cozied up on the couch next to Emma, with the arsenal ready. Candles are lit, two Mountain Dews front and center, Skittles spread out on a plate, a bowl of popcorn set between us, and Emma's thumb on the play button. Giving each other the chin salute, we open our mouths in unison, "Let's do this thang," right as the big red N appears on the screen.

As soon as the opening credits start to roll, Emma pauses and turns to face me.

"We need to talk about it, dude."

"There is nothing to talk about," I deflect, covering the lie. I want to talk about it badly, and she knows it.

"Don't play that with me. Look, I am far from being blind. And you have 20/20 vision."

"Meaning?"

"Meaning, I know you've seen it."

"Seen what?" In all fairness, I am playing dumb and pretending to be oblivious. I have seen it all: his beauty, his body, the way he stared at me; I was aware of it all.

"Fine, then let's go to the other problem."

"Look... I'll admit that he is hot, gorgeous, and sexy all wrapped in one. There were also glimpses of a nice and funny personality there, but none of that means anything."

"Dude, I love you, you know that I love you, but I hate this for you. I have never pushed you before, because frankly, none of the other guys had any effect on you... But him? Lord almighty!"

Understatement of the century.

"Not to mention how good the two of you look together,

and the dance… my God!" she exclaims, lifting her hands to raise the roof and actually drooling, literally.

"Just admit it to yourself, if not to me." Her knowing smirk is undeniable.

"What do you want me to admit exactly? That I'm scared? News flash-hell yeah, I am, and that's why I don't want to go there; I won't go there," I snap, making my point.

She knows dang well that it's not some pact I made with myself so I wouldn't get hurt. That ship has long sailed. Hurt happened, and everything related to the sport I once loved more than anything got all the hurt back. To any outsider, it would seem like I am being a stupid, immature coward, but it's the furthest thing from the truth. A coward is not a word I would use to describe myself. I am a strong, determined person who turned her whole life around and chose to be happy despite the pain that permanently resided within. I pushed through something bad, never looking back, and in doing so, I had to remove a part of me. That part is basketball and everything that comes with it.

"Whatever, dude… But just for the record, I have a feeling that Tyler is going to change everything," she says before she presses play.

That's what I'm afraid of.

"Is that him?" I ask, pointing at the picture that made Darla's whole body rigid. I skim through the page, reading his name: Carlos, age: twenty-eight. We've been at this for half an hour, flipping through all the DD drivers.

She nods her head, and my hand wraps around hers.

"Thank you for doing this. Don't worry, I'll take care of everything."

"Thank you, Maddie," she hesitates, "for believing me."

That one hits too close to home because I wish that once upon a time someone had believed me.

"Sorry to leave you, but I'm already late for work," I say with a lump in my throat.

"Yeah, no worries. See you, and thank you again."

I hug her tightly and grab my backpack, taking Carlos's file with me.

Being a scholarship kid is hard. I receive financial aid for the dorms, but I still have to work to cover the basics, such as food, clothes, and books. I work at a family-owned restaurant about a twenty-minute walk from my dorm. The owners, Tessa and Ian, an elderly married couple, gave me a job that lets me choose my work schedule, allowing me to combine it with classes and volleyball. I'm the diner chameleon, as in I fill in wherever I'm needed. Mostly, it's at the front, taking orders and serving people. On rare occasions, I get to work in the back of the kitchen, chopping, something I am not the biggest fan of, since it involves dealing with a lot of slimy seafood that makes me feel queasy. What's interesting about the place is that it attracts more people during the week. Lucky for me, it means generous tips and nice customers. Mostly, families and local seniors come in. Alcohol is not served, so thankfully, there are no drunks to worry about. Today, I'm here to help with the breakfast rush before I have to play the first game of the season.

Pulling my hair up in a bun, I tie my apron slash uniform around my waist and close my locker. Today's shift with Derek instantly puts me in a better mood. Working with him is easy; he is a whimsical person who constantly cracks jokes. A pretty ass man and very gay; in summary, the perfect coworker.

"Damn girl, something's different about you?"

"Nothing's different," I try to fake being unbothered by his revelation, knowing it was pointless.

"Yes, there is, but I can't quite put my finger on it." He places his finger on his full lips, tapping it slowly.

Please don't even try.

Chapter 5

Ben: *Where are you? Warm-ups are about to start ;p*

Me: *Who watches the warm-ups???*

Ben: *Bro, seriously, it's the best part. HURRY UP!!!*

Me: *Be there in 5*

Speeding up my pace, I enter the fully packed arena exactly 5 minutes after the last text. The Columbia sports complex is enormous. Each sport has its own hall, with one huge gym that we all share. The volleyball hall is right across from the basketball one, but I've never been inside it. Banners are held up by people wearing white and blue, plastering them on their faces, with matching hats on top. The atmosphere is on fire, and it surprises me. Music is blaring, and there is no sign of any players on the court.

Spotting my team, I go down the stairs to join them just as the announcer starts his welcoming rumble. After a quick exchange of head nods, I take my seat between Ben and

Jones. The announcer begins naming the players who step out of the tube on cue, forming a line.

"And wearing number 3, your LIONS Captain - MJ Stevens." The words echo, and the crowd goes wild. Every single person is jumping and screaming…

"GO MJ!"

"KILL 'EM MADDIE!"

"GET US THE TROPHY!"

"GO LIONS!"

All I can do is stand still, impressed by the girl who just ran out of the tube, high-fiving both teams.

"Oh, didn't I mention she's a beast and loved by everyone?" Colt closes in, and I hiss at him.

"No, I believe you didn't."

"Sorry, man," he shrugs his shoulders with a side of puffy lips.

Ben turns to face me, dragging out, "Sooooo. I kinda lied."

"Kinda?" I cock a brow, unamused.

"The girls' game attire is not the reason why we watch the games," he chuckles. "Don't get me wrong, it's an added bonus, but not why we're here."

"They're good, their game is fire," Colt bellows.

"For the record, she *is* a beast," Ben chimes in on my left. "Before she joined the team, there were barely any people rooting for them. She brought the crowd in with her game and attitude."

"Attitude?"

"Oh, you'll see," he adds and turns his attention to the court. I notice that all the front rows are filled with the male population, all of whom are gesturing and talking at the girls. Across the court, a couple of guys yell something, and the redhead gives them the middle finger. MJ's fists are clenched by her sides, and I zero in on the way her shoulders move up and down, like she is breathing heavily. Whatever the guys are saying, she doesn't like it. Something about it makes me tense up.

"What do you think is happening over there?" I nudge my chin to the action across from us. Ben follows my gaze and scoffs, "Same old, same old."

I stay quiet, giving him a look.

"Come on, you're not stupid. Look around, like 80% of guys are here solely to drool over the girls, mostly over the captain. Half of them are stupid enough to harass her with their words, and a small percentage are crazy enough to get handsy."

"Seriously?"

"Yeah, and she reciprocates by kneeling them in the crotch!"

Damn.

"Damn," I drawl.

"Yup, trust me, man, you have no chance. There is not a single person here who hasn't tried it out with her."

Trying to hide my grin, I turn my focus to number 3, wearing the team's tracksuit with her name and number on the back. Her hair is tied in a high ponytail, and her Captain C is stitched over her left upper arm. Stretching with her eyes closed, she mouths the lyrics of the song playing in the background. Focusing my ear, I register it's 'Someone To You' by Banners. She sings each word as she stretches her body from neck to ankle, and all I want is for her to sing it to me, for her to want to be someone to me. The team follows her every move, and her eminence is obvious. She has their respect, and she has also earned mine.

The next song makes MJ open her eyes, and the other girls scream, turning to the announcer. They all send him air kisses, undoubtedly for the song choice. 'I like it like that' by Alesso and Nate Smith blasts through the air. The Redhead starts to move, and MJ joins her as they dance into a line forming in front of the net. On cue, they jolt to the end line and back at full speed, then they side-step the same route before taking their spot. With the Redhead behind her filling her ear with something that brings out a loud smile, MJ bobs her head to the beat as they both do a ticking movement with their hips to the sides. Turning to face each other, the Redhead gives MJ a chin nod salute before MJ takes three steps, flying in front of the net with her hand in preparation for the smash. The hit is a straight, fast, and direct line that makes the sound echo over the music.

A beast was an understatement.

In complete awe, I fix my eyes on the alluring girl holding my attention. Continuing their warm-up, the Redhead follows MJ to the line, where they both pass the ball to each other while talking and laughing. The love between the duo is evident, and I conclude that the Redhead is MJ's best friend and a possible way in.

"Hey, number 3," a guy standing at the bottom of the stairs on our left yells, making MJ's face light up. Before I can even register anything, she's sprinting towards Mr. Tall, Dark, and Handsome.

"Oh my God, Damian, what are you doing here?"

She jumps into his arms, and they hug longer than any friends should, which I am not fond of.

"I couldn't miss this one, now could I?"

He looks at her with admiration, and she doesn't exactly return the sentiment, though she is genuinely happy to see him. He's wearing the home jersey with her number on the back and a pair of dark jeans with black Converse.

"You picked a good night; there's a team party later."

"What's the occasion?" he asks, tilting her head sideways, like the question is uncalled for.

"If we win - we drink, if we lose - we drink some more - what else do you want?"

Of course, she has to be funny and witty.

"Fair point. Now go and kick some ass." His eyes linger on her, making me question the status of their relationship.

"Hey, MJ," Ben screams out, and she jogs to the fence under us, placing her chin on the rail.

"Yeah, Ben, what can I do for you?" Her playful voice is as relaxing as it is cute.

"Is your redhead friend coming to the party?" he grits, and she shakes her head, a half smile lighting up her face.

"You mean the team party? Well, since she's on the team, I'm fairly certain she will be there. And you know her name, Ben, so use it." She turns around, her ponytail swinging high as she runs across the hardwood.

Fixated on the girl in the center of a circle holding the attention of her teammates with what seemed to be a pep talk, I fight a smile. MJ is nothing short of amazing, and with that thought, my heart stops as all the girls tear off their tracksuits, leaving them in spandex shorts and a tight jersey. Nr. 3 bends down to slide up her pads over the knees, and the sight ruins me. Built to perfection, with a tight heart-shaped ass, hourglass waist, and a set of what seem to be double D's - I am a done man. To make matters worse, she lifts the hem of her shirt to wipe her forehead, revealing the outlines of a six-pack.

The music stops, followed by the whistle's blow, marking the start of the game. MJ is the first one to serve, and the crowd goes mute. Colt whispers in my ear, "Just wait for it, magic is about to happen."

And so I do, I wait as MJ steps on the end line, prepping the ball for the blow. She performs the jump serve, and the ball hits the opposite side so quickly that I blink twice. The Lions do their middle ground huddle to celebrate MJ's ace. She repeats the same thing two more times, each one more majestic.

Ben gives me some insight: "She usually does it the three times, then shows them mercy with the normal serve."

And as if on cue, she sends the ball over with a normal serve and takes her outside hitter position with a ready stance. The following few points are made courtesy of the one and only captain who glides all over the court, catching the ball and sending it to the setter with such precision. Knowing only the general rules of the game, I quickly learned the terminology, such as "pancake" and "floater," which MJ used a couple of times during the first set.

The whole thing is hard to comprehend. How is it even possible? I've been playing basketball ever since I could hold a ball, and I've worked hard to get where I am today.

Meanwhile, she trained for one summer and plays like she was born for it. Pure art is all I can think of to describe the way she plays, not to mention the heart she puts into it, something that is very much obvious. She loves the game, and in return, the game loves her back, as does the packed arena.

The second set starts, and the Lions are in their starting formations. After a couple of rotations, MJ gets to the side right under where my team and I are sitting. The guy in the row below us shouts, "Come on, number 3, bend it down for me," making every hair on my body stand on end.

Chapter 6

"Come on, number 3, bend it down for me."

The mere voice makes my skin prickle, and not in a good way.

"Don't do it," Emma whispers as I tighten my fists, feeling my jaw tick. Sexual comments are a weak spot of mine, one that unleashes all hell.

"Don't be a tease, baby, show us that tight…"

"Dude, watch your mouth!" A familiar voice instinctively gets me to turn around, and boy, am I glad I did. Ty is standing in front of the presumable jerk, probably giving him a death glare.

The guy recoils, likely because of Ty's intimidating size and build.

"You good, 3?" He accompanies the question with a slight nod of his chin.

"All good, 7," I reciprocate with one of my own.

It's not lost on me that his jersey number matches the one around my neck. And yes, I looked him up, mostly his stats. Watching the sport that was once my everything isn't something I can handle, so instead I read updates on the games on the Lions' site. No matter how challenging it is for me to be friends with the team, I want to support them in the only way I can, by gathering information. I keep up with the scores, the standings, and the statistics of all my friends, down to the newest possible one.

"What was that?" Emma nudges me.

"I honestly don't know," I reply with a shoulder shrug.

"Well, I like it," she singsongs, getting me to giggle.

I giggled?

Giggling is not part of my makeup.

"It's weird, but so do I," I say sheepishly.

As true as it is, it scares the hell out of me. I can't remember the last time a guy made me feel this way, and it's all the more overwhelming. The moment I locked my eyes on his while we were doing the cha-cha, I was a goner. Even with the most common eye color in the world, he makes them look all celestial. The other parts of him are also on the perfect side of the spectrum. From his messy spiky brown haircut, thick brows and lashes, strong prominent jaw, down to his slightly disproportional lips - the lower one a bit fuller than the upper. Not letting out the defined muscles of his peach-skinned arms and the calves, my god, the calves. I never knew I had a thing for that particular part of a male's body, but after seeing the definition of his, down to the veins lining the curve, I became a calf girl. An honorable mention - the long, tapered fingers on his firm and smooth hands. The same fingers that look like they could do a whole lot of damage in all the right places.

A sharp, stinging feeling coming from my chest wakes me right up from my daydream.

Yep - I got hit by a ball-hard.

"Stevens, get your head in the game!" Coach yells, and I snap out of whatever that was, focusing on the now. The corner of my eye catches Emma's smirk, and I take a mental note to retaliate later.

With the scoreboard showing 22-15 for the home team, I step on the line to finish the third set and the game. We're up by two, and I am determined to make it to three and win the first game of the season.

Bouncing the ball, I straighten up, the sound of the ball hitting the wood like a song to my ears. Slowly rounding the ball, I throw it in front of me in the air just enough to impact it with two steps and the center of my palm. The ball flies, projecting a descending straight line barely touching the net right before it hits the floor-ACE.

"EEEEOPA," the six of us huddle in the middle, celebrating the point. I wipe the sweat from my forehead, inhaling and releasing a long breath. Back at the end line, I prepare myself for a repeat.

We win.

Jumping with excitement, surrounded by a screaming crowd, makes for an incredibly euphoric moment. Lining up, we salute the opposite team under the net before we huddle up in a circle.

Our regular post-game roundabout starts with the crowd joining us as we all sing our song. We stole some Katy Perry lyrics for this one, but the people love it.

"We got the heart of a lion, a fighter, dancing through the fire, 'cause we are the champions and you're gonna hear us roooooooaaaarrrr."

As the excitement dies down, I check the stance, one

corner in particular. I smile when I notice he's still there; the whole basketball team is. Emma comes to my side, waving at them, lifting my hand to do the same. They return the sentiment, and I feel it coming before she even opens her mouth.

"You are in so much trouble."

Don't I know it!

On our walk to the locker room, I hear my name being shouted.

"Steveeeens!" That would be Coach, with that harsh tone she reserves only for me. Lucky me. "My office, NOW!"

"Uuuuuuuu," the girls taunt.

With my tail between my legs, I enter Ms. Clark's office.

"Take a seat, Maddie." She points at the empty chair on the other side of her desk. She doesn't say my full name, the fact easing me in. I slide into the chair, glancing around the office. Nothing has changed since my last so-called visit. The walls are filled with the team's pictures dating back God knows how far. My hand shakes as I prepare myself for the worst.

"Duke called - again," she grits, her face locked on the papers in front of her.

"Oh," I gasp, wiggling in my seat.

I take a beat to look at her, the defined wrinkles on her face, and that smile that is a rarity to see. Coach is in her prime, looking fit in the team's tracksuit. The woman can outrun us at any given chance, despite being double our age.

"I am not interested," I repeat the same answer as the last time they called.

"I know, honey, but that's not all." She finally lifts her eyes

41

to meet mine. My heart jumps to my throat.

Oh shit.

I don't like that look.

"Texas called," she states, like it's no big deal.

"The Division 1 Texas? As in, the best team in the USA?"

"Exactly that, Texas." She bobs her head with pride in her eyes.

"Wow, that's big," I say under my breath, not sure how to react.

"There's more," Coach adds, and I blink.

"Should I brace myself?"

"Depends on your take regarding the national team?"

My heart stops.

"No?" I gasp in disbelief.

"Yes, honey, you got the formal invitation to join them for next summer's boot camp."

Mrs. Clark hands me the letter, and the words blur past, leaving me no chance to confirm what's happening. The national team wants *me?!* With a shaky hand, I grip the letter tightly, reading it over and over.

This is big.

I should be more excited about it, right?

So why am I feeling cold all of a sudden?

The national team was my dream once upon a time, except in that dream, I was holding a bigger ball and had four extra teammates on the court, not five.

"How long do I have?" I point my gaze at her.

"They gave you until the end of the year to give them a response. What do you want to do about Duke and Texas?"

"You know my answer; it still hasn't changed." I shrug it

off.

Duke was another lost dream, long forgotten. The big leagues never occurred to me before, so Texas did come as a surprise. I like the way things are now, comfortable, and I am as happy as I can be, so why change it?

"Maddison, you know I respect you, but I honestly think you should reconsider," she pushes again.

"Coach, you know me, probably better than anybody here," I state.

Coach Clark came through for me more than any adult ever had in my whole life. When I lost my love for basketball, I was afraid of losing my future. I had a scholarship based on my playing for the Lions, and I pleaded my case to the board, begging for a way to keep it. Coach found a way around it and took it upon herself to prepare me for the volleyball team's tryouts over the summer. I worked out three times a day, six days a week, ranging from basic to advanced conditioning. The shape and form I had from basketball came in handy as I kept up without a problem. The only thing that presented a slight hitch was ball handling. I had to transition from the natural handwork I was accustomed to with a size-six ball to handling a slightly lighter size-five.

During that summer, I got close to Ms. Clark, and she became someone I looked up to and could confide in. Though she is strict and firm, she has a heart of gold and roots for me every step of the way. The training sessions escalated from *'Come on, Stevens, don't be weak, give me two more!'* to *'You got this, Maddie, just one more!'*

I clear my throat. "You know how grateful I am for everything, but I want to experience the college life; I want to be a grown-up kid for as long as I can without the pressure a team of that kind of caliber would most likely put on me."

Coach lets out a breath, relaxing her shoulders, and gives me a warm smile.

"I get it, and I am so proud of you. I hope you know that."

"I know and will never forget it."

She gives me a nod, and I start to stand up.

"Is that all?"

"Yes, Maddie, that's all."

I head outside but stop when I reach the doorknob, turning to face her. "You coming to the party?"

"No, I've had enough of all of you for the day." She cuts her hand through the air.

A laugh escapes me, and I give her a disapproving head shake. "You know you love us!"

She winks and drawls, "No comment."

And with that, I leave straight for the locker room in desperate need of a shower. The second I step in, Emma and Kate rush to me with wide eyes.

"Well?" They both drag in unison.

"The national team called!" I squeal.

They start jumping up and down, and I join them, feeling all the feels with the people closest to me.

Chapter 7

Turning onto the street leading to the girls' dormitory, I point my question at Ben, "How are they allowed to have a party in the dorms?"

"Oh, right," he drags, scratching his forehead. "I keep forgetting you're fresh here. *Your* girl petitioned it, made a point of how it would be better and safer to allow supervised parties on the grounds with a handband system, and an on-call designated driver for the ones that are of legal age to drink."

The 'your girl' comment makes my insides flutter.

"Is she the student body president or something?"

"That's the funny thing; she's not even on the council. She just waltzed into a meeting, laid down her demands, and they somehow listened." He finishes, and I swallow a golf ball in my throat.

"I don't think I can handle any more of her praise, bro."

He doesn't respond, but I can see his grin.

We take the four steps to the double doors, and he gives me a look to let me know there's nothing that could prepare me for what's coming.

"She's good people. Red introduced us freshman year, and she clicked with the team easily. Though she doesn't go to our games, she keeps tabs on us, looks up stats, and shit. In her own way, she lets us know she's rooting for us."

We move through the crowd and join the rest of our team in the far corner of the room as I continue the conversation with Ben.

"You never told me you were friends," I glare at him, and he just smirks.

"You never asked. And seriously, how do you think I knew all the stuff?"

"I just thought it was general knowledge," I shrug.

Shaking his head, he takes the beer offering from Colt. Jones hands me a bottle, and I take it with a soft "Thanks."

"Well, it's not. It's an inner circle knowledge."

"Noted. Now tell me, how do *I* get in?" I put a bit of a kick on the I, taking a quick sip.

"The way she's looking at you right now, I think you're on your way there."

That one sentence comes at the exact moment I catch the blue eyes of the most beautiful creature I've ever seen. For a short minute, our eyes lock, and my heart does the now familiar upward jolt. She has a beer in her hand, leaning on the wall between the Redhead and another girl who, if I remember correctly, had the number 8 on her jersey.

The common area is enormous, overcrowded, and loud, with the music blaring out of a large speaker in the corner by the window. The room is on the darker side, with only two floor lamps lit; a large couch has been moved to the wall with the windows to make room to dance. Drinks are arranged on the kitchen island, with a keg positioned beside it on the floor. The overpowering smell of mixed alcohol fills the air. There are collections of photos covering every wall, but under the lighting, I can't see any details.

Lauv's 'I Like Me Better' starts playing, and the redhead screams, dragging one smiling MJ to the middle of the impromptu dancefloor. By the looks of it, the song is their anthem, and yup, there is a choreography to it.

Wearing a black t-shirt in combination with gray baggy sweatpants that are at least a size too big, and her hair loose down to her mid-back, MJ is nothing short of a vision. Swaying her hips, she shouts the lyrics to her friend and receives them right back from the Redhead. During the song, it's just the two of them, in their bubble, and I love every minute of seeing it. Unfortunately, so does every other testosterone-induced prick around. I tighten my grip on my bottle, my eyes not blinking. At the slowed-down verse, they hug each other and belt the words, showing their love for one another. As soon as the last lyric-less part begins, MJ closes her eyes and enters her nirvana. Her head tilts from one side to the other, all the while her hips make circular motions. Her shoulders join in. My mouth goes dry when she picks up her hair and drags it up, and up, and up. My eyes trace the movement, entranced. Releasing the silk-like strands, she lets them fall down her back as her arms stay above her head. Waving her hands one around another, she finishes in a nae-nae. Making the dance floor their bitch, they both welcome the upbeat of the next song and continue torturing everyone around with their sexy moves. The guy wearing MJ's jersey joins them, and I sip my drink, catching her eye, sparking a fleeting smile. The duo smiles at something the guy says, and I can hear MJ's laugh over the music.

God, she's breathtaking.

"You're staring." Colt nudges me with his elbow, and I flinch, turning to face him.

Am I that obvious?

Just as I was about to deflect, someone pats my shoulder, and I turn to lock eyes with the redhead.

"Well, well, well, if it isn't the man of the hour," she shouts, taking a bottle from Ben's hands, his blush obvious. The girl must read my confusion when she speaks out, "Back at the game, thanks for standing up for my girl."

I simply shrug, remembering how tense MJ's whole posture got at the idiot's remarks. "No problem, though I'm pretty sure she needs no saving."

"Oh, you have no idea, but considering she's one strike away from a suspension, you really did save her."

Suspension?

"Well, in that case, it was my pleasure." I tip my imaginary gentleman's hat, and she rolls her eyes.

"I'm Emma, by the way." She extends her hand, and I give it a friendly shake.

"I'm Tyler."

"Oh, I know, trust me," she says with a playful smile, turning her affection to Ben.

"So Benny, I believe you owe me a dance," she singsongs, making our playmaker turn crimson.

"That I do, Red, that I do." He bobs his head with the biggest grin.

Pulling his shirt, she reverses to the dancing crowd, dragging Ben with her.

My eyes search for the number 3, but come up short. Disappointment is not a strong enough word to describe the feelings I'm experiencing.

I engage in a discussion Colt is having with Chase, trying to divert my mind from the blond wonder. They keep fighting over who has better standing in rebounds, and I shake my head with the rest of the team following. The same team that welcomed me into their already-formed group the moment I stepped on their grounds. The only reason I accepted the transfer request was the fifteen hours less distance from my family. I was at the top of my game back in Tennessee, but Coach J was persistent in getting me here, desperate for a good shooting guard.

More than ever, I am happy for his tenacity; otherwise, I would've never laid eyes on her. My eyes scan the room once more, searching for the only person who ever made my heart skip a beat.

Chapter 8

"Can we talk? In private..." The mother of questions comes out of Damian's mouth, and I freeze.

Please don't do this to me here or now.

"Sure, let's go somewhere quiet," I gasp, and he nods in relief. I give Emma a reassuring nod and leave the dance floor, with my childhood best friend following me out into the hall. The entrance hall is occupied by a couple making out in one corner, so, wanting to give them their well-deserved privacy, I opt for fresh air. Thinking a walk would be a good idea, I wait for the shoe to drop, the one that has been flying above my head for about two years now.

"Look," he finally starts after five minutes of unpleasant silence, "I can't do this anymore."

"Do what exactly?"

"Lie to him."

Well, saw that one coming. I consider punching his beautiful face. Damian is your regular front-cover boy, walking dream. Even as a kid, he had a certain dominance about him, while I was a tomboy who lacked friends. And somehow, he wanted to be mine. Basketball brought us together, and we've been inseparable friends ever since.

High school was when it all started to fall apart.

"I never told you to do that," I lie, because sure, I haven't spoken the words, but my eyes did most of the begging and pleading.

"You didn't have to. I know you, Berta, I..." he trails off, dropping his head.

The old nickname feels like a punch right in the gut. There's this old movie, and one of the main characters, played by a young Christina Ricci, is practically a fictional reincarnation of me. If you were to change the hair color, shape of the face, and the eye color, we could be twins. The attitude's the same, so is the fashion choice, down to the taping of the breast.

"Damian, please..." I beg him, "I'm not ready."

Clenching my fist, I lower my hands to my sides, biting my tongue.

"I love you, Maddie."

"I love you too, D."

"You don't get it." He clears his throat. "I. Love. You."

The way he enunciates makes me stop, cementing my feet in the place of a long friendship's final resting place. Grabbing the hair on top of my head, I sigh, then growl, feeling the sweat escape my glands.

"You can't be serious right now."

Another thing about Emma, the bitch is always right. She called it... multiple times, while I was like 'No, he just sees me as a sister'.

Stupid, ignorant, fool.

"You don't love me, you don't even know me." I turn to face him and flare up, "Not truly. There is love between us, a

51

strong bond, but not a romantic one. You are not in love with me; you couldn't be."

"I know you, I know you better than anybody. And I've always been there. I've watched you with Jamie. Do you know how badly that hurt me?"

The reminder of my ex-boyfriend, slash his brother, makes me shiver - the one who chose a game over me, breaking my heart in the process. Jamie's face pops into my head, and I curse the memory.

"Please, don't do this. And don't ever mention *him* again."

He knows Jamie is the Voldemort of all topics; even Emma doesn't know the entire story.

"He knows I talk to you, and if you just…"

My hand flies in the air, the universal sign for him to stop. I can't handle this, not now, maybe not ever.

"He's miserable," Damian stutters, and I feel my face fall.

"D, you know what happened. You can't seriously ask me to forgive him."

Mute.

My best friend goes mute because he knows. He was there. He witnessed firsthand the intensity of my breakage.

"I thought you understood?" It comes out more as a question, a shaky, terrified question.

"I did, I do," he sighs, "and so does he. He knows he screwed up, and he wants to make it right."

"Nothing can make it right, Damian. He broke me. End of."

Scratching the back of his head, he looks at me with his brows drawn together. A car passes us by, and it's the only sound heard for the span of three minutes before he drops

lost it." His chin moves from me to Ty.

"Well, honey, you sure know how to use that pussy of yours, don't_"

All hell breaks loose. Ben appears out of nowhere, and they all start to push each other. Fists start flying, thankfully without a hit. I hear glass shattering, but I can't see anything, since they are all huddled up, obstructing my view. Fed up with the charade, I step between them, my hand on Tyler's chest. He is heaving. Loudly. But somehow, my touch calms him. It's when his eyes flip down at the contact that something in me springs to life.

His hand covers mine, but before I can register the warmth, I gasp, "Oh my God, your hand."

I take it gently, examining the spot where it's bleeding and swelling, a small shard of glass causing the damage.

"Come on, I have a first-aid kit in my room," I practically shout.

Without thinking, I start walking, and he seems more than happy to follow. Going up the flight of stairs, I keep turning around to make sure Tyler's keeping up. I stop in front of door number 17, my hands shaking as I insert the key and turn it. Once unlocked, I swing the door open, stepping aside for him to enter first. Closing the door, I lock it with a click.

What the hell am I doing?

"Sorry for the mess, Emma doesn't like to pick up after herself," I squirm, feeling my cheeks blush with embarrassment. I deep dive, sneering as I pick up Emma's bra from the floor and quickly tidy up whatever mess is lingering in the room. Every once in a while, I glance over to Tyler, who's taking in the space. I notice a grin covering his perfect face as he passes the PS5 on the sideboard beneath the TV. His eyes cover every inch of the room, from our three-seater red leather couch to the candles decorating the coffee table. He stops before the large pin-up board on the wall. I freeze as his nose dives closer, checking all the photos of Emma, myself, and the team, both the girls' volleyball and boys' basketball.

Something about him, not so subtly inspecting the ones with me, front and center, ignites a fire inside me.

I continue to 'clean up' the nonexistent mess to settle the fire rising. I hear a chuckle, which can only mean he landed on our Coachella photo. It's one of my favorites. The memory of all of us dressed up brings a smile to my face. The boys wore makeup under Emma's coercion, of course.

I sneak up to his side as he checks over the concert tickets pinned up around the photos, his head tilted to the side as he reads over them.

"Oh God, don't look at that," I quickly snatch up the photo of me doing the cartwheel over Emma, plastered on the grass, making the pin that was holding it fall on the floor. It rolls right under the couch.

"Why not?"

Because I look terrible in it.

I don't say that; I smile instead and pocket the Polaroid.

"So what's your favorite concert you've been to?"

I point at the LAUV ticket, hidden between One Republic and NF.

"Figures."

"What's that now?"

"I just figured since that little choreo you and Emma

56

performed earlier, that it would be your favorite one."

"You'd be correct."

"How did that thing happen?"

"Our dance?"

He nods.

"That's Emma for you. She said it was a rite of passage for our friendship. I kinda can't say no to her."

He chuckles, and I shrug, acting more confident than I feel around him.

With a shy smile, I turn on my heel and bolt for the kitchen, hollering over my shoulder, "Do you want something to drink?"

"Sure, whatever you have is fine," I hear him say from behind me. I grab two beers, closing the small fridge with my foot, then slowly walk toward him, my heart somersaulting at the sight of him in my space.

Chapter 9

Time stands still as I watch MJ walk straight to me, my lungs desperate for oxygen since I've managed to forget how to breathe.

"Your room?" I point to the one on the left.

"What gave it away?"

Both rooms are open, but my vantage point doesn't allow me the full view. I eye the bookcase filled top to bottom and designate, "Red doesn't really scream like a reader."

"Funny, usually people say that about a blonde," she retorts playfully.

"Well, not this one." With my good hand, I take a strand of her hair, locking eyes with hers. All the air in the room evaporates.

Jolting away from my touch, she averts her gaze. "You should take a seat. I'll bring the kit."

She hands me a beer, our fingers barely grazing, but I feel the touch all the way to my toes. I take the bottle, smiling at her before she turns away.

Like a good boy I was brought up to be, I take my seat on the couch and wait, my eyes focused on her as she disappears into the bathroom. A minute later, she's walking to me with a first aid kit bag in her arm and her beer in the other hand. She sets the bottle on the table and sits next to me on the couch. I watch her as she takes out a disinfectant and sprays it over my knuckles. Shit stings like hell, and I am so proud of my body for listening to my brain that ordered it not to react.

"You know you don't have to hold it in." She doesn't stop the torture, eyes focused on her task of cleaning by dabbing a cotton ball. "We're alone, and I won't tell anyone if you wince like a girl."

I can't stop it. A laugh escapes me, and she joins in, creating the most beautiful symphony.

"You didn't have to do that, you know," she mutters, "come to my rescue, I mean."

"I know. I just…" I swallow. "Wanted to!"

"Well, thank you." She looks up through her lashes, her head dipped low.

"Emma told me you are one strike away from suspension?" I pose it more as a question, leaving the rest up to her. It earns me a full-on face-to-face.

"So that's why you stepped in?"

"No, I learned that fact after my first intervention."

That confession causes her to blush, and I can't hide my stupid grin.

"What's the deal with that?" I ask, watching her get back to dabbing the cloth. She gently cleans the blood and blows a warm breath over my knuckles, making every hair on my body rise.

"What's the deal with what?"

"Why are you one strike away from suspension?"

"I have a temper," she says so matter-of-factly, but gives me a look, one that allows me to see beyond the words.

"I doubt that."

"Well, certain actions bring out a certain reaction," she deadpans.

"Like stupid jerks and their comments."

"Exactly."

"That doesn't mean you have a temper; it means you respect yourself and don't allow others to undermine that," I point out, noticing her deep blues searching for something in mine. When she doesn't find it, she carries on.

"That's a nice way to put it, but unfortunately, I don't respect myself enough to rise above it."

"That's overrated. Sometimes you need to kick a guy in the nuts."

"You heard about that?" She chuckles, taking a tube out of her small red bag. She uncaps it and drags a line of paste over her palm, then she dips her finger in the cream and massages it over my cuts ever so gently. I have to control the tingle. It feels too good.

"Not in detail, but I wouldn't mind hearing about it from you."

"Oh, it's not that interesting. Some asshole pinned me to the wall after a game and tried to grab my ass, so I kneed him in the groin—twice."

"He deserved it."

"Yeah, he did. But to my dismay," she sighs, "it turned out he was the son of the admissions director."

"Fuck!"

"Ding-ding-ding," she sings, the sound getting us both to burst into loud guffaws.

"There, all good."

She releases my hand and stands—I follow.

"Let me just find a bandage. I think I have some in my room."

She bolts to her room, my steps right behind her. Leaning on the door frame, I cross my ankles and take in the space, while she rummages through her bedside drawer. I don't know how I know it, but the room screams MJ. It's vibrant, just like her spirit, with a twin bed on the left wall, covered in blue sheets, and a nightstand on each side. The right corner is occupied by a desk, with another pin-up board above it, covered in photos and sticky notes. A small closet on my left is aligned with the door. There's school paraphernalia taped on the walls alongside framed pictures of the team and some of her and Emma. The faint smell of her cherry perfume lingers in the room. Inhaling deeply, for safekeeping, I focus on the bookcase. The angle of sight doesn't allow me to see all the titles, but I can see a couple of familiar covers, something that Sabrina, my brother's wife, made us read last year.

"You can come in, you know, get a better look." Her voice echoes, urging my eyes to snap in her direction.

"Sorry, I'm a nosy person." I shrug, zeroing in on the red rolled-up bandage in her hand.

"I can see that, and don't worry, it's an allowed trait."

She pulls another smile out of me, something she keeps achieving with ease.

"Let's take care of the hand first. Ok? Then I'll allow you

to snoop around some more. Take a seat." She points to the bed, and with my smile never fading, I sit down. The room shrinks when she joins my side, the bed barely shifting under the weight. Gentle in her care, she slowly wraps my hand, never lifting her gaze, allowing my eyes to roam around freely. This time, I got a good view of the books, and my heart jolts again when I zoom in on my favorite title.

"You found it?"

My gaze drops to her, and I find that she's staring at me, reading my expression. She knew what I was doing all along.

"Which one is it?"

"Care to guess?"

"How many do I get?"

"How 'bout 3?"

That one earns me a smile and a twinkle in her eyes. Focusing on the shelves, she bites the inside of her cheek. I notice her gaze being drawn down where the Tolkien collection is stacked, then she turns to face me, dismissing the thought with a hum. After a beat, she returns her attention to the books, eyes slowly moving to all sides of the case before they find their target. A slight curve appears on the side of her lips just as her eyes widen with recognition. She turns to face me, as if reading my thoughts, and in that moment, I know she has me; she knows me with that one revelation. She doesn't need to tell me her guess because her blues tell me she found it, found me.

"You know this book contains most of my favorite quotes." She stands up, takes two steps, and slides out my favorite book, Steinbeck's 'East of Eden'. Placing the paperback on her chest, she faces me. She doesn't wait for me to confirm. She just... knows.

"I bet I can guess it," I trumpet, "and your favorite book."

"That's mighty ambitious of you, but I'll bite."

Taking back her seat, she places the book in her lap and graces me with her full-on focus.

"Just a hint, I don't have a favorite book; it's more like three of them fighting on the podium," she confesses.

I give her a thankful smile and trace over her collection.

"One of them has to be *Persuasion*."

The Jane Austen classic is not as famous as *Emma* or *Pride and Prejudice*, but it is among the better-known works. MJ's copy of the book looks well-read; I can see the cracks on the spine, but it's still in pristine condition, like it has been cared for dearly.

"Huh," she snickers. "Now, that's just creepy."

"Not any less creepy than you guessing my favorite book on your first try."

I take out the golden-brown hardcover in an attempt to open it, only for it to be snatched from my grasp.

"That's cheating."

"Not true. I know that this book is important, but I need to figure out which story exactly." She hands it back to me with reservations, her brows furrowed. It is a book containing five short stories, and frankly, I can see her loving all of them, but I want to impress her.

Skimming through the pages, I stop when I land on the title '*The Remarkable Rocket*'. I skip to the last pages of the story and read aloud, "I am so clever that sometimes I don't understand a single word I am saying. I love this one," I say, her amazed gaze obvious.

"Ok, how did you figure that one out?"

"The spine," I note, "It looks like it was opened more than once, and I had doubts between the '*Nightingale and the Rose*' and '*The Remarkable Rocket*', but the pages of the last one are more yellow than the others."

"Observant." Her head tilts, her inner cheek at the mercy of her teeth.

"Deductive as well," I add.

"And the third one?"

"That's where I'm stuck. I don't think it's on the shelves. Maybe you don't have a physical copy, or you lent it to someone?"

"It's in my bag. I take it with me everywhere."

"I think I need to get to know you better to figure out which one it is."

With a shaky breath, she offers her copy of my favorite book, but I shake my head, not needing any help.

"I know it by heart at this point."

"How many times have you read it?"

"I stopped counting after the fifth."

She bobs her head with a low hum.

Clearing my throat, I start, "There's a responsibility in being a person..."

"It's more than just taking up space where air would be," she finishes, and it takes all of my willpower to restrain myself from wrapping her in a kiss.

"Are you a mind reader or something?"

"No," I gasp through a laugh.

But I'm an MJ reader.

And never in my life has anything been as easy.

Chapter 10

Mayday! Mayday!

I have a boy in my room.

I repeat, I have a boy in my room, and not just any boy—Tyler Hart. He is on my bed; the very place where I sleep, some nights, having wet dreams about the same man warming my comforter.

Wearing dark jeans and a black Air Jordan t-shirt, he sits comfortably next to me, all the while reading my mind. To take credit, I did read his first. It was as if some greater power drew me to that one title. I could practically see it calling for me, accompanied by a tingly feeling I felt the moment I read over the title, and I just knew. He does seem like a type who'd appreciate the complexities of 'East of Eden'. Technically, it's a hard book to absorb, let alone comprehend. I had to reread it myself to fully understand it. Tyler, on the other hand, gives the impression of being someone who would get it all on the first read. Not to mention, a person who'd love it.

When he guessed my favorite books and quotes, it not only blew my mind but also sent a shock to a specific part of my body. What can I say… Talking about books gets me horny. I think I'm developing a kink here…

He's a basketball player, MJ. You are not strong enough to go there.

I think to myself, jolting out of thoughts containing a number 7 jersey tossed on the floor.

"How old were you when you first read it?" I ask, curious.

"Um…" He hums, thinking it over. "I think seventeen," he says, uncertain.

"You?"

"Last year," I utter, not understanding why I am ashamed to admit it. With my mouth forgetting how to filter, I continue rambling on, "It was mentioned in one of the romance novels I was reading. Naturally, I got compelled into it."

The upper shelf of my bookcase calls out to me as I focus on all the titles. "Come to think of it, I read most of the classics after they were referenced in other books."

I take a breath, my confession hitting the realization.

"Huh." I tilt my head, laughing to myself on the inside.

Noting the sudden silence, I turn to face Ty, only to find his eyes already on me. For a brief moment, I forget how to breathe, the intensity of his glare too strong to handle. Still, my eyes stay locked on his, my heart drumming so loudly I fear he can hear it. Hating the quiet, I try to think of something to say, to blink the connection away—an impossible task. The pull is too strong.

Fun fact, I love talking; you're over the line, Chatty-Cathy right here. There's not a topic that can shut me up, except one. I have one wall around me that is heavily bricked up. No amount of huffing or puffing can blow it away, but this one boy denting my bed beside me… he makes me want to allow the smallest of cracks to form, making the whole dang thing

66

vulnerable. Honest to whatever force is out there, I am terrified of the probability. So I do what I do best—I run.

"We should probably get back," I blurt out, then stand - no, jump up, scaring us both a bit. He stays silent but nods and follows me out. He waits for me as I lock the door, then we're on our way downstairs, side by side.

Don't look at him, don't look at him.

Fuck, I looked at him.

I am so screwed beyond repair, and by the looks of his smirk, he dang well knows it. This guy intimidates me more than I care to admit.

"Finally!" Emma charges at me, wrapping her arms around my neck, then she... sniffs me?

"You bitch! You didn't have sex!" The room goes still, and I can feel my face turning red.

"Sorry to disappoint you." In horror, I look over her shoulder to face what's left of our friends spread out on the floor. Tyler chokes on air before Ben swoops in. "Well, now that we have established that, would you two like to join us?"

How long have we been upstairs?

Ben, Kate, Jones, Colt, and Chase are sitting in a circle playing UNO. Emma takes her place right next to Ben, and they all scoot over, making room for the two of us.

"What happened to the party?" I ask, sliding between Emma and Chase.

"Some idiot made a scene, so we turned off the music and made last call," Colt fills us in, and Tyler sits next to him, giving me the perfect view.

No view, MJ, you are not to look at him.

Fuck, I looked at him again.

Chase deals the cards, and we all get deep into the game.

"Ha! Suck it." Emma puts down the +4, making me lose my turn. Shaking my head in amusement, I take four cards from the stack.

"Pick your poison." Chase glares at her, but before she can even declare her color, he smacks a red number 6 on top of the pile. Emma cocks a brow, making Chase quickly put his hands up in surrender. "Don't look at me, he told me to." He nudges his head in Ben's direction. Emma's face softens, barely, before her expression turns deadly. My eyes keep playing ping pong between Chase and Ben, both scared, anticipating her next move. Even I'm surprised when she quickly snaps the same card on top of Chase's, giving him a witchy cackle.

"UNO motherfuckers," she squeals, leaving both guys stunned. I quickly top it with a red +2, and Chase curses, drawing two cards with his head bowed. Emma gives me a wink, and I blow out my tongue. Goosebumps erupt when I sense it. Every fiber of my body feels his stare, and I fight the urge to check. All the playfulness leaves my body, my eyes finding the courage to look up. I can lie and say I don't notice the way his jaw clicks, or the way he takes a shallow breath. I can even try to deny how my body shivers, locked in a stare-off. Although it lasts merely a moment, in my head it's an eternity. How can one simple look do so many wonders to my chemistry is beyond me, but here it is… wondering. Breaking the spell, I dive back into the game, my heart protesting.

During the next hour, bickering is the main event, cards fly more times than I could count, and swear words are tossed all over the place. All in all, it turned out to be a fun night.

Kate decides to sleep over in our room, Ben takes the downstairs couch, and the others go to their dorms, marking the party officially over. I brush my teeth and throw my tired body on my bed, eyeing the book next to my feet. I take it and dive in.

A loud racket outside my door gets the best of my curiosity, and I slowly crack the door open to find Ben and Emma in a lip-lock.

Finally.

Slowly backing away, I quietly close the door. Cementing my ears with my headphones, I pull up my Spotify playlist and continue to lose myself in the familiarity of the pages. My mind becomes my biggest enemy when it starts to play out a scene of a younger Tyler reading the same words. It gets worse when I join the scene, taking a space under his arm. I imagine the two of us wrapped in each other's arms as he reads the book out loud to me. His soothing voice is so vivid that I have to do the Stella double-tap. It's something I picked up from a Kate Stewart book. A forehead slap is a way to let someone know they are being an idiot. In my case, they are always self-inflicted. The double-tap means that I'm *really* being an idiot. And thinking about Tyler is definitely considered idiocy. I can't allow it, no matter how intense the pull is; I have to nip it in the bud.

Keep that wall up, Stevens. Everything depends on it.

I give myself a much-needed pep talk and get back into reading mode.

Chapter 11

This whole week was torture. Friday couldn't come any slower; it felt like the days were dragging on, getting longer just to spite me. I don't share any classes with MJ and haven't had any luck in coincidentally bumping into her in the courtyard or the halls. So I have been experiencing severe withdrawal.

The moment my alarm went off this morning, I was up and at 'em so fast nothing could stop me. Ticking the hours away, I patiently waited for the 6 o'clock, the same o'clock I would get to see and touch her.

Unfortunately for me, my friends sensed my desperation and took every opportunity to mock and rub it in my face. Jones, our center, had Statistics with her on Monday; she had her hair down and wore a red shirt with tights. Colt, our small forward, saw her at the gym on Tuesday, her hair in a high ponytail, wearing basketball shorts matched with a top. Ben, my so-called best friend, had two classes with her and met both her and Emma for coffee on Wednesday. The bastard didn't want to share any details on her appearance. That leaves me as the only person who hasn't seen her for five straight days. 135 hours of my nose trying to find the cherry sent, 135 hours of my eyes trying to find her oceans, 135 hours of misery.

At the sound of the coach's whistle, marking the end of our practice, I dart to the locker room. This time, I am faster than the guys, running straight to the shower all the while multitasking with impressive speed.

"My God, you are whipped without actually being whipped," Ben jeers loudly and proudly.

"That's just stating the obvious. Now come on, hurry the hell up," I snap back, finishing my scrubbing.

The whole team laughs, mocking my nerves, but keeps up their speed. My smile grows wider, and my steps feel lighter the closer I get to the studio. The moment my eyes land on her, my whole body relaxes, yet my heart pumps vigorously. I find her in the middle of the routine, turned sideways, facing Emma, doing all the steps, and mockingly laughing at her friend.

Something is different. I can't put my finger on it, but there's something new, something I can only define as a spark of some sort. With her eyes wide open and a full-on smile, she has this out-of-the-ordinary energy about her. Not that I can say what her everyday ordinary is, considering I'm still not a part of her inner circle. Regardless, every fiber of my body feels its anomalous, and it looks so damn good on her.

In the course of the last ten minutes, she looked up at me twenty-eight times, and yes, I counted. Each time lasted exactly seven seconds, not a beat over or under. I counted the mississippies and couldn't help but wonder if she, too, counted, making sure to stop and match the number written on my back. The thought, the mere chance of that premise, gives me an inkling of hope.

Rushing down the stairs with the rest of my team, we stop to a halt outside the door to collect ourselves to make a cool entrance. Ben knocks, then swings the double door open, yelling out, "Have no fear, the cavalry is here!"

The girls burst into laughter, and we all follow, scratch Ms. Lynch, who stands with her arms crossed over her chest and one foot tapping in annoyance. My eyes set and firmly lock on the blonde, still holding the summer tan, peachy-skinned beauty. And boy, are my eyes lucky to have the privilege of looking at her. This girl, this woman, should be enlisted for the 8th wonder of the world for her aura alone. She illuminates with so much purity, freedom, and spices it up with the right amount of spite.

Ms. Lynch claps her hands with the same intensity as always, and we all form a line at her demand. Ben gives me a winked smirk, taking his place next to a flushed-cheeked Emma. MJ is on Emma's other side with six people between us.

"Today, we will work on changing the formation stations. So remember, you will be moving clockwise for the first half and counterclockwise for the second." Ms. Lynch's voice echoes in the room, her glances switching between each of us as we all nod in compliance.

"Take your places. We will start in one minute." She claps again, and we all skedaddle to our assigned marks. With my heart spiraling, I close in on the girl who has invaded my every thought. I take my stance behind her back and warn in a hushed voice, "Heads up," before I place my hand on her stomach. She gives me the sideways glance, and even though her half smile lifts to the left and she's facing me over her right shoulder, I can feel the rise of that curve. I keep hoping she won't notice the racing of my heart. However, my sweaty palms are a dead giveaway. Her left hand covers mine, and we wait for the count. With the sound of the number eight, we sway. Mesmerized by her addictive scent, I stride after her.

The choreography is simple due to the team's lack of rhythm. The first eight beats consist of dragging steps forward with the opposite leg popping to the side. The same steps are performed backward for the next eight beats. That combination is repeated four times. This is where the formation stations make the switch, as the couple on the right replaces the spot of the couple on their left. The next phase is the cha-cha, which includes a sideways turn and a step forward. This is also the only phase in which the partners face each other, holding hands, with their elbows set at 90 degrees. The song we dance to is in a language I can't detect, but the melody is lovely and soothing. With my body so close to hers, holding something so precious, there is one thing beyond a doubt - it's definitely a love song.

Chapter 12

Has this been one of the longest weeks of my life? Sure.

Am I mad for not having at least one class to share with one gorgeous, tall basketball player? Of course.

Is there resentment pointed toward the threads of fate for not giving me at least one accidental run-in? Hell yes!

Somehow, Wednesday was the breaking point. After Econ, Ben invited Emma and me for coffee. For an entire hour, I was forced to listen to his praises of the new shooting guard. Don't get me wrong, I liked hearing about how Tyler was getting in sync with the team and how well he fit with them on and off the court, but it just made it worse for me. I mean, couldn't he tell that I was secretly scanning the crowd, hoping he'd miraculously appear?

And to top it all off, Ben and Emma were all googly eyes right there in front of me - sick, cute little bastards. God, you should've seen them. Trying to flirt while appearing cool. However, the blush on both their faces said it all. At some point, I mumbled out that they were adorable, and they sent me a death glare. They wanted each other, yet both played hard to get, even after hooking up three times since Saturday. Something told me it would be cemented on the night of

Ben's birthday. We discussed the party, for which he had rented out the entire bowling alley at Arcadia.

During Wednesday's practice, Emma and Kate talked about the color coordination for the bowling alley and the gift for Ben. We already got a signed jersey of his favorite player, Clippers point guard James Harden, but we wanted to add something personal to it.

For the first time since I enrolled here, I was happy with my tight schedule. It allowed me to focus, or better yet, refocus from Mister Nice Calves Dancer. Work was also fun this week, while simultaneously draining. After each shift, I would take the bus back and instantly crash on the bed without even putting on my PJs.

So when my alarm went off this morning, my excitement gave way to nerves. All of them disappeared the moment his perfect face came into view. We did the routine three times until Ms. Lynch was satisfied with the formation switches. There was no exchange of words between Tyler and me, just some intense stares, enveloped in silence. It was a comfortable kind of silence, one I wouldn't mind repeating or prolonging.

Sometimes there's no need for words, and with our bodies intertwined in rhythmic movements, we allow our bodies to speak volumes. Our stares remained locked, neither willing to look away the entire time we were facing each other.

With the last clap courtesy of Ms. Lynch, Emma and I bolt to the other side of the sports center, making it just in time for our pre-game meeting. Tomorrow is the away game against our biggest rivals, and we are in for a scrutinizing pep talk.

"Ok, girls, we all know what's tomorrow. We play NYU, and we need this win. So get your heads in the game and play your asses off, no mercy, girls. No mercy!" Our Coach speaks with a husky tone.

"Due to Tamara's injury, I need you all to step up, and yes, Kate, I am looking at you," Coach roars, and we all turn to face Kate, who simply nods. Then the coach's eyes lock on me, "Stevens, focus on the serve; it's our biggest weapon." The girls yell out a 'yeah', pumping me up. We finish with a huddle, palms topping one over the other. I count down from three, and on cue, we lift our hands in a quick whoosh, finishing it with jazz fingers and a loud shouted "Rooar!"

The boys also have a game tomorrow against the Bisons in Lewisburg. Their game starts at noon, giving them enough time to return for us to celebrate Ben's birthday. We play locally, so it isn't much of an issue for us girls. This will be the first game the boys won't be in the stands to cheer us on, and it makes me nervous. I like having their support, and with the addition of Tyler's sexy ass on the bleachers, it makes me feel unstoppable.

Emma and I exchange looks during the coach's monologue, both feeling the nerves. It's our second game of the season, one we need to win, and without the boys, there's a sense of void looming like a dark cloud.

Back in our room, Emma is slumped on the couch while

I'm getting dressed. I'm in the middle of tying my shoe when Emma shares her honest opinion. "You two looked good today dancing, you got a good one for a partner." There's a hint of jealousy there, and I know it has nothing to do with Tyler.

"Sorry that you got stuck with two left feet, Parker," I tell her with empathy, not a mocking tone in my voice. "But I saw you eyeing Ben the entire time, with claws out and ready to strike Lea; I think that's her name."

Yeah, so neither Emma nor I bothered to get acquainted with the other girls in class, since we're not on the same level. With Emma and Mua being goofy, as opposed to the other girls who give out that 'I'm better than you' vibe, which we're not the biggest fans of.

Red flushes over her cheeks, and I can almost feel the strength in the clench of her jaw.

"You mean the black goddess that couldn't keep her hands off him?"

"Oh, come on, you know all that boy sees is red. And trust me when I tell you that girl has nothing on you, none of them do."

"I don't know what's wrong with me. I never get jealous." She sinks deeper into the couch, her feet flying over the armrest.

"True, but you've never liked a guy the way or as much as you do Ben."

"You go, ok? I am not in the mood tonight."

Since I am the only one actually getting ready, it's pretty obvious she's not going to join me.

"I got that, dude. See you later. Don't wait up."

"Don't do anything I wouldn't do."

With that, I give her an air kiss and close the door behind me. Putting my earbuds in, I open my running playlist and press play, starting in a jog to match the beat. Five songs in, my pace a bit faster, I halt to a stop. An unexplainable feeling floods me, like the wind is blowing me to move in the direction my feet are now following. I was so immersed in the music that I deviated from my route without even realizing it.

A path I have never taken before in my run got me to a caged half-court hidden behind a thick set of trees. My blood runs cold at the sight, memories of a similar court back in Chicago invading my mind, of Jamie tossing me the ball, hearts in his eyes. Both of us shared a love of basketball with dreams of making it big. But for Jamie, basketball came first; I came second. So I took basketball out of the equation.

Flame ft. NF's 'Start Over' blasts in my ears the second my eyes land on the free-throw line. A black Spalding basketball with silver lines stands there, inviting me to pick it up. As NF belts out the chorus, compelling me to close in, I stretch out my hands and squat down. The chill spreads from my fingertips all over my entire body at the touch of the leather. The feeling is all too familiar.

It feels like—*home*.

The music dims out as I roll the ball between my fingers, getting reacquainted. I pocket my earbuds, and the next thing I know, I am throwing the ball, and it goes in with the sound of the swish - nothing but net. My feet move over the asphalt with my hands commanding the ball to bounce around me in such precision that it almost feels cataclysmic. Each shot I make goes through, giving me all the feels and chills. I thought basketball had left me; I thought I had lost it, forgotten it, but it has been here all along. It never stopped being a part of me, and my God, how I've missed it.

Chapter 13

Be still, my heart.

Maddison Stevens is using my ball to make magic happen. There I was, thinking that watching her play volleyball was something to witness, but boy, this girl keeps proving me wrong. Wearing dark navy basketball shorts paired with a gray sports top that exposes her lower back, she looks like a mirage. Her hair, pulled up in a high ponytail, sways as she zig-zags all over the ground. The way her body moves in tandem with the ball is pure art, and when her hand swings up to shoot, my heart stops when it goes through with such accuracy. The way her fingers follow through makes the ball rotate as it flies through the air in a perfect arc. The launch angle and speed of her shot are so impressive, and the way she owns the ball... Fuck me. She makes the ball an extension of her, not a part of her. It does her bidding, and she's in total control. Beautiful. Hypnotizing.

After her last shot, she retrieves the ball and places it at the exact spot I left it before. Seconds tick by while she stares at the hoop, her hands on the back of her head, fingers intertwined. I can't see her expression from this angle, but I zero in on the depth and speed of her breaths. When she turns around, a single tear falls on the side of her cheek, and when her eyes lock with mine, she drops to her knees, burying her face in her palms. The sound of her scream, followed by a loud sob, cuts me so deeply. Without hesitation, I charge, falling to the ground next to her. I open my arms, and she falls into me. Her cries get louder, and her shivers get more distinct. All I can do for her in that moment is hold her as tightly as I can without breaking her.

What the hell happened to her?

Curled up in my lap, I rock her back and forth, gently grazing her hair. The phenomenon of her being so vulnerable gets the best of me, and I finally break the silence, "It's ok, I got you." Somehow, those words soften her posture, causing her weight to drop, and an instant of relief eases the tension that has been controlling me. She feels so delicate, and all I want is to keep her safe and protected from the pain. The feisty, strong-minded, punch-throwing badass took a back seat, showing me a fractured side of her. A side that makes her one of us mere mortals.

I wish I could get inside her head to understand her better, to figure out how to fix whatever is holding her back.

Why would she back away from the game she was built to play?

What happened? What caused all this?

I have so many questions, but I choose to stay silent for her.

"I'm so sorry..." She moves away from my lap, taking a seat next to me, and wipes her face. "I-I don't know what came over me."

Her eyes widen when she looks at my shirt.

"Oh shit, I'm so sorry, I ruined your shirt." She frowns, which makes me laugh, so I take off my shirt and toss it to her. "No longer my shirt; meet your new handkerchief," I gush, and that causes her to chuckle, and boy, it's a sight for sore eyes. She swallows and gives my bare torso a once-over, sending chills up my spine. Clearing her throat, she averts her gaze and gasps, "I'm sorry."

"Don't. No reason to be."

"Doesn't make me any less sorry."

How does one respond to that? How does one feel about that? She already swept me off my feet; what more is there left for her to do to me? So, how does she continue to astonish me further? In great need of keeping her away from the dark, my mental light bulb lights up.

"Fine! How about a game of HORSE to make it up to me for the trauma?" I offer, my tone ever so eager.

"That's not fair, considering it's the first time I touched a basketball in over two years."

Two years?

I repeat it in my head.

"Sure as hell didn't look like that to me."

She glares at me, proving to herself my spoken truth.

Standing up first, I leave my hand open for hers, and she hesitantly takes it, allowing me to pull her up to her feet. She follows as I retrieve my bag, which has been tossed next to the backboard base. Quickly rummaging through it, I take out a spare shirt before I cover my skin with it. I can't decipher whether it's my imagination playing tricks on me or if a disappointed sigh escaped MJ.

I bend down to pick up the ball, then throw it to her with a bounce pass. Her ready hands welcome the impact, and the smile on her face widens. There's a twinkle in her eyes, and it is not from the street lamp.

"How is it that I have been living here for two years and never known this place existed?"

"Probably because you weren't looking for it."

"Fair point." She shrugs, scrunching up her nose.

"So what are we playing for?" I raise an eyebrow, and she replies by narrowing her eyes.

"Seriously, dude, it's not fair. You are an active player."

"And you just played like you never left, so do me a favor and state your claim."

Not knowing what I did to deserve her giggle, I walk under the hoop as she takes her starting position.

"Fine, if I win…" biting her lover's lip, she hums while contemplating.

Chapter 14

With my heart still pounding, loudly if I may add, I knock on Emma's door.

"You up? Can I come in?"

"Yeah, it's open," she yells from the other side, and I swing the door, finding her all cozied up in her bed, the lamp on her nightstand the only light illuminating the room. Her face fills with instant worry, and she sits up, screeching, "Oh, my god, what happened?"

I get inside, closing the door behind me, and start pacing.

"I need to vent," I gasp out, turning on my heel when I reach the wall, repeating the pattern over and over.

"Honey, I love you, but I can't deal with your book right now." Clasping her hands together, she points the tips at me, mouthing a 'please'.

"No book; real life." I shake my head; the floor creaks beneath me.

"Oh shit. Do we need alcohol?" Her eyes widen, and she stands up, brows spiked.

"Not a good idea, game tomorrow." I keep pacing, trying to figure out where to start.

"Right. So what do you need?" She rounds her bed and

sits on the side where I am continuously walking back and forth.

"I played," I marvel out.

"You played?" she gasps, placing her hand over her chest.

"I played," I chortle, still wrapping my head around it.

"Oh shit, seriously?" Her eyes start to fill up with water, and my God, how much I love her for it. It's like she's feeling all the feels right there with me.

"Yeah." I nod with a slight chuckle.

"And?"

"Like riding a bike, only… Better."

"How?"

"It was so weird…" I keep pacing; I have a good rhythm going. I'm still trying to understand everything. "I started running and, without even realizing it, I took a wrong turn. Then I came across this hidden half-court, and I saw a ball in the middle of it just as the right song started to play…" I take a deep breath. "So I just took it and—boom!" I exclaim.

"Boom?" She frowns, and I stop my movement, facing her.

"I don't know how to explain it; it was an explosion of some sort." I jab my chest, telling her where exactly the boom happened.

"Maddie, I don't know what to say. I am so proud of you."

Again, God, how much I love her.

"There's more." I lift a finger and then start fidgeting with the pendants on my necklace.

"There's more?" She raises one eyebrow.

"There's so much more," I gasp out, shaking my head,

and subsequently continuing on the pacing ritual.

"Ok," she hesitates, straightening up as if to brace herself.

"When I finished, I put the ball back where I found it, and there he was…"

"Tyler?"

Of course, she'd get it right, the clairvoyant little minx.

"You know it!"

"I told you, you two are so meant to be."

"Just wait for it."

"Oh shit." She slaps her mouth shut.

"Yeah, so… I broke down and ugly cried…"

She does the 'ugh' hissing through her teeth, wrinkling her whole face.

"What did he do?"

"He held me tightly while rocking me."

"Damn."

"That doesn't even cover it." The feel of his embrace still lingers. The scent of his sweat mixed with something spicy comes back to me like the air I breathe in.

"Ooooockeey, what happened next?"

"He gave me his shirt."

"Yaaaaaay." She claps her hands, but frowns when I continue. "Because I ruined it with my bodily fluids."

"Not yay."

"A bit of a yay; he was naked underneath."

"Whoohoo, what next?"

"We played horse," I reveal.

That one makes her jaw drop. Even though basketball is not her sport, being around the guys has made her an expert on the subject.

"I think I let him win."

"Why?"

"Well, we had a sort of a bet…" I stop again, taking a deep breath. "And if I had won, he was supposed to strip sprint through the girl dorms…"

"What?" she screams with piercing eyes and a threatening-to-kill-me expression all over her face.

"Sorry." I make a cross with my fingers, shoving it in her face.

"Unforgivable," she scoffs, the red of her hair matching the color of her cheeks.

"Ok, so what did he win?"

"Well…" I swallow. "My attendance at a game."

"No?" It comes out as a long, gasping breath.

"Yes." I shrug, remembering how his face lit up before he stated his claim. Something about the way he said it, the softness of his voice, made it clear he wasn't just a cocky jock asking to watch his game. It was as if he knew it was a step I had to take.

Emma jumps, wrapping her arms around me as tightly as she can. "Damn, that guy is such a smart-ass. I love him for you, Maddie, I really do."

"I know," I whine, both excited and scared by the revelation.

"And you let him win?"

"I'm not sure; I think so, like subconsciously." I shake my head over her shoulder.

He let me go first, and I was on fire, making shot after shot. When I got on the free-throw line, I stared at the hoop like we were in the middle of a conversation… My throw was short, and it hit the brim. Tyler took over and, in one go, won the game.

"Have I mentioned how proud I am of you?"

"On a regular basis."

"I love you," she whispers in my ear. Tightening my squeeze, I give her back her words, "I love you."

The hug lasts a long time with my best friend, waiting for me to be the first to break it, knowing how much I need it. Her support and her understanding mean everything to me. This kind of everlasting friendship is everything I hoped and prayed for. Not a day passes without my thanking God for sending her to me, especially when I needed her most. Behind her wit, smarts, and audacity is a heart of gold and an untenable amount of wisdom, one she shares only with the ones closest to her. For someone who grew up in a wealthy, loving family without experiencing any major drama, she somehow has a lifetime of knowledge about everything related to life. Guess her parents raised her right. Unlike me, a person raised thanks to the stories written by strangers. Books were my mother, and TV shows were my father. Heck, I learned everything by watching Disney and reading fairy tales. As I came of age, I evolved toward contemporary romances, romantasy, and thrillers. Emma keeps me connected to the screen, her sole goal being to get my nose away from my Kindle. Still, this girl, two months younger than me, is a smart ass of drastic proportions with her astonishing perception.

"So, what happens now?"

I shrug. "No idea."

"Scared?"

"Like hell," I admit, not a shred of hesitation with that one.

"Want my two cents?"

"Like I have a choice in the matter."

"Just go with it. As far as I can see, the cards are in your favor, and the way things are progressing, it seems to me that the path is already set for you to walk through."

"Ok, that was very perceptive and poetic."

"I have my moments."

"I hate you." I blow out my tongue, and she pinches it between her fingers.

"You love me."

"That I do, that I do," I mumble, my tongue still held captive. When she releases it, I give her a smooch, and she jumps on her bed, getting under the covers. "Ok, hit me!"

"Really?"

"Yeah, what the heck? I am wound up now… Let's do it."

With a silenced shriek, I get under the covers beside her and talk her ears off about the newest book that I'm in the middle of reading, and even though my mind is occupied with the storytelling, his brown eyes flash every couple of seconds.

Chapter 15

Game day is always a stress-filled one. Each player has their own pre-game ritual. There's not much insight into the details, but I was made aware of Ben's because he was extremely loud during it. On away games, he sits in the back, alone, talking on the phone with someone. There's an ongoing poll, and Emma is the top choice. I, on the other hand, have a book and noise-canceling earbuds with my pump-up mix blasting through.

A three-hour bus ride later, we're sitting in the Bison's locker room. They were third on last year's roster, one point above us. I wasn't part of the team at the time, so I have no personal grudges against them. I don't mean to imply I'm not fairly motivated to win. After our ears bled due to a long motivational speech courtesy of our Coach, we huddle up and head out to the court.

In the middle of our warm-ups, Ben starts his customary rant.

"So, you think the girls are gonna win?"

"I read the stats a bit on the drive, and honestly, I think it's gonna be a tight game," I disclose, starting with the A-skips.

"Yeah, NYU is their biggest rival; our girls are in for a tough game."

"Our girls?" I lift a brow, turning on my heel, picking up the pace on the jog back to the line.

"Damn straight, bro, *our* girls," he enunciates.

The notion plays on a loop in my head the entire time we do our suicides down the line, and when the sound of the beeping scoreboard marks the beginning of the game, my focus is all in it.

Jones catches the jump ball, sending it straight into Colt's hands, who gives us the head start with a dunk. The crowd's roar only pumps up the adrenaline rushing through my bloodstream.

We maintained our advantage throughout the first half, but kept it tight in the second.

The clock ticks down; 15 seconds left on the board, down by one. The crowd is a rumble of tension. Coach's voice echoes from the sidelines, "Run blue." My eyes snap to Ben, sweat dripping, palms slick as he dribbles just past half court. He signals the play, his closed fist in the air. I wait, watching Jones lumber up the post, planting hard at the top of the key, setting up the screen. Ben fades left, then snaps right, taking advantage of the wall. His defender clips Jones' shoulder, and he stumbles. The lane opens, just a crack, and Ben rises, one foot off balance, but he doesn't shoot. The gym feels small; everything tightens. His eyes go into scan mode and land on me, wide open on the three line, my hands already up. In a perfect spiral, he whip-passes, and my hands catch the ball. Without hesitation, I release it smoothly. The ball arcs, the buzzer goes off, followed by the sound of the swish.

The gym explodes, and my teammates start jumping. I point at Ben, who is fully grinning.

We fucking won!

As soon as we step back into the locker room, Ben starts working his phone. The girls are still playing, deep in the fifth set after tying the first four. The current score is 10:11, and our entire team is huddled around Ben's phone. A long play is happening, the ball just keeps crossing over the net, and you can feel the exhaustion on both teams. After a nice roll save from Emma, the score flips, and MJ steps on the serve line. Spending a whole week rewatching all the games on my laptop, I've picked up on her tells, and when I see the tip-toe flick, I know NYU is in trouble. A miniature version of the number 3 performs the two-step jump serve, sending the ball straight to the hardwood floor. With a silent fist celebration, we continue huddling as MJ repeats her action, making the score 10:14.

One more Feisty, one more…

With my eyes glued to the small screen, I seize my breathing, and I stop moving as MJ prepares the ball for liftoff. The stupid phone starts buffering, and we all argh in frustration. Colt quickly reacts by going to the home page to see the live results and starts screaming, showing us the score.

NYU 2:3 Columbia.

My team goes wild, and we all jump like crazy people, yelling and hugging.

Ben's phone rings, and with a full-on smile, he shows us Emma's name lighting up his screen before he answers.

"You're on speaker."

"You woooon," the girls yell at the same time we all do.

Taking her off speaker, Ben goes to the bathroom, and I go straight to the shower, flying with adrenaline from our wins.

Waking up to the blare of my alarm, I get up and start the morning hustle. Emma joins, and we head out for breakfast. Our game is scheduled for 11 o'clock, and we have to arrive an hour early to change and warm up. NYU is a thirty-minute subway ride away, so we have enough time to eat, gossip, get ready, and head out. Emma is on the phone the entire time, talking to Ben, a ritual they had whenever he was on the bus to away games. All our college games are streamed on our website, so she would always watch them in the common room while I looked up the scores online in my room. The boys also stream ours, and we habitually meet up after to celebrate or sink our sorrows with alcohol.

It's a different kind of atmosphere when we play away. There's no familiarity with the turf or the crowd, and it always unsettles me. Growing up, I never had a support system; no one there to root for me in the stands, to put their arms around me and offer congratulations or consolation. As the years passed, I grew accustomed to it, and it became a familiar comfort. However, when I enrolled at Columbia, everything changed. I got a team, an actual team of 12 girls who shared an unconditional love for the game and each other. Over time, the circle grew when Emma brought the basketball team into the mix. She's a longtime high school friend of Chase, so she got in with the team early on. After a lot of convincing, she got me to hang out with them, and we all became close, inseparable.

Today's game is an important one. We're playing the team that has been breathing down our roster-neck for the last two seasons, and each time we played against them, it was a close call. They have one of the best liberos in the league with the capability to catch any ball, even mine.

After a short ride, Emma and I meet the girls in front of the NYU gym, and we walk in with our hearts pumping. In the locker room, the team pump-up mix fills the silence from my phone while we change into our jerseys and shorts, bobbing our heads to the beat of Hush's 'Fired Up'. In the entire league, NYU has the best facilities, with a potent fresh floral scent filling the air.

The moment Coach steps inside, I pause the music, and we all turn our attention to her words, commanding us to do our best and win this game. Coach is not one for movie-worthy emotional speeches; she always leaves the words to me, and I try my best to deliver each time. My belief is that in the world of sports, when it comes down to that breaking point, the right combination of letters has the power to change it all, to break it or make it.

With the clap of Coach's hands, we exit the locker room and walk the tube until our shoes start scratching over the freshly polished hardwood.

Our warm-up routine is always the same: a jog, followed by stretching, running exercises, ball handling, and finishing it off with the serve. We try our best not to roll our eyes at the music choice, lacking a good rhythm to pump up a player; it's more like sending someone to sleep.

The game starts with a blow of the whistle, and I am on.

We lose the first set by two points and get yelled at. We win the second by three and still get yelled at. The third set goes on forever, never getting the two-point margin. We end the set with a score of 32:30. By the end of the fourth set, we are tied and exhausted.

With our strength on reserve, I gather the girls in a circle and assume my captain's role.

"Look, I know we are running low here, but we got this, we got each other. This is the time to step in for one another and communicate it loudly! No matter what happens, we played our best, that's all that matters, ok? That we do our best." I pause for the sole purpose of dramatic effect. "So let's finish this the best way we know how—together!"

"TOGETHER," we all shout, taking our hands in the middle right before we pull them up.

We win, and as soon as we get to the locker room, Emma calls Ben.

Chapter 16

Entering the bowling alley, Ben swings the door open with me by his side, followed by Jones, Colt, and Chase. Ben rented the entire area just for the eight of us for his birthday. Closing in on our lane, we all go static at the sight of Emma, Kate, and MJ jumping and laughing. On instinct, my eyes focus on the blonde one of the trio, wearing high-waist dark jeans, a tight white short-sleeved t-shirt, and bowling shoes. Her hair is let loose, falling down her back, looking damp, like she just stepped out of the shower.

And now I have that image clouding me…

The fabrics align with her figure, not leaving much to the imagination, and I wonder why she mostly wears baggy clothes with a body like that.

As soon as they spot us, they charge, jumping into Ben's arms, almost knocking him over. Pure, indisputable happiness is splattered all over his face as he laughs loudly like a madman. We all exchange our salutations and congratulate each other on our wins.

Taking the reins, MJ steps to the screen and suggests we divide the team alphabetically. At first, I get my hopes up, thinking MJ and I will end up together, but no such luck because she chooses our first names.

Teams are as follows:

1. *Blue: Adam (Chase) and Aron (Colt)*
2. *Red: Ben and Emma*
3. *Black: Kate and MJ*
4. *Green: Jones, aka Steve and Tyler, i.e., me*

The girls are already on their second cocktail when the guys order a pitcher of beer, accompanied by a side of shots for everyone. Clinking the small glasses, we yell out a loud 'Happy birthday, Ben', then swallow the liquor.

The party officially starts, and pins are flying. Ben reveals himself to be a pie-thrower on his first play, sending both balls to the sides. Chase hits eight pins on his first try and misses the two standing on his second. Kate knocks over three pins, then another two, and Jones makes a strike. The next round is the it round. Emma spares out, Colt follows, and MJ... Well, she sends the ball right out the center, knocking all the pins down. With the sound of the strike, she turns and bows, then walks past me as I prepare for my aim.

"Is there anything you're not good at?" My question makes her stop just as she reaches my shoulder, facing in the opposite direction.

"Physics, pool, and singing," she says with her nose wrinkled and her tone playful. I give her a wink and send my ball soaring, puffing out my chest when the bang of the strike fills the air. That earns me applause from her, and I'll be lying if I say it doesn't do wonders for my confidence.

The rest of the evening goes as such:

We play

Drink

Make fun of each other

Drink some more

The girls dance every chance they get…

I slum in the chair just as Ben, Jones, and Colt join the girls in a twerking session next to the ball return system. There's a disco ball right above them, spinning around in circles. A new song begins to play as Ben grinds with Emma, Kate with Jones, and Colt with MJ. His hand wraps around her waist.

Several things occur over the course of two songs, and some unwanted issues manifest. The way they smile at each other, how at ease she is around him. I want that. I want that smile, I want that touch. More than anything, I want to earn it. My breath grows heavy as I watch MJ sway her hips, Colt's hands slowly going down to her sides. Something inside of me ignites, a feeling I am not familiar with.

"You should blink every once in a while, you know? Try not to be so obvious." I turn in the direction from which the voice came, locking eyes with an overly amused Emma.

"What do you mean?"

"Your jealousy is showing; hide it better."

I huff, "I'm not jealous."

I'm not jealous. I repeat to myself. *Right?*

Is that what I'm feeling? It's not something I came up against before, let alone at this intensity, even knowing Colt has no interest in MJ.

"Sure," Emma drawls, "But for the record, you have nothing to worry about."

"I have no idea what you are talking about," I deflect,

wanting this conversation to be over so my head won't spiral further.

"Whatever you say," she taps me on the shoulder before she returns to Ben, leaving me with my thoughts.

I keep watching MJ dance with my friend, torturing myself.

Let the record show that Colt's got some serious moves.

He twirls and dips her with an enviable set of skills in his arsenal. With one flick of his wrist, he launches her away only to pull her back with a spring, making her crash into his chest. He towers over her and moves with her like the waves in the water.

"Maddie, come on, put him out of his misery," I hear Colt say, and that right there saves him from getting punched in that pretty-boy face.

I watch MJ as she strides to the table, takes a long sip of her red cocktail, and her eyes ever so slowly dart to mine. I know I sound like a broken record, but God, she's beautiful, fierce, and I can't look away, not that I ever tried to. Just as I prepare myself to stand up and go to her, she starts walking toward me, looking... nervous?

A new cocktail in hand, this time a blue one, she leans on the pole next to the table beside me, drinking through her straw. Her fingers graze over the slow droplets that drag down the length of the glass, and another knot forms in my stomach. Fuck, now I'm jealous of condensation. What's this girl doing to me?

"How's the cocktail?"

"Devious, sneaky little bastard," she quips, taking another sip.

"That's an odd description."

"It's the right one," she bickers, "I begrudge it."

I can feel my forehead wrinkle, so she goes on to elaborate.

"They lure you in with their sweetness only to fight off your inhibitions and any common sense."

"Is that why you finally decided to come and talk to me?"

"Maybe," she gushes, her cheeks holding in the blush.

Then she surprises me by offering her hand, and I take it without hesitation, an electric shock hitting me upon contact. Better yet, thunder strikes. She pulls me up, turns around, and places my hand over her shoulder, holding it tightly. I follow like a puppy, trying my best to keep my eyes up, respectfully. She guides us to the darkened side of the lane and presses her back to my chest, placing my hand on her stomach. A familiar melody fades in, 'Told You So' by Garrix and Jex blasts, like some sign from above nudging her. Responding to the lyrics, she leans her head on my clavicle, her hand slowly rising before she places it at the nape of my neck, all the while swaying her perfect body. My right hand moves from her stomach to the top side of her pelvic bone, and the other follows the motion on the opposite side. When I spot goosebumps covering her exposed skin, my fingers tremble as if they know the worth of what they are holding.

Her movements are pure torture, mainly when she ever so slightly grazes her ass over the part I try my best to keep hidden, but it's impossible. I am rock hard, and not a single thing that pops into my head makes my dick softer; nope, it only gets harder. When she moves to turn around, the music stops abruptly, making her pull back. At the sight of a cake shaped like a basketball being carried in by Emma and Kate, with candles already lit, MJ's face turns soft. We all erupt into the song for the birthday boy, and as I watch Ben make his wish, I can't help but send one of my own into the universe.

Her.

Chapter 17

Sunday went by in a blur. Emma and I slept most of it through, doing the opposite of powering through one hell of a hangover. Some parts of the night are missing from my memory bank, but Tyler's hands around me... Now that one is stored for safekeeping. Being in his arms, no matter the reason, is one of the safest places I have ever been.

Other things I remember are the shots, cocktails, dancing, and vomit, a whole lot of vomit. Mostly coming out of me, I think. I remember holding Emma's hair, so maybe it was she who was doing the vomiting. Ugh, I just smelled my breath, and yup, a lot of stuff came out of me.

Looking at the clock on my nightstand, I growl when I see it blink one o'clock. Dragging myself to the living room, I rub my eyes and open my mouth in a wide yawn. Someone is on our couch—naked. I think I'm going blind. Scratch that, all my eyes can see is a slightly hairy set of ass cheeks that belong to a blond person. "Dang it, Ben," I mouth, going straight to the fridge.

What's that smell?

Sniffing the air, I dry heave at the mixture of stale pizza and sweaty socks. Grabbing a Gatorade, I open the bottle and gulp half of it down, choking when Emma emerges from the bathroom, wearing nothing but a towel.

"Shit!"

"Shit's right. What the fuck, dude?" I whisper-yell. I'm mad, but I still have common sense not to wake someone up. Emma grabs my wrist and pulls me into her room, whisper-shouting, "Don't make a big deal out of it."

"If you tell me that you two had naked sex on our couch, I am going to strangle you!"

"Ok, first, come down." She grabs me by the shoulders and does the breathing exercise like we're in the middle of a birthing class. "Second, there was naked sex, but it was on the floor."

Okay, I can live with that. I never walk barefoot there anyway, so it's not a big deal... I take a deep breath; I'll allow it.

"He is still naked on our couch; his hairy groin is touching the leather," I point out, gagging at the visual in my head.

"Look, even full-on drunk, I had your stupid voice in my subconscious. I put a sheet under him."

Oh... thank my constant nagging. I give myself a mental high five.

"Well, I am flattered, you thought of me during and after sex. I believe we have embarked on new waters here, taking our friendship to the next level," I mock, my head still pounding.

She snatches the Gatorade from my hand and takes a long sip, leaving me with almost nothing, but I don't mind, and she knows it.

"My head hurts too much for your tone right now." She

hands me back the bottle and goes straight to her temples, massaging them in circles.

"Noted. Now please, details... I need details."

"We were drunk, but I remember everything," she gasps, the twinkle in her eye strong. I crash down on her bed as she drops her towel and starts getting dressed. "Maddie, I think I am in love with his penis."

"Of course you are," I snark.

"Seriously, it is so beautiful; you have to see it."

"Oh, no, thank you. His butt was enough to scar me for life." The Gatorade starts to sneak up on the memory, but I swallow it down.

"All joking aside, tell me," I prod.

She lifts her hand between us, showing off four fingers with a puckered lip.

"Way to go, Ben," I drawl, bobbing my head ecstatically.

Though happy for my friend, I can't help but feel a pinch of jealousy, because I haven't felt the bliss of an orgasm in what seems like forever.

"I'm scared," she discloses, and I notice her shivering.

"Of what?"

"Of what comes next. When he wakes up... Is he just going to leave, pretending it never happened? Or worse?"

"Come on, it's Ben. He's been pining over you since freshman year. He waited while you were on and off with Ted the jerk," I remind her, the mention of her ex making her whole face cringe. "He's not gonna leave you!"

A loud moan comes from outside the door, and Emma's whole body stiffens. Never, and I mean never, have I seen her so jumpy. I guess she's human after all. I was starting to have serious doubts.

"Reeeed?" Ben calls out, and Emma's eyes widen.

"Baby, where are you?" His voice comes out all raspy.

"*Baby?*" we both mouth out through a smile. I can see her turning into a puddle. Shrugging her shoulders, she looks at me, and with my nod, she opens the door.

Heart attack - I am going to have a heart attack.

"Dude, please cover your junk!" I scream, covering my eyes.

Delete—Delete—Delete!

Delete the image, mind; I'm begging you...

"Beautiful, isn't it?" I can actually hear the drool in Emma's voice.

"Shit, Red, I thought you left me."

"You are in *my* dorm," she points out, "You know that, right?"

There's a beat of silence, and if I have to guess, it's probably Ben taking in his surroundings.

"Right," is all he says, and I clear my throat, not hearing any movement.

"Dude, clothes, please." My hand is still glued over my eyes.

"Here," Emma yells out, hopefully tossing him something to cover up with.

A minute of silence later, Ben finally says, "Clear." With that, I release my eyes, happy with the sight of a fully dressed, somewhat groggy Ben. He closes in, swooping Emma in with impressive maneuvering. One grab of her neck is all it takes for her to melt into his mouth. It's a PG kind of kiss, but butterflies are undoubtedly flying around the room.

"I need coffee. What time is it?" Ben asks under his breath, his eyes never leaving the sight of Emma's lips.

"Just a little after one," I answer, and he growls.

"Shit, we slept through the day," he whines, "and through breakfast? I fucking love breakfast."

"You can go to Denni's; they serve breakfast all day long," I quip, which seems to get his spirits up. He looks at Emma. "Wanna buy me breakfast, Red?"

"Buy your own damn breakfast!" Just like that—there she is. Guess the scared part got bouldered over.

"Fine, then let me buy you breakfast."

"Much better." She gives him her signature grin, patting the top of his head.

"Coming?" Ben looks at me, and I answer with a head shake. "No, I'll leave you two with your post sex energy, thank you very much."

"Oh shit, we never gave you your present," Emma gasps, looking at me with wide eyes.

"Dang it!" I slap my forehead. "We are terrible friends!"

"Well, since today is my actual birthday, you can give..." Before he can finish, Emma is already rummaging through her room. A couple of seconds later, she hands him a big box.

He goes to the couch, fully clothed. When he opens his present, his jaw drops. A smile so wide appears on his face, showing all his straight white teeth.

"No way. How?" He picks the jersey up, reading the dedication written by the man himself: 'Happy birthday, Ben; looking forward to seeing you play for the NBA, JH.'

"How the hell did you manage to do this?"

Emma jumps in, "It was all Maddie. She has a couple of teams fishing her out, and she nonchalantly mentioned how her best friend had a birthday coming up and is a big fan of Harden."

I shrug. "One of the managers said they were good friends with Coach Lou, so he got it for me."

"I can't believe this, this is..." he trails off.

Emma and I share a look, both happy that we managed to leave him speechless.

"What's this?" he asks when he sees what's at the bottom of the box.

Emma blushes and stutters, like full-on stutters, "It... It's just... I just, uhm..."

Panic strikes, and her eyes scream for me to help her, so I do.

"We wanted to give you something personal, and Emma made that for you. I helped."

"You mean you hovered while I did all the work?"

"Hey. Someone has to do quality control," I retort, and she gives me a side glare. She tries to hide it, but I know she's nervous.

Pulling out the bracelet, he lifts it, turning it around to check each inch, and I swear I can see tears forming in his eyes.

"This is honestly the best thing anyone has ever given me."

Choosing not to disclose how Emma spent two weeks learning how to crochet a man's wristband, I focus on the details, as if seeing them for the first time. It's a simple white and blue armband with our numbers embroidered on it. Ben's a bit bigger than ours. He pulls us both into a hug, his voice cracking, "I am so lucky to have the two of you in my circle."

"We are the lucky ones," I counter.

"Dido," Emma jars, trying hard not to show too much emotion.

"Ok, so breakfast? I'm starving." Emma stands up, and Ben follows.

"You want us to bring you something?"

The smile on Emma's face in response to the "us" part melts me. "Sure, I could go for a croissant."

"Noted, see you later," Ben says, taking Emma's hand before they leave.

Happy with the afterthought of my two best friends starting their story, I toss myself on the bed and enter a fictional one. Two pages in, I fall into dreamland.

Chapter 18

I couldn't wait for Friday. Somehow, that one day became my favorite, most anticipated day of the week. Why? Because of the 10 minutes spent with Tyler. Crazy is not even close to describing the state of my mind. Obviously, I can get his number, ask him out, and end this torture, but there is this invisible force blocking me. So, Friday is all I get—my consolation prize. Ten minutes out of 10,080, and I am breathing for that limited amount of time. Forgetting about the world, the pain, the past, the future... just everything, except the two of us. Those ten minutes give me something to look forward to and make me happy about what's coming, even if they last just 600 seconds. And God, how I need those seconds. Especially since last Friday fell on a national holiday, meaning no classes. Fortunately, my jam-packed schedule worked wonders, and the days just blipped by.

The air around the dance studio shifts the second the doors swing open. Enter Tyler, wearing black basketball shorts paired with a gray sleeveless Nike shirt, showcasing his defined biceps, and sporting a messy hairdo that reveals growth over the two weeks I've been deprived of him.

Lord, almighty.

I think as I gawk at him, striding toward me with those brown eyes, the same eyes I dreamt about every single night. Ms. Lynch has already made her threats and claps, so we are all just waiting for the music to start.

The imprinted spot on my stomach eagerly waits for his touch. My heart stops when I feel his breath in my ear. He gives me a heads-up, something he has been doing ever since our first practice together. I'm not sure if he knows how much that little whisper means to me, what it does to me, but I'm sure my body can't hide the sensation.

With the first beat, we go into our bubble, and when the song finishes, there's an undefinable expression on Ms. Lynch's face. Upon inspection, it seems that she is actually content with the outcome, with us. Is she even capable of that?

"Great job, everybody."

Guess she is.

"Miss Stevens and Mr. Hart, you two especially."

"What do you mean?" I blurt out, my mouth somehow taking control.

"Great job! You two have found a nice rhythm and go very well together; it was flawless."

Is this really happening, or am I dreaming? No way in hell did Ms. Lynch actually give me her praise. For crying out loud, both she and the TA hate my guts. Ok, strictly speaking, the TA does most of the hating, giving out a vibe that's almost always directed at me. On the other hand, I'm not her biggest fan either. She says one thing only to do the opposite, like switching the coreo mid-dance, or misstepping, and even doing some moves on a different beat.

"Thank you." Tyler comes to my rescue with his good manners and an elbow nudge to my ribs.

"Right, thank you," I gasp out, blinking.

"That will be all; you are free to go."

With the sound of her clapping hands, we all take flight. Filling my ears with my earbuds, I cover them with my beanie and head outside into the cold November evening, Emma and Ben in tow. Ben is now a permanent resident in our dorms, and I love having him there. He's good for Emma, and they make each other happy, which makes me the best roommate-slash-friend for sharing her. Slowing my pace to give the couple their 'privacy', I take out my phone and pull up my playlist. But then I hear a familiar voice behind me.

"Wait up, Feisty!"

I hate to admit it, but I really like that nickname.

Turning my right bud off, I look over my shoulder and find Tyler trotting in my direction.

"Mind if I walk with you guys?"

"You do know that we are going in the opposite direction from your dorm, right?"

"Yeah, but I don't want you walking alone at night."

"First of all, it's not even that dark. Second, I am not alone." I point at our friends who are somehow walking and making out at the same time.

"And third, I can take care of myself, thank you very much." I give a bit of a kick to the last part.

"All three are valid points, but you forgot the fourth, which happens to be the most important one."

"And that would be?"

He leans over a bit, then whispers, "I want to."

A minor heart attack occurs, but I recover quickly.

"You want to what exactly?" I bite the inside of my cheek, trying hard not to pull out a smile.

"Walk you home, maybe share some words." He finishes it off by giving me a lopsided smile. Taken completely off guard, I gawk at him, my eyebrows pressed together while my heart keeps jumping up and down, full throttle.

"You know, walking me home is a privilege, something I am not sure you have yet earned."

"Oh, we both know I've earned more than that."

"Cocky now, are we?"

"Right back at 'ya, Feisty, right back at 'ya."

The power his voice has over me makes me want to shatter into pieces.

We start to walk, catching up to the love fest in full PDA.

"I bet you're happy about that." Tyler nudges his chin in their direction, and I can't fight my smile.

"Of course I am, it's been a long time coming."

"Well, good thing you intervened."

"Whatever do you mean?" I bat my lashes, giving my most innocent smile.

"Oh, don't you even dare. Miss Let's-divide-teams-alphabetically," he mocks in a not-so-bad impression of me.

"You caught that, huh?"

"Yeah, but at the time I was hoping it was for my benefit, that was until you called Jones by his first name and shattered all that hope away."

He wanted to be on my team?

Commanding my heart to act cool, I shoo the thought far, far away.

"Sorry I burst your bubble, but there was more at stake than having the best bawler on your team."

"Well, since I have never seen you play before, I can say with all certainty that was not the reason I wanted to be on your team."

Am I blushing? I can't tell over the cold, but it feels like I am blushing.

My side glance catches him shortening his strides to match my tempo, his hands deep in his jacket pockets.

"But I'm not complaining. At least I got a dance out of it." It's a mixture of playful and somewhat flirtatious tone, I sense, right there with his stare.

"We dance every Friday," I point out, but he quickly retorts. "Not like that, and you know it."

His hand goes to my beanie, lifting the side slightly, revealing an earful of bud. I get on the offensive quickly, "I turned it off the second you approached."

I watch in slow motion as he takes it out of my ear and presses the side button, his smile beaming. The small light blinks blue, indicating that the power is on, before he sticks it in his ear, and the current song fades out. Seeing my expression, which probably shows a lot of confusion, he shrugs. "What? I want to hear your soundtrack."

"Soundtrack?"

"Yeah, the songs that make you tick."

"Soundtrack," I repeat in a hushed tone, "I like that." Nodding slowly, I face forward, taking my steps and raking my lower lip.

Never in my life have I cursed on the faiths, or whatever forces rule over the momentum of fortuity. That is, until now.

For reasons unknown to me, something decides to mock me, because as soon as Tyler's ears are free to listen to my playlist, the worst song comes to play. My cheeks blush at the sound of Ava Max singing the opening chorus of 'Into Your Arms' by Witt Lowry. Wishing for the ground to open and swallow me whole, the corner of my eye catches a smirk forming on his face, and all my nerves unsettle at the sight.

"Stop it!"

"Stop what?"

"The smirk. It's a coincidence," I point out, "My phone is in my bag and set on shuffle."

The campus's chilly air does nothing to cool down the rising temperature under my skin.

"I never said it was your doing."

"Then what's with the smirk?"

"Because I believe there is nothing random about this."

I gape at him, ice probing through my eyes.

"You know the eight ball, where you ask a question, and it answers?"

"Yeaaah?" I stretch it out.

"Well, Sabrina does this thing with the radio…"

Just as panic starts to rise at the mention of another girl, he adds, "That's my brother's wife. Anyway, she asks a question, then the song playing answers it."

"That's from One Tree Hill," I reveal, making him skid to a halt.

"What?" His shock is genuine, causing my feet to hit the brakes.

"Yeah, it's from a TV show. Brooke, one of the main characters, does it."

"Oh, Sabrina is never going to hear the end of this." Rubbing his hands, a mischievous grin emerges.

"You are close with your family, aren't you?"

The question comes out of nowhere, but I want to know more about him. I want to know everything, regardless of how heavy the topic may be for me personally.

"Yeah, I have four brothers; we were all fostered."

"You mean adopted?"

"No, I mean fostered. Only one of us could've been adopted - Tristan, the youngest. He refused out of solidarity."

"I don't get it. Why couldn't the rest of you get adopted?" I shudder a bit, like my mouth is scared to ask the question, but Ty starts talking without missing a beat. "We all have family or parents that just didn't want us, and the system doesn't allow adoption without the relinquishment of parental rights. When we all came of age, we legally changed our last names to match our Mama's."

The way his eyes light up at the mention of his mother feels like my lungs are drowning. And the way he said Mama, with so much endearment, makes me want to scream. Guilt comes next, shame follows, and I want to crawl into a hole. There Tyler is, sharing something I asked him about, and what do I do? I get freaking jealous.

Idiot.

Putting on my unemotional mask, I dry my sweaty palms over the fabric of my leggings. One quick inhale is all it takes for my fake smile to emerge.

"So it's just your mom?"

"Yeah. She lost the love of her life back in college and chose to give us all the love she had left."

"Wow, she must be an amazing woman." I swallow a golf ball that keeps materializing in my throat.

"She is all that and so much more. What about your family?"

"You're looking at it." Taking my hand out of the warmth of my pocket, I point to the two people who are rarely coming out for air.

"Would you mind sharing some more?" The softness of his voice feels like a plea, as if he's trying to tell me I'm safe with him, just by his intonation. Even though I am messed up in my head and keep putting up fences, I cross my arms over my chest, holding myself, and give him a piece of me. "Nothing much to share. My father left when I was three, and my mother and I…" I swallow, contemplating how to explain that I have a person who birthed me, but no mother. I drop my head, focusing on the ground. "We don't talk much." My voice cracks at the understatement.

My entire life, my mother has been disconnected. She never truly cared about me. We just coexisted… then I left, never looking back.

"I'm so sorry."

The quiet hum of the world seems to fade as he stops beside me, the sky around us slowly surrendering to dusk. My eyes fall to his hand, the barely noticeable twitch of his fingers, like he's hesitating. Above us, leaves rustle almost as if they're whispering all the things in our heads. My arms drop to my sides, inches apart from his. The distance nearly non-existent. He lets the moment stretch, but I have a feeling it's for my benefit. And then… He moves.

His fingertips brush the back of my hand before he turns

his palm upward beneath mine in silent invitation. My fingers hesitate, just a flicker, then settle into his. Our palms meet with quiet finality, his fingers gently curling around mine, not gripping, but holding. My eyes focus on my responding fingers, intertwining with his until the space between us vanishes. So much is said in this one simple act. Even more is felt. The warmth of his touch is immediate, soft, grounding… Real—a perfect fit.

Chapter 19

Earth stopped moving…

Never in my wildest dreams could I have imagined that a simple act of hand-holding could feel so… life-altering. One touch of reassurance, adding to a moment of stillness, as if the act were made to ground you. The gesture, one I wanted to make for her, is to let her know she's not alone in the world.

I want her to feel it, to hear all the unspoken words.

I'm here.

You matter.

The rise and fall of her chest is my focus; everything around us ceases to exist.

And then the bubble bursts, or rather, Ben pops it. "Yo, Ty! What are you doing here?"

MJ pulls away a bit too quickly, and my hand protests at the loss.

"Seriously, you just now noticed me?" I glare at him. Emma's intense gaze is on us, reading the scene just as 'Let You Love Me' starts playing. MJ looks like she wants to kill Rita Ora, and I fight the urge to mock her for it. I didn't even register that we were at the bottom of the girls' dorm stairs. With a fleeting smile, I take out the little black piece of electric equipment from my ear and place it in MJ's waiting palm.

"So, guess I'll see you next Friday?" There's a query in my question, but before she can decode it, Emma interrupts with a cheer.

"No, you won't. Miss Thang has a meeting with the National team next weekend; she leaves for Colorado on Thursday." The pride in her voice is so loud that it is impossible to miss.

"What?" Ben and I both squeal.

"Yeah, I got the official invitation last month." MJ puffs out her chest.

Ben gives her a high five, but I stand there, hands hidden in my pockets.

Two more weeks, I am in for another two weeks of not seeing her, and it's already killing me.

When I finally do speak, it is with marvel. "Good luck with your meeting, not that you need it."

"Thanks, I guess I'll be seeing ya."

I watch MJ disappear inside, Emma in tow. Ben lingers, a pointed look in place.

"You could ask her out, you know?" he prods.

"She's not ready," I falter, kicking one foot in front of the other.

"And how would you know that?"

"I just do."

It's the truth; she's not ready. I see the hurt in her eyes, and I know I have to build up trust. I have to keep my patience in check, following her pace, waiting for her to be

119

sure. There will be no pushing on my end. The control and the decision are hers and hers alone. No way in hell am I going to jeopardize any of it, no matter how badly I want to, and trust me—I want to. There's something, like a strong voice telling me to be strong for her, to have fortitude. In all honesty, as hard as it is, I know she's worth it. The distance, the waiting, not to mention the temptation; it consumes me, makes me enfeebled.

The way she disclosed the fact about her family, as if it's nothing important, keeps me up most of the night. I could feel the strength of her shield, the wall she had built up around herself for self-protection. I want to be the one to break, to tear it down and smash it to the ground. More than anything, I want to keep her; I want her to be my everything, knowing she already somehow is.

On the cold Sunday morning, I sit on my bed, phone in hand, thumb hovering over the green phone icon. O is the first to answer, Sabrina in his lap, waving. Tristan, Luka, and Mak still live back home, while Mateo moved in with Sabrina at the beginning of the year. I live on campus, but we never miss the scheduled video conference.

"Hi, lovebirds, how are you?"

"We're good, little brother. You?"

"I'm good."

Something hits my chest at the sight of them. Never have two people been more made for each other than those two were from the get-go. The Romeo to his Juliet, without the death part, the Clyde to her Bonny, it was inevitable. Different backgrounds, different upbringings, different lifestyles, total opposites in every way on the outside, but so much alike on the inside. Their love is greater than anything I have seen on screen, better than any story written or read, better than any love song out there, and I crave that kind of love. Not just that, I crave that love with the one person I couldn't get out of my head. The one person who possesses my mind, body, and soul. Drawn to her, I am falling, crashing, burning... She's my breath, everything I can feel, everything I could ever want.

"Oh my god, there's a girl," Sabrina half-cheers, half-screams.

"What? No? What? How do you know?" O stutters, turning his head back and forth between the two of us.

Of the five of us, Mateo and I share actual blood, though it doesn't make any difference. In our heads and hearts, we are all true brothers in every sense of the word.

"Just look at him, there's a glow, the girl kind," she says the last part in a whisper.

"Is it true?" Mateo's eyebrows come together.

"Kind of." I shrug my shoulders, something they can't see since it's just my head in the frame.

"Details, now, I need to know eve—" Sabrina's thoughts are cut off by a new window joining the screen.

"Oh great, there was a glitch; I couldn't click the green thing," Mama yells, her nose zoomed in on the camera.

I swear, every single time.

"Move back, Mama, they can hear and see you from afar. Do we have to go over this every time?" Tristan draws a frustrated breath.

"Hi, Sabrina, sweetie, how are you?"

"I'm great, Eva; you look good."

"Oh, you flatter me."

Sabrina clears her throat, getting everyone's attention. "Guys, we have something to discuss."

Everyone stays quiet, anticipating.

"Tyler is in love," she squeaks.

All eyes, everyone's attention shifts toward me, and I feel my Adam's apple jolt.

Luka covers Mama's ears, and then the ritual starts.

"Hair?" Tristan's question comes first.

"Blond."

"Eyes?" Luka with his usual.

"Blue."

Which leaves Mak. "Mouth?"

I avert my gaze to Sabrina, and she shakes her head, gleaming, "Oh, shit, you want to say something dirty, don't you?"

She looks behind her to where Mateo is trying hard to bite off a laugh right before she hits him in the gut.

"What was the description of my mouth, Babe?"

He covers his face, scrunching down as she pounds him with her hands.

"Say it! Come on, you little wuss, say it," she yells, all the while smacking the top of his head.

"Damn, O, whipped looks good on you," Luka teases. The

second Sabrina turns around, he freezes, dropping his gaze. If there's one thing that scares the hell out of Luka, it's an angry Sabrina.

"Say it," she threatens. We can't see what she's doing to him because her back blocks the view, but from his expression, I think she's twisting his nipple.

"Fine, I said they were fuckable," he utters.

"Oh." She moves away and tilts her head. "Hm, I like that."

And just like that, she turns in his lap, facing the camera. These two are something else.

"Shrek, uncover your mother's ears," Sabrina orders, snapping her fingers.

"Now that was just mean," Mama scolds, shaking her index to the sides. "You do know you don't have to censor me; I have been there, done all of that way before any of you were born."

Tristan shoves his fingers in his ear, singing, "La La La La La, I don't need to hear this."

"Oh, don't be dramatic." Our mother waves her hand in front of him.

Her gray eyes turn to me, "What's her name?"

"Maddison."

"You should bring her for Thanksgiving."

After what I've learned about MJ's family, I like the idea, but don't know how she'll take it.

"We're not together, so I don't know how that would work."

"What do you mean you are not together?" Sabrina shrieks, and I'm pretty sure it bursts my brother's eardrums.

"We're just friends; I think."

"You think? How do you not know if you're friends or not?" Mak gives me a pointed stare from behind his glasses.

"It's complicated; she's not really..." I can't finish, I can't explain any of it, so I drop my head.

"But you like her?" Mateo asks, and I look up with a nod.

"More than that?" This one comes from Mama.

I don't need to elaborate. She can see it in my expression.

"Well, whatever she is, the invitation is open, and I can't wait to see you. Are you eating well?"

"Yes, Mama, I'm eating well. I cook as much as the schedule allows me to."

"Good. I am so proud of you."

"I love you, Mama, all of you."

"Love you," they all said in unison.

"But I love you mostest," Sabrina jumps in, then she rubs her palms together and orders, "Now, let's discuss the week's read, shall we?"

And so we do, we discuss another one of Lee Child's thrillers, and when we end the call, Sabrina stays on the line.

"You're one of the good ones; you know that?"

"What do you mean?"

"You're waiting for her to be ready, aren't you? She was hurt somehow, and you are waiting?" Well, I'll be damned. O is so screwed if she has the ability to read minds like that. Unable to utter a single word, I bob my chin.

"She's a lucky girl."

"Not really, I'm the lucky one here."

"Well, then it's a mutual luck." Sabrina smiles and then

Nothing's fair in Love & Basketball

sends me an air kiss before hanging up.

Chapter 20

How does one explain the feeling of being excited at the same time as being somewhat depressed? For the past week, I've been cooking up these types of emotions, something between jitters for my meeting, and misery over the Tyler withdrawal.

Colorado Springs is cold/er, but I welcome the ice breeze, my every step making the crunching noise over the snow. When it comes to NY, the first snow usually arrives in January, so it's nice to get a taste of it in mid-November. With my meeting set for the late afternoon, I spend the day just taking in the city, trying to imagine myself living here.

When my nose gets beyond frozen, and I can't take the cold any longer, I walk back to the training facilities to snoop around and get the feel of the place.

The gym is state-of-the-art and so big, like three times bigger than the one the Lions share. Two players are inside, spotting each other over a bench press. When I realize who they are, I jump in silence. The number one outside hitter and the best setter on this side of the earth are right there, lifting weights and laughing. They look so normal, like two regular girls, not the best players of the generation. The metallic clang of the weights ceases.

They're waving at me.

Now, they're motioning me to come inside.

WTF do I do?

You go inside and introduce yourself.

So I listen to that little voice and step in, waving my hand before I shy away. "Hi. Sorry to interrupt. I just wanted to snoop around. I'm Maddison." Then the smell hits me, citrus… a lot of citrus in the air. It's beyond me how a gym smells so good, but I take it in, committing it to memory.

"Oh, we know," the setter drawls, "we've seen your tapes, you are fire."

"I am?"

"Well, duh. Anyway… I'm Tessa," the other one stands up, and dang, she is gorgeous - long brown hair, green eyes, and a lot of toned muscles. "We know your story. Is it true that you only trained for three months before making the team?"

"Yeah, I played basketball prior and needed to switch."

"That's amazing, and I'm Lena." The hitter places an elbow on Tessa's shoulder, showing off her height. I have to look up to face her.

"It's nice to meet you both."

I must look scared because Tessa places her hand on my shoulder.

"We're a team here; you have nothing to be nervous about."

"I know it's just…" I take a deep breath before I confess, "I don't know if this is the right move for me."

"Look, full disclosure, you probably won't get much

playing time your first year, but you will acclimate, see how this kind of game works, and then you'll be ready to dominate the court," Tessa speaks with so much reassurance in her tone that it is impossible not to soak the words in. I mean, she is the team captain after all.

"You left out the best part, though," Lena chimes, "we also have fun." Her brows dance while she continues, "We do a lot of bonding on this squad, and I don't mean trust exercises." The two of them share a look, and I giggle like a freaking two-year-old.

Guess I'm a giggler now.

Still, there is something so natural about our interaction.

"Does it involve alcohol?" I probe, and they break into laughter.

"You'll fit right in," Tessa concludes, and I give them a shy smile.

"Any advice?"

"Control what you can," Lena shares her insight first; Tessa finishes, "Resilience matters, don't get cocky, and keep earning your spot."

I thank them with a nod and an honest smile. Looking at my wrist watch, I mumble a curse, not wanting to leave.

"I have to go, but thank you."

"Good luck!" both exclaim, and I walk out, leaving them to it.

Even though I have about twenty minutes left before the meeting, I want some time to clear my head.

That's how I find myself in the practice arena. The place is small, with polished floors that are painted in the colors of the nation, surrounded by red walls. There are no bleachers, no seats, just walls that somehow look like they are closing in. I can't shake this feeling, can't help but wonder if this is where I belong.

Playing for the big leagues was once the goal, and even the Olympics made it onto the dream board. Alas, all those hopes and dreams got squashed. After all, my life does like to bite me in the ass daily. Mulling it over, I find doubts overshadowing my thoughts. I feel like an outsider; the sense of not belonging overpowers everything, and I need to take control of it… I need it gone. Phone in hand, my fingers do my bidding, typing out, then deleting. It takes about four tries, but I finally hit send.

Me: *Hi. I got your number from Ben. I hope that's ok?*

My foot taps nervously, waiting, anticipating. I smack my forehead when I realize I forgot to sign my name. And just as I unlock the screen, my phone vibrates.

7: *Hi, Feisty. Perfect timing, I was just about to send you a good luck text.*

How did he know it was me? Did he already have my number? Is my heart beating? I can't tell.

Me: *You were?*

7: *Of course I was! Today's a big day for you, and I wanted to give you a boost*

Me: *I'm scared*

The dots come and go, then return, only to disappear again. Then, my phone rings, displaying Tyler's name on the caller ID. I blink. My heart somersaults. I blink again. I answer. Blink, then the world goes quiet, singling out his husky voice.

"Sorry, I just thought this was a phone call kind of conversation."

"Ok," I mutter, wishing I could see his face.

"What are you scared of?"

"I don't know, this is all wrong. I don't think that I belong here," I admit, my heart racing.

"Of course, you don't belong there, because you belong here. But come next summer, you will belong, you will own that place." The way he says it, so sure and confident, makes me believe him. I play with my pendants, rubbing them between my fingers.

"How can you be so sure?"

"Hey. Where's the Feisty MJ we know and love?"

"Hiding," I murmur. His chuckle reverberates over the speaker, the vibration going straight to my toes.

"Well, tell her to stop hiding. Tell her that she earned it, she worked hard, and she deserves to be there."

I shrug my shoulders, staying silent, not even realizing he can't see it.

"MJ?"

"Yeah?"

"What's this really about?"

"I don't know…" I sigh, "The truth is, I never saw myself

here; I saw myself in the adjoining building."

"That can still happen, you know? It's all up to you."

Is it a possibility for me? It has been so long, and I have nothing to show for the time lost. Swallowing the lump, not allowing it to grow any bigger, I walk through the big hallway and stop before the double door. When I swing it open, I am instantly hit by the smell of wood polish. And just like that, it all clicks into place.

"My God, Tyler... You should see this place; it's..." I trail off, trying to find the right word, taking more steps, and looking around.

"Like home?"

"Exactly," I gasp, feeling the pumping in my chest intensify.

"Look, whatever you decide, you know that you have all of us here. We will support you no matter what, but please do me a favor..."

"What?"

"Don't think with your head; follow your heart."

"I don't know how to do that, don't think I got one." I try to pass it off as all playful, but the crack in my voice is audible.

"Considering I felt it beating, I'm pretty sure you have one hell of a heart."

Well, that settles it. I am doomed. The way my body reacts to his voice, his words, the raspy breaths he takes... It sends me into shock. I feel like I can fly, knowing the distance of the fall. Still, I trust him so much that I don't need a safety net.

"Thank you."

"No problem."

Wanting to keep the conversation going, I blurt out the first thing that pops into my head. "So what are you up to?"

"I am just walking to practice," he pants.

"Oh, sorry, I didn't mean to..." Before I can finish apologizing, he cuts me off. "You're not. I still have about five minutes, and I want to spend each talking to you."

Can a person suffer from a heart attack after hearing something so soul-stirring?

"Well, I can't think of a better way to spend mine."

There's a pause, no sound on the other end, but the weight of a grin is there. I close my eyes, trying to picture it. God, I wish I could see it.

"You're smiling, aren't you?"

I shake my head when I notice I've crossed my fingers, as it would somehow affect his answer.

"Ear to ear, Feisty, ear to ear."

I press my phone closer, focusing on the sound of his breathing.

"You always go quiet when you're trying not to laugh."

No, I don't.

Before I can voice my protest, he chirps, "You've got that look. I can feel it."

"What look?"

"The *no I don't* one."

How does he know that?

"Anyway, as much as I want to prove you wrong, we both have places to be."

I check the time. It flew by.

"Right. Well, thanks for the boost."

"My pleasure. And Feisty?"

"Yeah?"

"Your heart is your biggest weapon; use it, trust it. You got this."

"I got this," I repeat, lingering. Three breaths later, I hang up, his words playing on repeat.

Follow your heart.

World - meet my new mantra.

Chapter 21

During practice, I was flying. Hearing MJ's voice and having a conversation with her felt like I was on cloud nine. My feet were quick, and my hands handled the ball precisely as I wanted, maneuvering each dribble with ease. The feeling kept me on a high during the entire practice, only to knock me down when I got to dance class. Dancing without her was a special kind of torture, one I never wanted to experience again. My hands felt empty, my feet felt out of place, and my mind was anywhere with her instead of here without her.

"Ok, that was great. Casey?" Ms. Lynch snaps her fingers to her TA. "You do the next round with Mr. Hart here."

Something wrenching happens deep in my gut as I look at the TA closing in on me. She steps before me, taking MJ's place, and it is all kinds of wrong.

Casey is a senior, a beautiful, tall dance major, wearing pink tights and a matching top that reveals too much skin for comfort. The tone of her skin is not peachy, her hair is not blonde, and she smells all wrong. I hold my breath, trying to trick my mind into somehow manifesting the cherries, but fail.

Keeping my distance, I leave my hand hanging, only for it

to be taken by the TA, who then places it on her stomach. Even my palm feels the discomfort. I am sure my face pales with unease.

Just as the music starts and we move to take the first step, a loud thud echoes in the studio.

"Oh my God, Red, are you ok? What happened?"

I can hear Ben yell. Then I see him tearing through the crowd to Emma's side. He slides his hand under her and picks her up, bridal style, in a quick swoop.

"I'm fine; the room was spinning."

"Ok, let's call it a day, kids, leave Miss Banks some breathing room."

I come to their side just as Ben settles her on her feet. She straightens her posture, dusts herself off, and runs a hand through her red hair. Then she winks at me. I gawk at her, confused. Passing me by, she whispers so that only I can hear, "You owe me big time." It hits me then - she faked it to save me—one hell of a friend, that one. I mouth a thank you, and she gives me another wink, making it our little secret.

On my walk back to my room, I pull out my phone and type out a text.

Me: *How did it go?*

Nothing. A minute later, still nothing. Ten minutes later, I enter my room and still nothing. Twenty pages of the second half of the book and—you guessed it—still nothing. An eternity later, my phone chimes and I jump up. Fine, it was only an hour, not an actual eternity.

Feisty: *Sorry, it lasted longer than I thought it would. Can I call you when I get to my room? In about fifteen minutes?*

Me: *Sure, I'll be here*

My eyes are glued to the digital alarm clock on my nightstand, counting down the minutes, seconds, milliseconds… When my phone rings, thirteen minutes later, I sit up and steady my breath before I answer on the second ring.

"Hi."

"Hi."

God, I've missed her voice.

"So how did it go?"

"It was…" she pauses, "interesting."

"I'm kind of gonna need more than that, Feisty."

"I met the whole team, and they were great; taller and so much more intimidating in person, but kind and nice, a real team."

"Sounds great."

"The director offered me a four-year contract if I finish the summer boot camp."

"So… you'd get to play for the Olympics?"

"Yeah, if I make it through?"

"That's a non-issue if it is something you want." Although I didn't phrase it as a question, I still want her to bite. She doesn't.

"I told them I needed more time to decide."

"Smart."

"They gave me until the end of the year, so I guess it leaves me enough time to brainstorm."

"No brainstorming, heart-storming."

She chuckles, and I melt at the sound.

"That is not a thing," she rebuts, and I hear rustling in the background.

"Well, I am making it a thing."

Another pause, a long sigh, followed by a quick throat clear.

"I asked them about basketball."

My heart skips a beat at that, and my knee starts to shake nervously.

"And?" I drawl.

"They said I have time to make a name and build a strong profile, that I am still young." She sighs, "No guarantees, though."

"There's never a guarantee."

I hear a squeaking sound, then water running, ending with the same squeaking sound again. I imagine her washing her hands in her room, getting dressed for bed, and I get hard at the mere thought. There's a creaking sound that I can only assume is her getting into bed, followed by a loud exhale.

"I don't want to let volleyball go."

"What's holding you back from doing both?"

"I never even thought about it. Could I?"

I can hear the uncertainty in her voice, and I want to wipe her doubts away. It amazes me how she dominates the court, only to become a shell of herself whenever she is off it.

"Why not? Anything is possible if you just believe."

"Did you just quote 'A Cinderella Story'?" Her snicker

ends with a snort, and I can't hold in my laugh.

"Maybe"

"Didn't peg you for a rom-com guy?"

Now that's a lie, and she knows it.

"You're a terrible liar."

I know there's an eye roll on the other end of the line.

"I mean it, though. If anybody can do it, you can. And if you need someone to train with or stand there and pass you the ball, I volunteer as tribute."

That earns me another chuckle.

"Thank you, seriously. For everything. For listening while I babble, for being there, for..." she wavers, "You know?"

"I know. And no thanks necessary. I like your babble, and I like being there. I like *you*, period."

Silence. Nothing on the other line. I have to check if the call is still ongoing—it is.

Shit. I spooked her, didn't I?

I should not have said that.

No! Fuck it, it's done, and it's out there, in the universe.

"I like you too."

Oh, thank you, Morgan Freeman.

My heart races, and I fear it will explode.

Then I sense it, the hesitation.

"I feel a 'but' coming?"

"It's just that..."

"You don't want to like me," I cut her off.

Not knowing her story is taking its toll right now, but I have to keep my head in the game. Not that this is a game. It's a serious matter, and I respect it. I do. It's just that I want to do more, but I don't know how, and it's killing me.

"It's not like that..."

"Don't worry, I get it. I really do."

She needs more time. I know she's fighting the connection, no matter how obvious it is. So I swallow all the words I desperately want to say, knowing they would scare her away.

It's ok. I'm here—waiting. Patiently.

Chapter 22

I like you.

He said it. I said it. And then I practically took it back. What's wrong with me? Two crucial parts of me are at war right now. It's like my body is trying to decide whether to have a stroke or a heart attack. One thing's for sure: hurt is inevitable.

"What's Colorado like?"

Thankful for the gear switch, I release a breath and relax my shoulders. He still wants to talk to me.

"Cold, there's snow and a lot of it here." I smile, looking out the window to see small flakes flying around in the air.

"You like snow?"

"I like everything nature gives me."

"Well, color me wooed," he gushes, and my heart skips a couple of beats.

We are definitely turning toward the heart attack lane.

"Seen anything interesting?"

"I mostly walked around the training center. My camera roll went into overdrive."

"I bet. What was your favorite part?"

"The Gift Shop."

He snickers, and my stomach gets all tingly.

"Don't laugh. I spent way too much money."

Meaning I'm banned from bookstores for the foreseeable future.

"Got me anything?"

Yes.

He's the reason I went inside in the first place. Emma will kill me if she ever finds out she was not at the top of my priority list. I sure as hell can't admit that to him, so I chicken out.

"I got everyone a little keepsake."

Then, he chuckles. And it isn't your regular chuckle... It's the '*I call bullshit*' one. Choosing to rise above it, I go on with my itinerary.

"Tomorrow, Coach is taking me to see the Garden of the Gods, and I'm excited about it."

She invited herself, ignoring my every protest. In doing so, she also missed our game, leaving our team in the capable hands of our assistant coach. I'm beyond grateful for her support, even if sometimes I feel like I don't deserve it.

"Random question. What's your go-to ice cream flavor?"

"Don't mock, but it's vanilla."

"Why?"

"I recall specifically saying not to mock."

"I'm not; I genuinely wanna know." The sincerity in his voice is loud and clear, and it spikes up my body temperature.

"Vanilla is underrated."

"Please do elaborate."

"Just think about it. It's the only flavor that is always

gonna be good, whether it's from some gold star Gelateria…"
I do my best Italian accent, shaking my hand with my
fingertips pinched together… "or a dumpster ice cream shop."

"Puf," he makes the explosion noise. "Mind officially
blown."

"You're welcome."

"What if you happen to find yourself in the best ice cream
shop in the world? What flavor would you get?"

"If they have it, Double Trouble."

"What's that?"

"Brownie and cookie dough."

"Never tried it."

"Well, you should. Every time I eat it, I feel like a
mischievous kid."

The memory of my grandma baking flashes by, and a
smile creeps up. My mother never baked or cooked, so my
nana filled that void. She also taught me how to make my
favorite food.

"Sneaking, stealing the sourdough, licking the spoon?"

It never ceases to amaze me how he gets me,
understands me like it's second nature to him.

"Exactly, you get it. What's your go-to flavor?"

"Mint chocolate chip."

"Of course it is," I sneer, and he turns on the offense.

"What?"

"Nothing. I listen and don't judge."

"Hey, there is nothing wrong with having nice breath."

And now his breath is all I can think about. Great, just
what I needed.

"When's your flight back?"

"Sunday morning."

"Are you alone there?"

"Yeah, I got my own room."

"You don't mind it, do you? Being alone?"

"I spent most of my life alone, so I'm pretty used to it." I shrug, knowing he can't see me, but it is more for my benefit. Being alone is a comfort that never makes me feel lonely.

"Shit, sorry." There's no pity in his voice, and I appreciate it.

"Nothing to be sorry about; I had books keeping me company."

"What are you reading now?"

"It's called 'Torment', the fourth book in a series. I thought every book was a standalone, but I fucked up. It turns out that the first four books are about the same couple, while the last two are about a different one. So it was hard not to binge one after the other."

I take in a breath, since I didn't inhale throughout that whole babble.

Dial it down, MJ, you're going to scare the guy away.

"That's intense."

Tell me about it. Still, the series is addictive, the reason why I'm lacking sleep.

"Yeah, what are you reading?"

"The newest from Lee Child."

"I haven't read any of his books yet, but he's on my list,"

"If you want, I have all the physical copies. I can lend them to you," he offers, and for the life of me, I don't know why the space between my thighs starts to throb.

"That would be amazing," I gush, "thank you."

"Don't mention it," he deadpans, then inquires, "So what's your book about?"

God, why is that so sexy? A man wanting to talk about books?

"Well, it's about next-door neighbors who torment each other, trying to mask the love."

"Classic."

"He comes from a mobster family and fights illegally to keep his mom safe. So they get together; he almost dies, she almost dies—it's suspenseful."

"Naturally," he comments in a bit of a teasing tone.

"So after the near-death experience, they decide to run away together, but she finds him in bed with someone else, and she runs away with her best friend to Ireland."

"Sounds about right."

"Are you mocking me?"

"Not at all, keep going."

"You sure?"

"You know the answer to that."

The flutter in my stomach is untameable, a reminder I don't wish to restrain. Not when it comes to Tyler.

"Ok, so the first book ended when she left, and the second book is eight years later."

"When they meet again," he jumps in.

"You know it. So she ran away, and he went to prison. Right, sorry, I never mentioned that." And so I babble on and on about everything that happened in books two and three.

"Ok, I need to know what happens next. Mind reading out loud for me?"

"You want me to read to you over the phone?"

"Well, I'd rather listen to you in person, but I'll settle for this," he slurs, and my cheeks blush.

"It's just weird," I confess as I start to sweat for some reason.

"Why?"

"Because… That's a lot of my voice."

"I happen to like your voice, so it works for me."

This person holds the record for raising the hairs on my body. I lost count of how many times his voice has given me goosebumps.

"You're weird," I blurt out.

"And I own it. Now open your Kindle and read."

"How'd you know I'm reading on my Kindle?"

"Because you don't have any space left on your shelves," he says, and my heart warms. The way he's so observant about me gives me chills, the good kind.

"It was a gift from the team when I was made captain."

"Smart team you've got there."

I can't help my giggle. I'm sure he hears it even though I tried to cover it. I want to keep talking to him; I want him to stay on the line… to be there. Always.

"Come on, Feisty, read to me."

Fuck me, that's hot.

Getting under the blanket of my hotel bed, I take out my Kindle and start reading out loud, while he listens. It takes way too much effort to steady my voice, not to mention my heartbeat. Something about this feels intimate. It's the closest thing to the dreams I have of us reading together, me wrapped in his arms. And even though he's miles away, it feels like he is right beside me.

Every once in a while, he asks me to clarify something he didn't understand because it was mentioned in the previous books. He listens to every word I say, read, and some I even think of.

When I wake up in the middle of the night, my Kindle is off, my phone is still counting the minutes of the ongoing conversation, and the sound of Tyler's cute, barely audible snore pierces through the speaker.

I bored him to sleep

I lower my head onto the pillow and place my phone next to me, then I go back to sleep with his snores for a lullaby.

Chapter 23

In all my twenty-one years on this earth, I don't think I have ever talked to someone as much as I did in one night with MJ. The way she lost herself while reading aloud to me, not even realizing I was on the other line, made me want to invent teleportation. There was something about how she felt the words that made me desperate to see her expression. When she finished the book, we both fell asleep without commenting, and I have never slept better. I could hear her breathing through the speaker, my phone set on the loudest setting for the full effect. I spent the night wishing I was next to her... that I could touch her, feel her, kiss her.

She's not ready, and she refuses to confront her feelings. The same feelings that make me hers, wholly, desperately—hers.

When I wake up in the morning, it's next to my dead phone. I curse the battery life, then myself for not plugging it in. I hope she won't think it was me who disconnected on purpose. Okay, I'm being oversensitive right now, and it doesn't sit well with me. Ben was right; I am whipped without even being whipped. My whip has no owner, but she owns my heart.

Dammit, there I go again.

There's an inner discussion between the badass in me and the lovesick puppy, and somehow the latter is winning. And I allowed it—me...

Shit.

I get up, toss a shirt on, and go to the bathroom to brush my teeth when my phone pings.

Feisty: *Thanks for last night.*

I reread the text twenty times. Nothing special, it's nothing special, and yet it feels like so much more. Naturally, I see it as a sign. I have a question at the ready, just hovering above my head, and it's time to set it free.

I look at my reflection, pump myself up, and press the dial button.

"Hello?" She sounds surprised.

"Hey, what are you doing for Thanksgiving?"

Yup, I just went for it. Straight up.

"What?"

"Thanksgiving? Any plans?"

There's a pause filled with a long hum.

"Uhm... I was thinking about pulling out an extra shift. My boss always pays extra on the holidays."

"Wait. I've known you for over a month now. How come I didn't know you worked?"

"Never came up, I guess."

"Where do you work?"

"A diner in Brooklyn."

"How do you do it all?"

"Barely. But I've got a good boss and mostly work during the week, so I have weekends off to recover."

I'm at a loss for words. Honestly, she might be an actual superhuman.

I cross my middle finger over my index for good luck and go for it.

"Would you like to come with me to Boston?"

"Boston? What?" I can hear the confusion in her voice, but there's something else there. Excitement, maybe?

"Thanksgiving, come spend it with my family and me."

Say yes. Say yes.

I have to be very careful not to push too hard.

"I don't need your pity," she hisses, causing my breath to hitch.

I run my fingers through my hair, trying to smooth out the strays.

"Do you honestly think that's why I'm asking?"

A short beat, then a whispered, "No."

"Good. Now what do you say?"

"Oh, I don't know, uhm—it'll be weird, right?"

"Not any less weird than spending it alone."

"I'm not," she counters, but I know better. Ben told me Emma is going somewhere with her family, and I'm pretty sure MJ won't be spending the holiday with her mother.

"Don't lie, not to me, ok?"

I open the drawer in my nightstand and take out my earbuds.

"How do you do it? Even over the phone?"

"The same way you do it," I reply through a snicker.

"You're better at it."

That's debatable. Our souls know one another, and I honestly feel like we're written in the stars.

"Agree to disagree."

"What will your family think?"

My family will love you—is what I want to say, but take a different approach.

"It was my mother's idea."

"You told her about me?" she stammers, like she can't believe I'd do such a thing.

"Yeah, I tell her everything."

She mumbles something I couldn't quite hear, but I don't ask her to repeat it. It sounded like she was telling it to herself, anyway.

"Look. My Mama is a mean cook. My brothers are fun, mostly, and Sabrina is cool. Don't read too much into it. It's just a friend inviting a friend to Thanksgiving."

My body cringes; the word tastes sour, bitter... wrong.

There's a moment of silence, her breathing being the only thing I can hear. Then it stops. I press my phone between my shoulder and ear so I can put on my pants.

"I'll think about it."

"Good enough for me."

It feels like a win in my book.

I retrieve my bag from under the bed and start tossing in my towel, bottle, new socks, and my jersey.

"You ready for the game?"

I remember Ben and Colt telling me how she keeps up with the score and stats and how much she supports the team. I wonder if I am now a part of that whole thing.

"Yeah, we're pretty confident."

We are playing the Bears, and they are next to last, so we're more cocky than usual about the game.

"I heard Brown got a new center; supposedly, he's good."

"He's got nothing on Jones."

Jones is a fantastic player, third-ranked in the league, and he's only a freshman.

"True. True. Still. You all might want to prepare yourselves."

"Don't worry, captain, we've got our heads in the game."

"I have no doubt," she chortles.

"Sure sounds like you do," I say sarcastically.

"Full disclosure, even though you only have four games behind you, the team has improved. Like a lot."

"Want to add something there?"

"Remove the smirk, and maybe I will."

"Consider it removed," I lie.

"I still hear it."

"No, you don't."

"I do, it's right there, pursed a bit more on the right."

Biting my inner cheek, I fight the urge to giggle like a schoolgirl.

"Keeping tabs on my lips?"

"No," she snorts through a huff.

"Come on, Feisty, just say it. My ego won't implode... that much."

"Fine. The team has improved since you joined the roster."

At that, my chest puffs out, and I pat myself on the shoulder.

"Now, was that so hard?"

"You have no idea."

I just know she's shaking that beautiful head of hers.

"I think you'll be just fine."

"I'm not so sure. I think I flatlined for a minute."

And I've been flatlining ever since I first saw you.

My knees weaken at the thought, but I swallow the words. Then I hear a knock on the other side of the line.

"That's Coach. Sorry to cut this short, but I have to go explore the city."

"Have fun."

"You too, and good luck at your game."

"Thanks. Oh, and MJ?"

"Yeah?"

"Thanksgiving, think about it."

"I will. Bye."

That's all I ask.

"Bye."

There's a long beat of silence, neither of us hanging up. Another knock, and the line goes dead. The fact that she lingered, even if just for a moment, speaks louder than any words could.

She's getting there.

Chapter 24

"You were missed. We could've used your pep talk when it got heated in the third set," Kate speaks first, stretching her neck. We're in the middle of our warm-up before practice officially starts. The girls caught me up on the game I missed while in Colorado, and even though I watched the live stream, no footage could capture the chemistry or the vibe.

"Guys, you were amazing. It was beautiful to watch."

It was my first missed game ever, and watching my team play without me was unsettling, to put it mildly.

"Did you watch the guy's game?" Emma asks enthusiastically.

When I got back from Colorado, I was ambushed by a very motivated Emma who sped me up on everything I had missed. The disclosure that Tyler got rattled when paired with the TA in dance class was by far my favorite story. The second one was Emma saving his ass. I was now officially in her debt, one she'll cash in soon, no doubt about it.

"No, I wanted the first one to be a live one." I get on the line next to them and start stretching.

"What? You're going to a basketball game?" Kate shrieks.

"Yeah, I lost a bet, so I kind of have to..." I say with a noncommittal shrug.

"But she also wants to," Emma points out, her brows dancing up and down.

"Is that true?" Kate gawks at me, stretching her upper arm.

"Yeah, it's true." I start rotating my shoulders, and the girls follow suit.

"Oh my God, this is huge," Kate howls right before she and Emma start clapping and jumping.

"No, it's not. Let's not make a big deal out of it, please," I beg, snapping looks between them.

"Dude, you can say whatever you want, but it *so* is a big deal." Emma places her hands on her hips with a pointed look to match.

"If you make a production out of this, I will not go, mark my words." I raise a finger in threat.

"Ok, cap, ok." Kate waves an imaginary flag. "Calm down, sheesh."

The whistle echoes through the gym, causing us all to freeze momentarily. We are in so much trouble.

"You three on the line!" Coach points her finger between the three of us, and we jolt to the outline. The usual punishment for talking during practice are suicides, so we already know the drill. The whistle blows, and we sprint. The sound of sneakers squealing against the wood reverberates through the gym. My heart pounds in my ears as I touch the far line and pivot, legs burning already. Emma is right behind me, pushing hard, arms pumping. We run three sets, then four. Coach watches us like a hawk, clipboard under her arm, eyes never leaving the court.

When the final whistle blows, we all stumble into loose formation, red-faced and gasping. Kate keeps her hands on her hips, forcing her chest to stay open, and I know her lungs are screaming, just like mine.

"Give me five laps," Coach says before the whistle. With me up front, we start the slow jog over the out line, a snake forming behind me.

With every lap, I increase the speed; the girls follow, every step in perfect unison.

"You want endurance on game day? Then earn it now!" Coach barks, and we sprint the last lap.

"Water break," Coach shouts, and half the team bolts. Emma walks instead, slow and steady, grabbing her bottle and gulping like it's the first drink she's had in a week.

Practice goes on… The team keeps moving, ball after ball, dig after dig, as the sun sinks lower outside. Light from the tall windows cuts golden lines across the gym floor. We're all tired, sore, and sweating through our T-shirts, but no one dares to stop. Because that's what we do; this is how we get better. And as I'm standing in the center of it all, I take a mental picture.

After practice, I take a shower and rush to work, arriving two minutes late after the girls in the locker room interrogated me about everything Colorado.

"Sorry I'm late," I gush, trying to catch my breath. Tessa is on the counter writing off last week's checks, just like she has been doing every Monday since before I started working here. Tessa is a strong-willed, warm-hearted woman in her late forties. Her wavy black hair is pulled up in a messy bun, with a few grays peeking through. Her face is that of a beauty in her thirties, and every woman who comes through this place wants to know her secret. She once told me that it was all about the water; that she doesn't use anything, no creams, no facial care, nothing, just pure H2O. Beautiful light green eyes and full reddish lips rounded her pointy nose, all framed with a square face. She is beautiful inside and out. One sad thing about Tessa and Ian is that they were not blessed with children of their own. Still, she kept her faith and made the restaurant her baby. They both give back to the community, providing free food every Tuesday to those who cannot afford it and sending their signature pies to the nearby shelter.

"Oh, honey, it has barely been a minute. Anyway, the evening rush still hasn't started, so take your time." Tessa waves her hand and gets back to writing, and I go to the staff room to change. This week I am working with Lisa. She's one of the quiet ones, so we never exchange many words and usually stick to our sides. The vibration of my phone in my pocket gets all the jitters going. Taking out the phone, my smile is instant when I see his name.

7: *What have you done to me?*

Me: *Care to be more specific?*

7: *Noah and Teagan, I'm deep into book 1*

Oh my God, oh my God, oh my God!
Breathe, dude, just breathe.

Me: *You hooked?*

7: *Understatement*

Me: *Well, happy to be a bad influence on you. Enjoy the book. I have to get to work.*

Placing my phone in my bag, I close my locker with the biggest smile. He's reading the book that leads to the one I read to him out loud over the phone two nights ago.

The entire shift I'm flying. Honestly, I don't think the tables have ever been this shiny because I keep polishing them over and over, daydreaming about Tyler; beaming.

An hour later, we're in full rush mode.

The bell above the door jingles for the seventh time in twenty minutes, and my feet ache like I've been walking barefoot on broken glass. The stain from bacon grease clings to my apron, and there's syrup on the bottom from a spill that happened an hour ago. It was an accident; a toddler knocked over the bottle. His mother kept apologizing, but I kept saying it was nothing, giving them an honest smile. When I finished cleaning up their table, I ruffled the little boy's hair playfully, and he giggled.

The place is alive with its usual hum: silverware clinking, the old jukebox in the corner playing Dolly Parton through the static.

"Table six needs a refill," Lisa barks, not looking up from the chaos behind the counter.

"I've got it," I call back, grabbing the coffee pot and weaving between tables like a tightrope walker.

At the end of the shift, Lisa and I count our tip jar and split our winnings, both satisfied with the amount. I rub my sore shoulder as I take my steps to my locker. It takes more effort than usual to change, but I manage to do so. I shove the dirty clothes into my bag, take out my earbuds, and stuff them into their respective holes. When I pull out my phone, I forget how to breathe upon seeing the notification.

7: *Just to let you know my progress... Started the second book, one chapter in already*

Somehow, my smile grows even bigger; the muscles in my cheeks can barely handle it. I open my Spotify playlist, press play, and start typing.

Me: *Progress report?*

The three dots appear the second I send out the text, making me giddy, and I wonder if he has been waiting for my reply. I am too tired to walk, so I get to the bus station and wait. The bell chimes with a side of vibration, and my insides explode.

7: *Halfway through, right about where Noah confesses what Reese has done*

Knowing what's about to happen in the book, I start wondering how guys react to reading spicy scenes. The bus pulls to a stop, and I get in. With a variety of seat choices at my disposal, I opt for the window seat at the far back.

'Number 1' by Nico Santos drums in my ear as I wait eagerly for the next little ping.

7: *I'm blushing now*

My cheeks reciprocate, and I quickly reply.

Me: *I was just about to warn you*

I look at the city lights blurring out in passing. This city never ceases to amaze me. How alive it is at any given hour.

7: *These two are crazy*

Me: *Understatement ;P*

7: *You got home ok?*

Something strange forms in my chest. It's a simple question, probably a passing thought, but to me… It's everything. Growing up, I never had anyone keeping tabs on me, so I don't even know what to think about Tyler's thoughtfulness.

Me: *Not yet. Two stops away.*

7: *Are you tired?*

Yes. So freaking tired, but I don't care. My finger hovers above the phone icon, but the bastard chickens out.

Me: *A bit. It was a heavy shift. Mondays are usually packed. I think I'll start snoring after a couple of pages.*

7: *Are you reading now?*

Me: *No, I need a shower first. I think I have noodles stuck in my hair.*

7: *I didn't need that visual*

Me: *Ha ha, very funny.*

7: *What happened?*

Me: *Food fight between a mother and a very frustrated toddler*

7: *You got in the crossfire?*

Me: *More like I tried to intervene, making the kid angrier*

7: *What did he do?*

Me: *It was a girl, and she made a ball of spaghetti and tossed it in my face.*

7: *Shit*

I send him a photo of the chunk of my hair with spaghetti

straps glued on.

7: *My new screen saver*

Me: *Be my guest. No one can tell that's me*

7: *True. And that was mean, by the way.*

Me: *What was?*

7: *Sending me a photo without your beautiful face in it*

I dropped dead for a second there.

He thinks I'm beautiful?

And why is my chest burning right now?

I don't respond, having a shortage of words. So, I get home, take a shower, and fall asleep rereading his last text.

In the morning, I wake up to another one. The same thing happens every day of the week. It's a simple 'Good morning, hope you have a great day' text. I reply with the same sentiment.

By the time Friday comes, I am over-pumped to finally see the man who occupies the entire thread of messages. One quick peek at his last text lights up my whole world. I can't contain the butterflies.

7: *See you later, I'll be the one with the biggest smile*

Chapter 25

Texting with MJ on a daily basis is a whole mood for me. This girl challenges me, makes me laugh, think, and question everything. There are muscles on my face that I've never used before, and they hurt from all the smiling, making me feel like a stupid teenager falling off cloud nine.

Through our thread, I've learned that she is good with numbers, majors in statistics and data science, and hopes to one day become a sports statistical analyst—slash —agent. The idea came to her after watching Moneyball. She guessed on her first try that I'm a Kinesiology major. I had trouble believing she hadn't fished out the information before our exchange. She denied it, and I was forced into letting it go. She broke her first bone when she was 3, falling from a tree—the femur. I never broke a bone, but had a couple of wrist fractures in my early basketball days. Her favorite movie is 'Now and Then', which I find endearing, and she laughed my ear off when I told her mine is 'Little Rascals'.

I learned her favorite song is Kelly Clarkson's 'Breakaway', and I revealed mine to be 'M.O.M' by Will Roush, which is pretty much the same song if you think about it as much as I have.

When Friday finally came, and she was back in my arms, everything was right with the world. The choreography was the same, the song never changed, but something was different. There was a new vibe between us, a shift in her behavior.

"The TA keeps eying me," MJ whispers over her shoulder, "She's totally giving me the death stare."

"I think you're imagining things," I lie through my teeth. She is, in fact, giving her the kill eyes.

"Maybe I should fake an injury so she gets to dance with you," MJ tweets, and every part of me stiffens.

"So you've heard?"

"Whatever do you mean?" she mocks, trying hard to contain her laugh.

"I didn't peg you for a rude one, Feisty."

"But seriously, I am fearing for my life now."

"Don't worry; I'll keep you safe." I press my palm on her stomach harder to prove my point.

"Aaaaaaaa, my hero. Let me return the favor." With mischief in her voice, she lifts her finger and opens her mouth, but I close it shut, whispering in her ear, "Don't you dare." She giggles in my palm, and I can feel the vibration she makes as her body shakes through the laugh. Then, without warning, she bites my skin, making me yelp, "Auch, what the fuck!?"

"Mr. Hart! Miss Stevens! What do you think you're doing?"

Bowing our heads, we both utter, "Sorry, Ms. Lynch."

"Don't make me separate you, nearly a month before the

big event."

My whole body tenses up at her threat, and by the look on MJ's face, she has the same reaction. She wants to dance with me just as much as I want to with her.

"Sorry, Ms. Lynch, it won't happen again," MJ gasps out, locking eyes with one angry dance professor.

"Final warning, you two." She does the two fingers in the eyes thing, turning them to us, then back, letting us know she's watching us.

"Yes, Ms. Lynch," we say together on cue.

Getting back to the routine, we stay perfectly civil and silent. Three repeats later, we're dismissed, Ms. Lynch giving us one last 'watch yourselves' glance.

The studio smells like a mix of sweat and soap. I yank my shirt over my head and toss it into my bag—missing the shot. And I am supposed to be the star shooting guard.

Fuck.

"Bro, what's the hurry?" Colt asks, sprawled across the floor like he has nowhere better to be

"Places to go, people to see," I mutter, digging through my duffel. My good shirt is crumpled at the bottom, wrinkled as hell, but I don't care. I shake it out, sniff it - it's passable. Finger-combing my hair into something vaguely normal, I scan the room. MJ's already gone.

I run out of the building, catching up to the well-known trio. Emma and Ben are walking in front of MJ, holding hands, and MJ bobs her head with each step she takes behind them. Suddenly, she slows down, like she's sensing me coming. The next thing she does makes my heart jolt to my throat, a well-known reaction... She takes out her right earbud and extends her hand, holding it out for me. I run to her, take the offered bud, and shove it in my ear, joining her side.

A song I've never heard before starts to play, and I tune in, fully focused. Every once in a while, I turn to look at MJ to find her focused on the path ahead, mouthing the words. I can't shake the feeling that this song's important, like she's trying to tell me something with it. So I store the lyrics about distance that grows and silence that remains, so I can Google them later.

When the song fades out, it's replaced by an upbeat sound of Mark Ambor's 'Belong Together'. Now that's some poetic justice right there, the universe paying her back for the taunting during class. All the proof I need, I get when I see her head turned away from me. She's blushing and trying to hide it, but it's pointless. My inner self is dancing on the inside—gloating.

When 'Stargazing' by Myles Smith starts to play next, we are already outside the dorms. I take out the bud and hand it back to her with a smile. Her fingers graze my palm when she takes the small contraption, and I feel the jolt of electricity. She must've felt it too because she snaps her hand away with impressive reflex.

Ben presses Emma against the streetlight pole and sucks her face with a loud groan. The sound makes both MJ and me burst into laughter, and my God, is she beautiful when she laughs. The sight of her rattles my nerves, making my mouth speak out, becoming my best ally.

"We're leaving on Wednesday afternoon after class."

"Okay," she drags it out, her brows furrowed, but I bypass it.

"The train leaves at 3."

"You're losing me here." She tilts her head, and I have trouble staying confident.

"Thanksgiving weekend, I already bought your ticket. So we can either meet up here and go to Penn Station together, or meet up there. Your choice."

The confused look on her face is too cute; I have to restrain myself from pinching her cheeks.

"It's about a three-and-a-half-hour ride, so bring your Kindle."

She opens and shuts her mouth four times before she finally speaks, "I have a job, you know? I can't just leave everything and go with you to meet your family, Tyler."

My name slipping out of that beautiful mouth of hers is like a melody made to lighten up my core.

"That's the only thing you could think of?"

She didn't refuse it, didn't reject it, and it feels like I have won the lottery.

"Well, I... I... You confused me," she stutters through it.

"Glad I have that effect on you."

Sticking out her tongue, she blows out a loud raspberry in my face. I'm tempted to capture the muscle between my fingers, but she's too quick to retract it.

"You can take time off, right?" I raise a brow for emphasis.

"Right?" Like she's unsure, she makes it into a question

"So just do that," I simply state, and she shakes her head.

"But I..."

"But what, Feisty?"

A frustrated breath comes out of her, causing me to grin.

"I don't wanna go," she whines, not all that convincing, if I may add.

"You are such a bad liar."

"Fine, whatever. I still think it's weird."

"Weird or scary?"

"Both," she pouts, and fuck me.. why is that so sexy?

"None of us bite, and we are a pretty weird kind of family, so it's not a real excuse."

She crosses her arms over her chest and works on biting her inner cheek. I wait for a reply, but when I get none, I finalize with a simple "Meet me here at 2.20?"

"Tyler." There is a plea in her voice, my name a prayer.

God, I want her to keep saying my name over and over.

"Feisty?"

"Fine," she says through gritted teeth.

Yes!

I discreetly pump my fist behind my back.

"Come on, Ben, get your tentacles off the girl," I shout, slowly backing up.

"Bye," Ben hollers, walking backward, his eyes glued to his girl.

"Bye, guys," Emma yells, hooking MJ's arm, who waves while biting her lip.

I wave back before turning in the direction of the boys' dormitories.

On Monday morning, I sent her a text, not giving her a way out.

Me: *Don't forget to ask for time off*

Feisty: *I hate you*

Me: *Such a bad liar*

Feisty: *Whatever*

Me: *See you Wednesday, 2.20*

Feisty: *Yeah, yeah, yeah*

Wednesday can't come any sooner.

Chapter 26

On a chilly Wednesday afternoon, I nervously step outside the dorms to find Tyler already waiting for me. My heart somersaults at the sight of him leaning on the lamppost, ankles crossed, hair messy, begging to be touched.

No touching of the hair!

"You pack light." He checks my duffel with a sly side-glance.

"I honestly don't know how to respond to that."

A twinkle lights up his eyes, adding to his chuckle.

"I can bet you Sabrina comes with three suitcases."

"Your brother's wife?"

"Yeah, Mateo's."

I nod slowly, mentally committing the names to memory.

"Do any of your other brothers have significant others?"

"No, just Mateo," he says, followed by a wink, then a whispered, "For now."

"Oh."

Now, why did that come out all excited and shit?

What have I gotten myself into?

"Don't worry about it, Sabrina's good people, and so are my brothers."

We start walking to the subway station, and I can't help myself, my fingers fidgeting over the grip of my duffel. "This is gonna be awkward, isn't it?"

"Only if you make it."

"Smart-ass," I huff with a puff.

"Come on, Feisty, just relax, what's the worst that can happen?"

Everything.

Half an hour later, we board the train, and Tyler lifts my bag into the compartment above our seats.

"Window or aisle?" he asks playfully, and I bat my lashes. "Window, if you don't mind?"

"Not at all."

"Thank you."

As I pass by him to take my seat, I inhale his essence, which is heavenly; a mixture of ocean and sandalwood, I gather. Getting comfy in my seat, I take out my Kindle only to be surprised by Tyler's hand, holding one earpiece in front of me. I turn to face him, question marks circling my head.

"Think it's time I share my soundtrack."

With a wide beam, I take the earpiece and stick it in my eardrum, averting my gaze from those gorgeous brown eyes. The opening melody of 'Can't Be Touched' by Roy Jones gets me choking on air in a loud chuckle.

"I had it before I read the books," he goes on the defensive, and it only makes me laugh louder.

"I said nothing."

"I know what you were thinking."

It's the song mentioned often in the books we were reading—the coming-out song of the main character before his fight. The song gained fame long ago, notably in the movie Undisputed, which, ironically, also features a fighter.

"Boyka?"

Shaking his head in disbelief, he gives me a lopsided smile.

I light up my Kindle, and my head starts to bob to the beat as I silently rap out the lyrics.

The rest of his playlist keeps the same tone:

*Fort Minor—Remember the name
*Grits—My life be like
*Maclemore—Can't hold us
*Eminem—Till I collapse
*NF—Oh lord
*Neffex—Unstoppable
*Kid Ink—Ride out
*MGK—Invincible
*Flo Rida—Game Time (and yes, this one made me blush, and yes, I failed to hide it)

Just as I am fake belting out Kanye's 'Stronger', tapping my feet to the beat, I feel Ty's stare.

"What?"

"How is it possible that you know every single song?"

With a loud chortle, I get my phone out of my jacket pocket and open my workout mix containing the same songs. Handing my phone to Tyler, I rake my lower lip, waiting for his reaction. He takes the phone and scrolls, his jaw doing this sexy little tick with each move of his finger. A couple of eyebrow twitches and hums later, he gives me back my phone without a single comment.

"Cat got your tongue?"

"You just keep on doing that."

I cock a brow in question. "Doing what?"

"Blowing my mind."

I don't know what he means by it, and the only thing I can think to say is: "It's unintentional; I assure you."

"Oh, I know." His tone is a bit hostile, unsettling even.

"What's that supposed to mean?"

"Nothing," he actually huffs, then turns his attention to his book. Spitefully, I do the same, all the while mouthing NF's 'When I grow up'.

The rest of the ride, he full-on avoids me, something I honestly don't understand. For some reason, unknown to me, he is angry - and by the looks of it, his anger is pointed right at me. My nerves take over, and I keep biting my tongue to avoid saying something to piss him off even more, which gets me pissed instead. What is it that he wants from me? I am here, going to his house for fuck's sake. I am the one going out of my comfort zone, not even knowing why. Ok, I know why. I want to spend time with him, meet his family, and learn more about his background so that I can better understand him.

A low sigh escapes me, and with one inner 'fuck it', I take out his earpiece and replace it with mine, needing a genre change. My elbow nudges him gently, my open palm between us, his earbud right there in the middle. He stares at my offering for a beat, his nostrils flaring, before he takes it and stuffs it in his ear.

Still mad? Duly noted.

Why am I feeling guilty? Can someone explain it to me? I must've said something wrong, but what? His coldness stings more than I expected. At a loss, I turn off my Kindle, not able to concentrate on the words. So I focus on the trees outside as the train passes them by at full speed. My gut is in complete and utter turmoil. I can feel the turbulence inside me, and the ride is not the culprit.

Hours tick by before the train pulls into the last stop. In absolute silence, Tyler hands me my bag, and I follow him outside to the parking lot filled with cars. We walk toward a huge Hulk-looking dude, leaning on the tailgate of a green pickup truck, looking like he has all the time in the world. He has a crooked grin, a fascinating square face barely hidden behind a beat-up cap pulled low.

"Been a while," Tyler says, opening his arms.

The Hulk pushes off the truck, nodding once. "Too long."

"Missed me?" Tyler asks, both locked in a hug, each doing the tapping on the back with one hand.

"Eh." The guy lifts one shoulder, turning his attention to me. His smile is genuine as he steps toward me, his hand extended. "You must be Maddison. I'm Luka." I shake his steady hand and return a smile of my own. "Nice to meet you, Luka. Thank you for picking us up."

"You see, baby brother, that is a proper way someone shows their appreciation," Luka mocks, ruffing up Tyler's hair.

I watch their interaction with the eyes of an only child. I try to kick the jealousy out of me, but it's useless.

"Oh, come on, you know I appreciate you."

There's an eye roll before Luka takes both our bags and tosses them on the truck bed. He also proves to be a gentleman by opening the passenger door for me to slide in. Taking the middle seat, I mumble a thank you and get stuck sandwiched between two Hart brothers.

What fun.

The truck sparks to life, and we're off into the unknown.

"So, Maddison, first time in Boston?"

"She prefers MJ," Tyler says abruptly with a harsh tone.

Choosing to ignore him, I answer his brother, "Technically, not my first time. We played in Boston a couple of times, but I only saw the insides of gyms."

"Well, we have to remedy that. You should take her to see the city, little B."

Luka glances over at his brother, who has suddenly gone mute.

How rude!

"That's not necessary, I am more than happy to do it alone." Though I try to be nice, it comes across as malice. Tyler's response is a scoff.

What the fuck is his problem?

"Well, if you want company, I am an ok tour guide," Luka offers, focused on the road ahead.

"Thank you, I don't wanna put you out."

"It would be my pleasure." Luka winks at me, stopping at the red light. The brothers share a look, and those are the last words spoken for the remainder of the drive.

When Luka parks his truck in the driveway, I honestly have to catch my breath. A small two-and-a-half-story house with an elevated front porch stands there before me. A tree at the end of the driveway with a tire swing and a big yard spreads to and around the house. It has a yellow exterior and wooden, white-colored windows with matching shutters. Luka and Tyler get out, and I follow. I reach for my bag, but Luka nudges me away. Tyler finally speaks, a playful jab at his brother. "What, you're not going to carry mine?"

"Carry your own bag, princess." Luka tosses Tyler's bag onto his chest, and he catches it with an oomph.

I snort. Loudly.

The front door swings open. An older woman, whom I can only assume is their mother, stands there, a beaming smile lighting up her face. She opens her arms, and Tyler runs right into her embrace. Technically, he's the one doing the embracing, given that she's a petite woman. Sentiments I can't quite pick out are exchanged, and Ms. Hart takes her time giving him a once-over. Staring like a freak, I stand there at the bottom of the steps. Then I feel a hand cover my lower back. I flinch.

In moments like these, I hate my body betraying me the way it does. Even after all this time, extensive therapy, and soul-searching, it still displays fear. The worst part is that it can't register the good ones. The same reaction happened with Ben, Colt, the rest of the team, and now Luka. I hate it. I hate the power it has over me.

I don't even notice the hand retrieved until Luka comes up beside me. With a reassuring nod, we both take the stoop. Luka's boots make each step vibrate with his stomp. He clears his throat, and the woman turns to face me. I offer my hand for a shake, but she waves it away, opening her arms.

"You must be Maddison…"

I practically leap into them before we lock in a tight squeeze.

"Hello, ma'am, I mean Ms. Hart. Thank you for having me."

"Oh dear, don't you dare. It's Eva."

Every nerve, the uncertainty, not to mention all the panic - it just goes poof. All gone, demolished by the warmth of her arms. I want to stay here forever, all wrapped up and safe.

Chapter 27

MJ is ambushed before she gets to blink. My brothers, sans Mateo, go full throttle, invading her space. Fun fact: The Harts are a hugging family. I have to hand it to her; she's keeping her cool, reciprocating every embrace like a champ. The lines on her forehead wrinkle with each new piece of information thrown at her, but she absorbs them all.

I feel bad about my behavior on the train, which was petty and childish. I was frustrated over nothing, I know that now, but back then... I just couldn't handle it—her. The way she made a point out of unintentionally impressing me was like a blow to the chest. My mood went on in the cab of Luka's truck, his knowing look pointing it out every couple of seconds. By the time we got home, I cooled off, realizing I was blowing the whole thing out of proportion. I made a promise to be patient, only for my mind to turn against me.

With my head finally screwed into place, I stand like a bystander, gaping at the way MJ interacts with the people closest to me. My brothers completely ignore me as they all get lost in their infatuation with our guest.

Mak, my oldest brother, is the first to acknowledge me.

Though by the looks of him, he'd fall better as the youngest due to his height, the short Filipino brilliant ass doctor with a heart of gold.

"What's up, Doc?" I open my arms, towering over him. He snorts, squeezing the air out of me, "Hi, Bugs. Welcome home."

Tristan steps in next and pulls me into one of those quick, two-pat-on-the-back hugs, all firm and solid. The kind that says *I missed you*, without actually saying it. He has also grown since I last saw him, almost two months ago.

"Mateo and Sabrina will join us in the morning. Come in, make yourself comfortable," Mama interrupts, taking MJ's hand and gently guiding her further inside.

"Thank you so much for having me. I hope it is not an imposition." MJ has that shy thing about her, but it doesn't look like she's uncomfortable.

"Nonsense, sweetheart. I was just about to make us coffee. Want some?"

"I would love some coffee; thank you."

The more I watch them interact, the more I soften; the sight warming my insides.

"Luka, take MJ's bag to your room," Mama commands with her sharp tone. Before Luka fully bends down to grab the handle, MJ yells, "Oh, please no; I can sleep on the couch, I don't want to take anyone's space..." She waves her hands with wide eyes, holding her duffel with a tight grip.

"No worries, Maddison, I am more than happy to lend you my room," Luka offers, keeping up with her full name, despite my earlier remark.

"Honestly, I don't think I will be able to sleep knowing I

kind of kicked you out. And I don't mind the couch. Please?"

Mama debates, but eventually caves. Guess MJ has a hold on her as much as she does over me.

"You can give the room to Mateo and Sabrina, and you can sleep in Mateo's bed." Mama quickly shuffles the sleeping arrangements. Luka is the only one of us with his own room and a king-size bed. The rest of us have bunk beds. I used to share the room with Mateo, and Tristan still shares his with Mak. Luka tosses MJ's bag on the couch, and the two women head into the kitchen. I notice some hesitation in MJ, but she quickly recovers, easing into the seat at the end of the dining table.

Looking at her talking to my mother is nothing as I'd imagined. It's... Better. So, why the hell am I still mad at her? In reality, there are no reasonable or rational grounds for me to feel this way, but here I am, mad, maybe even a bit hurt. The reason? Her, just her. The fact that she's all kinds of perfect makes me so angry and agitated that I am acting like a spoiled little brat.

"Bro, you are so toast," Tristan whispers, stepping to my left. Mak comes to my right, stating the obvious, "She's gorgeous."

"Most importantly... Mama seems to like her." Luka comes behind me, leaping over my shoulder.

In this house, our mother's stamp of approval is everything. She has a unique ability to read people, which she calls "reading the soul." It has a 100% accuracy rate. I take another minute to look at the two women in the kitchen, my entire focus on their exchange. One thing that sticks out is how animatedly MJ talks to my mother, her hands flying as she explains something with enthusiasm. I can't hear a thing, but I don't care. Knowing Mama took a liking to her and seeing MJ so relaxed in my home is all I need.

I am about to join in on their conversation, but a shoulder grip pulls me back. I know the grip well. Luke leans in, whispering, "Come on, let's get you settled and give the women some privacy." Dropping my head, I walk behind my brother, Mak, and Tristan in tow. As soon as the door to my room closes, all eyes are on me.

"Fine," I let out a sigh, "let's get this over with." I face my palms up and curl my fingers repeatedly in challenge.

"Where do you two stand?" Tristan takes the first question.

"Still just friends," I state, a bit of a bite to my tone.

"Nothing happened between you two?" That one is from Mak.

I shake my head, choosing not to disclose some intense hand-holding, a mere moment that lives rent-free in my mind.

"Nothing?" Luka with the double take.

"Nothing."

Luka squints his eyes, trying to catch the lie. A perceptive glare indicates he has succeeded, but he doesn't share it with the others. Thankfully.

"Mind if I try my luck?" Tristan speaks with a clear death wish. All I have to do is stand up with clenched fists for him to retrieve, hand lifted in surrender immediately. "Bro, you never called dibs."

"Color it implied," I bite, causing a proud grin on his smug little face. Despite being the youngest, Tristan has the entire high school football team captain going for him. He's popular and cocky. Worst part, he's not afraid of us anymore. Not even Luka, who's a tank of a person.

"Stop it, you two," think of the devil, who steps between us, pulling out his referee card. "Seriously, little brother, what's the deal with you two?"

"I like her, I know she likes me, but she had some shit happen to her, so I am trying really, *really* hard to be respectful and patient."

Luka gives me a knowingly approving look, and it's exactly what I need.

"What happened to her?" Both Tristan and Mak ask. Luka remains silent. All three have the same worried expressions.

"No idea." My throat bobs. "It has something to do with basketball, I think." I glance at my brothers, who all listen closely. "But there's something else, something more."

"What?" I am too far in my thoughts, replaying the past month, to figure out who asked.

"I don't know exactly, but I see it in her eyes, something I can't quite figure out."

"Maybe you're not supposed to figure it out," the doctor in Mak emerges.

I drop my head, "I just want to be there for her, whether she tells me or not."

"I never thought I would say this, but I'm proud of you, Bro." My jaw drops. It's Luka who says it, a sentiment he shared with all of us on all the big milestones. I never would have guessed that falling for a girl and giving her the time she needs would become one of those milestones. I puff out my chest because it feels that good.

"She's worth it," I mutter, but point my look to Luka, who

bobs his head. "I know."

"Dinner!" Mama's voice reverberates through the house, making all of us spring into action. We are out the door in under a second and downstairs in less than three. There's some heavy pushing and pulling on the way down, but we make it in one piece.

Everything happens way too fast; I don't even have the time to reflect on anything properly. I am still way up in my head, the insides of my brain all tangled. One second, one look changes it all. There she is, setting the table like she has been doing so her whole life. Her smile reaches her eyes, and it's the first time I've ever seen it. I melt at the sight.

"Can I help with anything?" I ask. Mama answers, "Just sit and wait, all of you."

Like little puppies, we plant our asses on our seats, hands in our laps, stomachs growling loudly. MJ smiles with her head dropped, but I can still see it, feel it.

Mama lifts a finger before she takes her seat. "Guests first, boys. We will be civilized."

We all nod, knowing she means business.

Chapter 28

Everything I know about faith, I learned from my grandma. After she passed, my connection with the Almighty started to weaken.

Seeing this family together, praying, is comforting, yet it also has its drawbacks.

Am I a believer? Sure. Am I a person who prays? Not really, not anymore.

Glancing around the table at the family, their heads bowed, hands clasped together, eyes closed, I feel out of place but oddly soothed by their quiet. I follow their lead, sending a silent "thank you" into the universe.

When I open my eyes, they go straight to Tyler, his frown upside down, making the flutter in my stomach go whoosh. And trust me, being a Dominic girl myself, I know the power of the whoosh.

"It's make-your-roast-beef-sandwich night," Tristan explains, sporting a prom king vibe, a heartbreaker in the making.

"Since you're our guest, you get first pick," Mak continues, explaining the rules to me. And there are plenty to go through, such as the number of condiments per take, the ratio and volume of scoops, and the most important rule: no double-dipping. The middle of the table is colored with ingredients and toppings.

"If I may offer my expertise…" Tristan's voice stops my mouth from drooling at the spread. "If you have never tried it, I would recommend going North Shore 3-way. It's a tradition here."

My expression must give away my lack of knowledge at the name drop, because Tyler finally speaks directly to me, "I can make it for you if you want?"

Goosebumps spread across the entire surface of my skin. I forget how to function; all I can do is stare at him.

"Any allergies?" he queries, his soft eyes never leaving mine. I shake my head, my tongue obviously bitten away by some phantom cat.

"You trust me?"

His expression is hopeful, and it lets me know he's not talking about dinner, not entirely.

"Yes," I hush, the simple three-letter word lighting up his face. I watch as he carefully selects a toasted onion roll, a slice of cheese, and mixes a teaspoon of extra-heavy mayonnaise with barbecue sauce over the top of the bun. With a pair of tongs, he delicately picks out the most roasted slice of beef and spreads it over the roll. He does a double-take, checking if everything is up to his standards before he slowly slides the plate in front of me. I lick my lips and then turn to face him. "Thank you."

He says nothing in return, just glares at me. Never in my life have I experienced performance anxiety, and I have played in packed arenas. So, how did I end up having stage fright over eating a freaking sandwich? Every single person at the table is anticipating the reaction to my first bite. My stomach gives a low, traitorous growl.

Please taste like heaven.

I really don't want to lie to them.

Both my hands wrap the entire thing, still warm, and bring it to my mouth. The first bite is a revelation. The bread crackles under my teeth, crisp on the outside, yet squishy on the inside. Then comes the beef, all tender and impossibly juicy. It practically melts over my tongue.

I close my eyes.

The world could end right here, and I might just thank it.

My fingers, slick with grease, clutch the sandwich as if someone might try to steal it; no, like it's a lifeline. I'm not even sitting in the Hart home anymore; I am floating, drifting into taste bud heaven. I open my mouth to take another bite, but a distinguished sound of throat-clearing brings me down to earth.

"That good?" Tyler gently tilts his head, a slight twitch on his lips.

I answer by taking another bite, and the room falls into laughter.

By the time the rest finish their build-a-sandwich, I am already halfway through mine.

"So, Tyler tells me you play basketball." Ms. Hart gives me a sincere look, and I return it.

"Oh no, ma'am, I mean, I used to..." I mumble with my mouthful. "I'm sorry," I swallow, "I play volleyball now."

"Do you like playing volleyball?"

"Yeah, I like my team and our coach is amazing."

"That's good, but it is not what I asked you," she deadpans.

As I try to tuck away a nonexistent strand of my hair behind my ear, I take a deep breath. "I *do* like it," I admit.

"More than you did basketball?" Tristan quips from across the table.

"I don't know, it's not the same," I confess.

I give Tyler a side glance, but can't read his expression.

"How do you mean?" Luka, who is sitting next to me, turns to face me.

I wiggle in my seat, thinking of the best way to describe it.

"It's not the same kind of love, I don't know how to explain it." I take a deep breath just as the right analogy hits me. "It's like when you read a romance novel, and you love it, but you also love a thriller. There is no way you can love one over the other because they don't go into the same category."

"Ok, I can understand that," Luka notes as the others nod in understanding.

"How do you like school?" Mak, who is obviously the scholar of the family, changes the subject, and I'm thankful for it.

"I love it," I say with too much excitement, "I love all my classes and get along with most of the professors." Though it's weird on some scale to be in the middle of an investigation, I'm not nervous about it, nor do I feel pressured.

"That's good. Have you picked a major?" Ms. Hart inquires without actually prying.

"Oh yeah, I pre-declared Statistics and Science."

Even though I am facing his mother, I can feel Tyler's eyes on me.

"She wants to be Brad Pitt and Jonah Hill from Moneyball all smashed into one."

The memory of us texting about the subject and him instantly getting the reference puts another smile on my face. I scan the bunch, all sporting impressed expressions, which makes me all giddy.

"You like reading?" Miss Hart asks, pouring water into her glass.

"Oh yes, very."

It's my favorite escape from reality.

"That's good, it is an appreciated quality in this house. What do you like to read?"

"Everything, I don't have a specific taste. If I like the storyline, I just like it. Some books I devour in a matter of hours, others take time because of the lack of connection, you know?"

"That I understand perfectly."

She takes my hand and looks me straight in the center, deep, as far as it takes for her to see everything. I allow it. Something pierces my heart, her hand covering mine, her warm, deep gaze, just her overall. With nothing better to say, I go to the first compliment that comes to mind.

"You've made a lovely home here, Miss Hart."

"Please, call me Eva," she demands for the umpteenth time.

"I'm sorry. I should've warned you. It will take some time until I can make that switch. It's a player's hazard, the constant of ma'am and sir's; it's hard to lose."

"Good manners are also appreciated here, so don't worry about anything, and please make yourself at home."

Don't mind if I do.

Is what I want to say, but I choose to alternate with "Thank you for having me."

"I think it's safe to say that you are always welcome here."

God, I hope she means it; please let her mean it, because I need her to.

Chapter 29

A true hallmark moment gets interrupted by Tristan's shout, "Not it!"

On instinct, my arm flies up, and so does Luka's. Mak and Mama follow right after, all of us repeating the same two-word save. Mama shakes her head, dropping it with a disapproving grin before she gives MJ her most sincere apology. "Sorry, sweetie, should've warned ya. You have to do the dishes now."

"I was gonna offer to do them anyway." MJ shrugs and stands up, going into action, stacking up empty plates.

"I'll help," I offer, taking the stack and carrying it into the empty sink. She says nothing but comes to my left.

"You wash, I'll dry," I nudge her side with my elbow. We both dive into our tasks in silence, but it's the good kind, comfortable. She works on each plate with the foamy sponge, rinses, and hands it over to me. Her eyes dart up to meet mine for a beat before she goes back to work. I soak each glance, the weight of it running through my bloodstream like wildfire. What is it about a simple chore that makes me feel so alive? Is it her doing it with me? Or is it her smile, unfaltering?

All I can think about is how I want to do this forever. Mostly, I wonder if she feels the same.

When the last dish is dried and safely put in place, I feel the need to keep the comfort going.

"Want to see the best part of the house?"

She stares blankly at my hand in offering, taking her time torturing me. With a quick nod, she finally takes it, the electric current of her touch stretching from my fingers straight to my heart. I guide her out back, where she reluctantly lets go of my hand before leaning over the wooden railing. We stand on the back porch, enjoying the cold air. With her eyes fixed on the fenced yard, I catch her profile indirectly. We didn't bother putting on our jackets, thinking it would only take a second or two to show the back of the house, but she doesn't seem to mind. Unfazed by the cold or my presence, she continues to stare at the emptiness before her. She breaks the silence with a whisper, "I don't know why, but I can see younger versions of the five of you playing here."

"We lost so many balls over the fence," I say through a laugh, "our neighbor, Mr. Tucker, has made a nice collection for himself."

"He never gave them back to you?" she gasps in shock.

"No, he hated kids and hated stuff or people getting onto his property."

"That's just mean." She shakes her head in disbelief.

"Tell me about it," I mutter, thinking back to those days. "Did you ever watch the old Dennis the Menace movie?"

She nods, though her brows make the deep V, waiting for me to elaborate.

"You know the mean neighbor who hated his guts?" I

forgot the name, but she nods anyway.

"Well, just give him a round bear belly, and you have Mr. Tucker."

"Thanks for the visual. I'll be sure to keep an eye out so I can give him my best mean mug."

I chuckle despite being 99% certain she's being serious as fuck.

"Don't take this the wrong way, but I kind of envy you."

I gape at her, mouth open and all, with a side of sweaty palms. I guess my nerves go hand in hand with her talking.

"Being an only child was boring. We lived in a building on the third floor; no yard, not even a balcony."

Trying hard not to react solely so I don't spook her from sharing further, I feel all the feels at her finally starting to open up.

"It was a bad neighborhood, and most of the neighbors were loud and moody, always screaming at each other. When I was around eight, I saw this house for sale from the bus on my way from school. It had a mounted hoop over the garage door."

I swallow, listening carefully, reading her body language for any discomfort, but all I see is her faint smile.

"I went home, smashed my piggy bank, and bought myself a basketball. I spent every day after school trying to get it to fly high enough to go through the dang hoop."

I fight off a chuckle, trying to picture a young MJ holding a ball that was probably too big for her little body. Her eyes go to the floor, and I notice her breath getting heavier. The urge to take her hand is strong, but I manage to keep it in check.

"One day, a family came to check it out, and there was a

little boy with them, my age, but with dark skin. I asked them if I could come and play if they moved in. The boy said yes, but only if he and his brother could play with me. That was the day Damian became my best friend."

The dots connect, the dark skin, the name; it's the guy who came to her game.

I swallow again, not liking the direction the story is heading.

"I begged my mother to sign me up to play, but she just brushed me off. Damian's parents ended up paying for me to get into the peewees."

Her fingers play with her necklace, rotating between the numbers, giving each the same care.

"Why did you quit basketball?"

I curse my tongue the moment I say it, because that question ruins the moment. As soon as the words slip out of my mouth, she retreats into herself.

We both stay quiet, MJ refusing to look at me, until I can't take it anymore.

"Come on, let's get back inside; don't want us to freeze."

I open the door for her, and she walks past me, her head dropped.

When she gets inside before me, she stops in front of a framed art piece covering the wall. I put my palm over my chest, over the pendant hanging from a long chain around my neck, remembering last Christmas. It belonged to my mother; she never took it off. I was too young when they died and couldn't remember much, but I remembered the necklace. After entering the foster system, we lost all our belongings. Sabrina went snooping to find Mom's favorite book for Mateo, and in the process, she stumbled upon the necklace, giving it to me with a long-lost memory.

"Sabrina got one of her friends to draw that for Mama."

MJ finally turns to face me, making me realize why she has been avoiding doing so before. So much sadness and pain, it's all I can see in her eyes, and it kills me. She turns her focus back to the wall, and I stare at her while her eyes go over every single detail.

"It's so beautiful and perfect for all of you."

You have no idea.

Chapter 30

Art is not something I'd say I'm acquainted with. Come to think of it, I can't remember ever setting foot in a museum, let alone an art gallery. And I never thought that stargazing at something generated by someone's creative power would be so enlightening. Out of breath, I can't unglue my eyes from the five small hands in different sizes covering a slightly larger, more feminine one. The hands are drawn in the background with an illusion of transparency, allowing the front text to be focused on. Words that describe the same feeling I got as soon as I stepped inside are written in bold over the said hands, stating:

NOT STEP
NOT HALF
NOT FOSTER
NOT ADOPTED
JUST FAMILY!

So perfectly put, so simple, so them.

Until today, I have never felt like something was missing in my life. After dinner, I found myself jealous of something

I've never had the chance to experience.

I watched from the sidelines as they got caught up, blessed to witness their dynamic and connection. You could feel the love, support, and respect they have for one another.

It's late evening now, all the guys have gone to their rooms, and Ms. Hart stayed to help me get the couch ready, over my every protest. I must say, I love their living room. It's specious, yet cozy; the heart of this house. The hardwood floor is covered with a colorful, round carpet spreading from under the large, brownish couch, the table, and the two mismatched armchairs. There's also a rocking chair on the side, with a basket of yarn on the floor next to it.

I watch as she takes slow steps toward me, sadness screaming out of her, and I just know that it's pointed at me. For me.

"Now that we are alone, I want to tell you something."

I take the deepest of breaths, preparing for whatever is coming.

"Come here, sit." She sits down, tapping the spot next to her on the couch, and I do as I'm told without hesitation.

"I was in the system most of my childhood." The struggle in her voice is obvious, and I remain silent, listening intently.

"Tyler and Mateo were the first kids I got to foster. The moment I saw their sad eyes, all I wanted was to take their pain away."

I place my palm over her warm hand. It's a simple act, but I want it to convey something along the lines of 'it's okay' and 'thank you for sharing, please continue'.

"Tyler didn't speak to anybody for an entire month. He had nightmares so intense that he would wake up covered in sweat. Mateo coped better, but only because he had his memories. Tyler couldn't even remember his parents' faces. He ran away one day, and Mateo, that smart little boy he was, figured out exactly where he had gone. We found him on the front steps of their childhood home, holding this."

Why do I feel like my heart is burning?

She slides a Polaroid out of her back pocket and hands it to me. The white frame around the photo has turned brown with age, but the image itself remains remarkably clear. A beautiful Latina woman with dark, curly hair that reaches her thighs sits next to a tall, handsome man with round glasses and a beaming smile. You can feel their love from this small piece of glossy paper.

"How he got there on his own, only three years old…" she trails off, shaking her head.

"Why are you telling me all this?"

"My Tyler is a persistent boy, and when he sets his heart on something, he always goes all in."

My eyes widen, not because I was unaware of the fact, but because I realize where this is going.

"From what I've gathered, you are no stranger to pain, and I…" she hesitates for a moment, contemplating. "I want you to know that with Tyler, you get all of us. You have me. Anytime, anywhere, I am here for you. I will listen, hold you, guide you… whatever you need."

Though she said all the right things, making me feel like I could trust her, I am just not there yet. Not ready. She wouldn't understand. No one could. I tried it once, sharing, only for it to backfire. So I chose to hide certain parts of me behind a smile.

"Thank you" is all I say. She doesn't push further, but I know I can come to her if the time ever comes.

"Good night, sweetie."

"Good night, Eva," I gasp, and she pulls me into her arms. I linger a bit longer, feeling all the comfort before she goes upstairs.

Whenever I enter the state of a nightmare, it's always the same one. A blurry face, a firm hand, and a basketball going into flames. And it plays on a loop, repeating endlessly. The dream itself isn't anything gut-wrenching, but it makes my body react as if it were. It's been a while since I last woke up covered in sweat.

Panic attacks, on the milder scale, are something I have been prone to since the first nightmares started. The problem is that I have never had said attacks in front of witnesses, and now I have two distraught, confused ones staring at me.

Eva takes a seat next to me, and I can see her mouth opening and closing like she's talking, but I can't hear a thing over my heartbeat.

I feel like I am choking on nothing.

One thing I should probably confess to is how much I welcome the panic. It's the only time I get to actually physically feel the pain. Real somatic hurt, not the imagined one I feel when surprised or angry.

When a sense of warmth wraps around me, something

impossible happens: all the pain ceases to exist. Just like that. One hug - it takes one hug from a person I met mere hours ago to shut it all down. It's honest, sheltered, motherly. Is it sad to say that it's the type of hug I never had the privilege to endure? It's not a poor choice of words, if that's what you're thinking, considering all the forced embraces I have faced while craving this very one I am currently wrapped in. So yes, hugs were something I endured, not something I experienced.

It dawns on me... I am breaking down in a stranger's arms, in someone else's home, and I don't know how to stop. My throat closes up. Somehow, I feel Tyler, somewhere close, making it worse.

I am on a roll here.

Can a person die of embarrassment?

Is that a thing? I sure want it to be.

When I finally emerge from Eva's hold, I am met by new sets of eyes, all differently shaped and colored.

When did they all get here?

"I am so sorry that I woke all of you up. This doesn't happen often. It hasn't in a long time. I am so sorry." And now I'm babbling. "I am so sorry, I think it's best I leave."

The words leave my mouth, but my body makes no action to indicate their intent.

"I am sorry to disappoint you, but that is not an option." Eva places her hand on my knee, the sentiment making me lift my gaze.

"You haven't woken anybody up; it's already morning," she states, making me turn my head to look out the window, and sure enough, the sun is beaming through the shutters.

"Do you get panic attacks often?" Mak asks, his glasses nowhere to be seen, with a worried expression on his face.

"It was a nightmare, not a panic attack." I am lying through my teeth, guilt rising as soon as the words leave me. Believe it or not, I don't like lying to people.

"Sorry to break it to you, but I'm a doctor, so I know what a panic attack looks like."

"Oh." I drop my head. I lied to Tyler's brother to his face and got caught.

"Yeah, oh." He crosses his arms over his chest. "Now, tell me, do you get them often?"

"Not really. I haven't had one in..." My eyes immediately go to Tyler. "Two months or so." Since my first dance with Tyler, to be more precise.

"Here." Luka offers me a glass of water, which I take, emptying it in one quick tip. He takes my empty glass, and I smile at him, saying, "Thank you." He gives me a quick nod before he goes back to the kitchen, probably to wash it.

I don't even notice Tyler move, not until he's kneeling next to me. My God, those eyes. It's all I can think about, staring like a danged fool.

No! No! No!

Not here, not now, not in front of him. But the will gets stuck somewhere between my chest and my throat, and before I can stop them, the tears spill. Then I feel it, the shift.

"Hey," he says softly. Just that—a three-letter word, but the kind that makes me want to collapse into it. His arms brush mine, all tentative, like he's asking permission with the simple touch. Before I can stop myself—or maybe I don't want to —my body leans in. He wraps his arms around me, quiet and steady, as he did at the court, which seems like a lifetime ago. I didn't even realize how badly I needed it until this moment. My heart wants to jump out of my chest, but Tyler's embrace keeps it situated, beating only for him. Here, in his arms, I don't care about the rest of his family, probably staring. I don't care that I have water running out of my nose. It's only the two of us, lost in time and space. His chin rests gently on the top of my head; he stays there. And somehow, in that silence, I start to breathe again.

Chapter 31

We're settled around the table, plates cleared. Breakfast gone. Comfortable silence. Until my hand flies up in the air. "Not it!"

Laughter spreads around the room, the sounds pumping up my chest. The last hand up belongs to Mak, who is obviously stunned by my action. Eva gives me a wink, one beaming with what I can only gather as pride.

"What's up, family?" The front door swings open with a thud, and all the faces around me light up. Standing up, I stare at the beautiful-looking couple, the woman vaguely familiar. Eva jumps to her feet and goes to hug, my guess, Sabrina, first, while the brothers all huddle up in a group hug.

"Oh my God, you didn't..." The woman, whom I can still only presume to be Mateo's wife, gasps. I gawk at the goddess beaming at me with bright green eyes. My throat bobs, but her smile never falters.

"Hi, I'm MJ." I wave my shaking hand.

"Yeah, you are," are the last words I hear before I am oomph-ed into a crushing hug. Trying to get out a mouthful of hair stuck to my tongue, I hear her whisper in my ear, "I am so happy you're here."

Speechless and a tad bit frightened, I return her squeeze and whisper out a *'thank you'*. When she pulls away, she places her hands on my shoulders to take a good look at me, the assessment kind. That's when I realize that I am in the presence of greatness. Wearing leather pants tucked into high boots that match her motorcycle jacket, she is a vision. Her hair is braided to the side, a few loose strands framing her face. Green piercing eyes, one signature beauty mark under the left one, and full lips that produce a wide smile.

"OH, MY GOD! You're Sabrina Furst!" There's some screaming involved; it's not my proudest moment.

The room falls silent, then erupts in laughter. "So you know who I am? That's refreshing." Sabrina points her dancing eyebrows at her husband. Obviously, it's an inner joke I don't get.

"My roommate is a huge fan of yours… She has a wall covered with your posters, top to bottom!" I exclaim. A genuine smile lights up her features, no smugness or egotistical tendencies in sight. I take a step back, feeling like I have just committed a crime. "She is sooo gonna kill me," I say in horror.

"You are so cute, it's priceless." Sabrina Furst, the supermodel-slash-entrepreneur-slash-big-shot lawyer, is saying I am cute—out loud, to my face. And here I am, messy hair, oversized hoodie, and my favorite pair of joggers. Emma would have a field day.

"Hi!" A tall guy with short hair in a biker attire gives me a wave, stepping in the line of sight between Sabrina and me. The resemblance between him and Tyler is uncanny.

"I'm Mateo, and it's no longer Furst; she's a Hart now," he

corrects. I smack my mouth shut, mumbling over my hand, "Mmm, so souwe..."

Sabrina whacks the back of her husband's head with a splat. He says nothing, doesn't even react, as if it's totally normal for them.

"I am MJ, nice to meet you." My smile is apologetic, my hand extended, but, as expected, he ignores it, going in for a hug.

"Why is MJ sleeping on the couch?" Sabrina fixes her gaze on Luka, who appears frail. Her hands are on her hips, waiting for him to respond.

"I begged, I wasn't comfortable kicking someone out of their room," I intervene, going right into folding the blanket that covered me during the night.

"Well, I am." With a pointed finger in the air, she commands, "Luka, you give your room to the girl right NOW!"

"I-I-I..." The human tank actually stutters at a girl who is one-third of his weight and two-thirds of his size. "I already moved to Mateo's bed."

"What?"

"Yeah, honey, you and Mateo can sleep in Luka's room," Eva points out.

That seems to settle the veins that were on Sabrina's forehead three seconds ago.

"Ok, you're off the hook." She pats Luka's chest and beelines toward the kitchen, then yells over her shoulder, "Who wants coffee?"

Six hands fly in the air, and I slowly lift mine, feeling categorically confused.

The whole dynamic has shifted now that Sabrina and

Mateo are here. Can you keep a secret? I am totally fan-girling. But not over the model—no... It's over the person. Honestly, if Emma hadn't been filling my ears about her constantly, I don't think I would've known who she is. Now, this girl, woman, cracking jokes from across the table—*her*, I'm in love with.

Mugs empty, we're deep into the retelling of Sabrina's latest conquest. Frankly, I am a bit lost trying to keep up.

"And then he said that he was gonna make me pay..." The whole table simultaneously combusts into hysterical laughter, and I just sit there, my head swinging, trying to get the joke. Sabrina is the first to look at me with her eyes narrowed, right before she stands up and smacks Tyler over the head. "You didn't tell her?"

Tyler makes the cross with his fingers. "Sorry, I wasn't sure if I was allowed to."

"Of course, you are allowed to tell about my evil genius, awesome, sparkling self," she says in one breath, all the while batting her lashes at him.

"I am so confused right now," I speak out, letting everyone know where my head is at.

"Of course you are, because Ty here is an idiot. Plus, I thought you already knew; otherwise, I would've caught you up with everything beforehand." She turns to face me, demanding attention.

"Tell me, have you heard about the Boston take-down that happened last year?" There's an almost dramatic pause, as if she is giving me a minute to rewind. It clicks rather quickly.

"The district attorney, all the CEOs, and that judge?"

"Yeah, well, that was all Sabrina," Mateo lets it out.

"What do you mean it was all Sabrina?" My execution of the questions comes out as a shriek.

"She took them down. The judge, that's her father, and he had his hands in everything, so she exposed it all to the public," Tristan explains, and I take in all the information.

"Oh, my God. That's amazing."

"Oh well, I had some help." She looks at Mateo with a loving smile.

"Anyway, I'm kind of a badass, so that's why it was funny that the guy thought he could threaten me!"

Somehow, I get even more starstruck, unable to form words. I just peer, jaw remaining dropped.

"You ok?"

"Yeah, it's just that I was kinda in love with you already, and now I believe I'm terminal." I pop one shoulder, and the room fills with a new set of ha-ha's.

"Oh, I knew I was gonna like you. Ty, you did good." I turn to face Tyler only to find his eyes already set on me. That all too familiar ping strikes, spreading through my cells.

Sabrina comes from behind me and places her chin on my shoulder, wrapping her arms around me. I am getting used to all these hugs; they're warming up to me.

Luka stands up, clasping his hands. "Ok, boys, game time!" Chairs are sliding out in an instant, followed by all the brothers standing up, Luka leading them outside. Yes, I watch Tyler leave… Yes, he turns around to look at me at the last second… and yes, my heart flatlines. It stays that way until the door closes behind him.

"Game?" I grill, looking between the two women left.

"The boys play football outside while we girls drink, talk, and prepare the food."

I eagerly stand up, rubbing my hands with a clap. "So what can I do?"

"You can peel the potatoes," Eva offers, bending down to open a cabinet. She fills a large bowl before handing it to me. It takes three drawers till I finally find a scraper and get my ass to work.

"You drink wine?" Sabrina asks, opening a cabinet above my head. I watch as she takes three glasses out, but before I can answer, she returns the last one with a side glance. "Nooo. You're a beer girl, right?"

"I'm not that picky."

"Oh sweetie, no. That is not allowed. You should be picky," Eva advises from the corner.

Opening the fridge, Sabrina yells over her shoulder, "Oh my goodness, we have to make that TikTok!"

Aside from Booktok, I'm not much of a TikToker; it's mostly Emma's territory. Unfortunately, I do know the trends, had to do a couple with her, so I think I see where this is going.

"The owner of this house?"

"Oh, I love that we're on the same level. I believe this is the start of a beautiful friendship."

Then she squeaks while clapping her hands. She's excited for this, and I don't know what to do. If Emma finds out, she'll kill me, bring me back, and kill me all over again, so I am a bit scared. With that said, Sabrina freaking Hart wants to be my friend. Sign me up.

"We need to seal the deal. I'm going to my friend's club's

reopening in town tomorrow. Wanna join me?"

"Really?" I jump, almost cheering. Dancing is just the getaway I didn't know I needed.

"Yeah, if you want?"

"I think the jump gave me away. But just to be clear - yes, I would love to go, thank you."

"How much do you love me now?"

"I think you ruined me for anybody else."

"I doubt that." She shares a look with Eva, and it ignites a fire that spreads across my cheeks.

"Potatoes are peeled; what else can I do?"

"You can put them in a pot of water and put them on the stove."

Sabrina takes out a pot from under the sink, gives it to me, and I fill it with water.

"Go, join the boys. I will call you when I need you." Eva winks and shares another look with Sabrina. A different kind of ping hits deep, like it's labeling me an outsider. I want to know what those looks mean. I want to have those unspoken conversations.

My eyes are blessed by the view I will hardly ever forget: five brothers, all hot in their own way, playing football, grunting, rolling on the grass…

I am in heaven.

Sabrina and I are sitting on the back porch, wrapped in a warm blanket, enjoying the view, and gulping our second beer.

"You wanna show them how it's done?" Sabrina gives me a winking smirk, and I give one right back, excitement filling me. "Oh, hell yeah!"

"That's the spirit." She lifts her arms above her head, fists pumping the air.

We both stand up and charge toward the ball. She steals it first and tosses it to me to catch mid-run. I smash the ball to the imaginary touchdown line, and Sabrina whistles with a loud 'whohoo'.

"That's not fair, you weren't playing," Luka protests, but is silenced as soon as Sabrina's hands are on her hips. I guess that's the pose that says, *'You better think about your next move, big fella'.*

Someone touches my lower back, and on instinct, I turn with a swinging elbow, hitting a nose, hard. Tristan falls on the ground, and I grab my face, dread flooding me. "Oh, my God. I am so sorry; you scared me, and it was a reflex. I am so sorry."

"My fault, I shouldn't have snuck up like that. Sorry," he heaves, both his hands hiding what I can only presume to be blood.

"No, I am sorry." I offer him a hand, and he takes it; I pull him up. The others join in around him, asking what happened. I can only offer my sincerest apologies. "I am sorry, I am so sorry."

"Stop apologizing," Tristan orders. "For the record, that was one hell of a strike."

"And a nice aim," Luka jumps in.

I know they're saying it for my benefit, to ease whatever is culminating from within. It's not until Tyler joins them that I finally alleviate.

"Damn, Feisty, that was beautiful," he says, doing a slow clap. Mak whistles low, stepping between Tristan and me, nursing what is probably going to be a nasty bruise.

"I give it a solid 9," Luka deadpans, "point off for not punning before the kick."

"I wasn't planning it," I snap, still breathing hard. My elbow is throbbing.

"Oh come on, just admit it; you've been dying to hit him ever since you met him," Mak mocks, squeezing Tristan's nose. I don't say anything, but I might've smiled… just a little.

Chapter 32

Thanksgiving lunch was, for lack of a better description, special. Tears were swabbed and dried; uncontrollable shakes were punctuated by laughter, with togetherness as the all-around theme.

Having MJ here gives me a sense of comfort, but the constant, dejected look on her face leaves me with an unsettling feeling in the pit of my stomach. As much as I am glad to have brought her here, I feel like the worst person in the world for doing the same. I can't shake this feeling like I'm rubbing my happy family in her face when all I want is to share my world with her. That pained dullness in her eyes overpowers the smile her lips produce, and it guts me.

"I am so thankful for my boys. I hope you know how proud I am of all of you." Mama is on her feet, her wine glass in hand, a smile covering her beautifully aged face. Her silver eyes roam the table and the people around it. "And I am incredibly thankful for the two of you," she says, lifting her glass towards Sabrina and then to MJ. "For being here and allowing us to share it all with you."

Subtly, I glance at MJ, noticing her throat tightening. With watery eyes, Mama raises her glass, and the table follows, each taking a sip of the drink of their choice. Luka stands up next, saying he's thankful for the family, followed by Mak with the same sentiment. Tristan adds his awesomeness to the mix, and Mateo adds Sabrina, who then stands up and brings everybody to tears. "I never thought that I would experience the true definition of a loving family or feel the kind of love all of you gave me."

My focus is back on MJ, her hand gripping the glass. I wish I could get inside her head.

Sabrina's voice snaps my attention to her. "You accepted me for me and loved me through my worst, and I am so thankful for all of you." She turns her loving gaze to Mateo. "Now, you, there are no words to say how much I am fucking thankful for you. My life was so empty, and I didn't even realize how much until you stalked the hell out of me. I love your family, but I love you the mostest!"

I'm not crying; there's just something in my eye. There must be something in the air because everyone is crying, even Sabrina.

"Dammit, I'm leaking again!"

That statement gets MJ to release a chuckle, and the sight, accompanied by the sound, relaxes every muscle in my body, and when she stands up, the jolt of my heart follows.

"Uhm, not to be a buzzkill, but aside from my best friend, I don't know the last time I felt thankful for anything. But today, I get to say that I am thankful for many things…" she takes a long breath. "This delicious food, the cook who made it. I am thankful for the warmth you all showed me…" She darts her eyes to mine. "I am thankful for you, Tyler, for somehow knowing what I need when I need it..." Then she turns to my mother. "Eva, you raised not one but five incredible people, and I am so honored to have had the chance to get to know all of you. Thank you for having me, truly."

Before MJ has the chance to sit down, she is wrapped in a family hug. I join, still bewildered by her words. My mother grazes my hand and gives me a genuine smile, letting me know I've done well and that she's proud.

Sabrina lets out a dramatic cough, overplaying it a bit. "I believe you forgot about something, or someone..."

"And I am most thankful for the badass I now get to call a friend," MJ tweets, and Sabrina sweeps off her shoulders. "Damn straight!"

The mashed potatoes have just made their second round when I glance at MJ again, sitting between Mak and Sabrina, two very different energies around her. Somehow, she manages both like she's been doing it her whole life. She smiles politely at Mak's endless stories about the difference between 'Grey's Anatomy' and real-life residency, while also fielding questions from Sabrina about zodiac signs. Frankly, I don't even know if she believes in that stuff, but she's answering as if it all matters. Her hands fidget with the edge of her napkin whenever they aren't holding a fork.

She's nervous.

I catch her eye for a flicker. Long enough to let her know she's doing fine. Truth is, I can't stop watching her, noticing... The way she nods when Mama goes on about brining turkeys versus deep-frying them, as if it were the most crucial information. The way her eyes light up when Sabrina and Mateo share a look. Or the way she passes the gravy boat to

Tristan before he even asks. Little things. All it is, really—a string of small, human moments that add up to something bigger than I've expected.

She's not trying too hard; she's not performing. She just *is.*

When everyone is stuffed and too lazy to move, I lean back in my chair - the only one with the squeaky leg that likes to make itself known. My stomach is full enough to make breathing feel like a chore, and somewhere in the background, Tristan is still going on about the moisture of the turkey, like he was the one who perfected it. Without looking, I can tell Mama is giving him a death glare. The table looks like a food bomb has gone off, with empty plates, gravy boats with dried edges, and crumpled napkins trying to hide all the evidence. Everyone is slumped and blissed out, unmoving. Well, all except for MJ, who volunteered to clean up. Mama sits across from me, swirling her wine and smiling softly at nothing in particular. Her hair has come loose from her tight bun, revealing her exhaustion. Tristan moves to the couch and works the stereo, putting on some old mix.

"Alright," I say, clapping my hands together with zero conviction, "Who's helping with the dishes?"

A chorus of groans answers me, followed by a few mumbled excuses. I wave them off, already heading for the kitchen sink. I don't mind doing the cleanup, knowing who I'll be standing next to. I come to MJ's side just as she opens the tap. Gently shoving her out of the way, I frisk, "You dry this time." She nods, and we get to work.

From the sink, I can hear the family's hum, laughs, and light arguments. I glance out the window above the faucet, the sun finishing its ascension. The last of the November wind is brushing against the trees, as if it has somewhere else to be.

"Thank you," MJ's whisper prickles my ear.

"For what?"

"For bringing me here."

"Thank *you*."

"For what?"

"For coming with me."

Wash—rinse—hand over—watch her dry—repeat.

Chapter 33

The house quiets into the post-lunch hush, dishes done, energy gone. One single sunbeam slants through the living room window, casting a golden line across the hardwood floor.

Sabrina and Mateo went to her brother's place to spend the night with his family. Tyler disappeared right after we cleaned up, saying he needed to lie down. I believe his exact words were 'deflate the stomach'. Soon after, Luka went for a walk.

Mak speeds through the house in a blur, grabbing his keys and jacket, muttering something about being called in. The door clicks shut behind him, and then there are three. Tristan is stretched out on the couch like he owns it, remote in hand, eyes locked on the football game. Every so often, he curses something at the screen, apologizing to his mom for his language. And then, there is sweet, kind Eva, curled up in her rocking chair with her knitting needles moving like clockwork. I sink onto the edge of the armrest next to her, tucking my feet under me. She looks up and smiles, as she expected me to be there all along.

"What is it?"

"They all just… scattered."

"They always do." Her needles clack gently, but there's content in her voice. "Five boys mean five exits. But don't worry, they always come back."

I glance around the room, the only sound coming from the TV; the faint smell of apple pie hovering.

The comfort gets me thinking.

Is this what it feels like to be part of something that breathes even when no one is talking?

Maybe, if I'm lucky, I'll get to be a part of it too.

I take out my Kindle and dive back into the book I started on the train ride here. I can't tell how much time has passed, nor how many chapters I've crossed, until I get stuck. Clenching my Kindle, I stand up, trying not to spiral out of control.

"Sorry, Eva? Is it ok if I go upstairs? I need to talk to Tyler?" There is a crack in my voice, but she doesn't seem to notice it.

"Of course, sweetie, you don't need to ask," she says, like it's a normal thing. I give her a shy smile and head upstairs, one slow step at a time.

A brown door in front of me, the wood just staring back at me, freezes my hand pre-knock. Digging deep, I find the courage I need and flick my wrist for the strike. The second the door swings open, I start rambling, "I'm sorry, but Emma isn't here, and I need to vent…"

Ty steps aside, with his wide eyes, giving me the space to storm in. Passing around his bedroom floor, not bothering to look up, I go on, "She's my vent person, and it's bad!"

"Ok, calm down and talk to me; I can be your person."

216

That does it. Those words do it; that one declaration stops the world from spinning. I cease moving altogether and take a deep breath, meeting his eyes. "It's... I can't turn the page... I... I... I know what's coming, and I can't turn the page." I'm stuttering, my heart is beating so fast that you would think something horrific happened. "It's a thing with me, one of my many crazies..." I find a spot on the floor, a small dot to focus on. "Emma does this thing, she holds my hand while I read. She hates it, but she does it anyway, and she's not here, and I can't turn the page..."

"I'll hold your hand," he whispers, but it's loud enough for my entire body to ignite.

"You will?"

He frames my face, and despite his warm palms, I shiver. With his eyes intensely focused on mine, my body submits to the weakness.

"I'll do whatever you want and need."

Oh, my...

"And what if I wanted you to kiss me?"

What just came out of my mouth?

"Then I would kiss you."

Breathe, you stupid woman, breathe.

"And if I wanted you to do more?"

"I'd do more."

My lungs are out of control. Breathing feels like an impossible task. There is motion, oxygen goes in, but my lungs don't register any of it. There's no air getting through to me, and my chest starts to burn. Other parts join in the beautiful agony, and against my efforts, there's a crack.

"In case you didn't pick up on any of that, I want you to

kiss me."

He doesn't move—just stands still, his eyes never leaving mine.

"Preferably *NOW*," I yell the last part.

That is the only warning before I tug on his shirt and pull his lips to meet mine. That one collision blows up all the pain, all the fears, all the insecurities...

PUF!

Everything ceases to exist; nothing but the two of us, alone in the universe, and it is paradisaical.

Why did I wait so long?

Why haven't I done this the first time I saw him?

Because you're scared.

My inner voice answers me, knocking me back to reality. The aftermath, the potential hurt, all come crashing in. So, I do the only thing I can think of—I deviate from this being *something.* Opening my mouth slightly, I invite it to go on deeper, welcoming whatever is coming. His tongue plays around mine in perfect rhapsody, making me desperate, itching for more.

I cry out, "I need your fingers inside me."

Without hesitation, he drags his hand inside my underwear, all the way to that sensitive spot desirous for his touch. The moment his finger slides inside, my body momentarily shatters.

"Is that ok?"

"Please restrain yourself from asking stupid questions. Now, give me another one," I snap, demanding and needy.

He delivers, pushing another finger inside, and the sensation is glorious.

"Your tongue on my neck, now, please!"

"Damn Feisty, you're a bossy one."

"Not that bossy, more like starving."

He sinks to my neck and circles his tongue, covering every inch of my skin he can reach. His fingers dig deep, penetrating at the perfect speed, all the while leaving my clit at his thumb's mercy.

"Fucking magic fingers..." I babble in delirium as tension rises in my core. It's right there, but still out of reach... Before I can get in my own head, it's his voice that gets me out.

"Let it go, Feisty," he demands with a slight quiver.

"Let. What. Go?" I gasp, taking short breaths between each word.

"Control!" He claims my mouth and curves his fingers, introducing them to that spot that makes me rapture. Somewhere between heaven and hell, that's where his fingers take me—into a state of bliss and misery. An orgasm unlike any other, one that tears my body and soul in half. He keeps moving, helping me ride it out all the way. As I calm down, my body becomes greedy, wanting more.

"I need you to replace toes fingers with my future best friend down there." I slide my hand inside all the barriers and grab his hard, way-too-big a cock, shivering at the feel of his pre-cum. There's a groan, maybe even a whimper, and I can feel the slight tremble in his lower stomach. But then he pulls away, a pained expression on his gorgeous face.

"As much as I want that Feisty, I need your heart first."

And with that, he leaves.

What the fuck just happened?

My heart wants to jump out of my chest, and my eyes

start to well up, but I close them shut, backing up until my ass falls on a bed. My hands welcome my face, and I sob like a stupid little girl—not because he rejected me, but because he wants me.

The thing is, I'm pretty sure he already has my heart, and I didn't even get the chance to tell him that.

Chapter 34

It takes me about five minutes to function enough to face whatever is behind Tyler's door. I know he's there; I feel him.

I stand up, inhale, and count.

In for four.

Hold for four.

Exhale for four.

As soon as my lids fly up, I go into snoop mode. The room is small, with a bunk bed covering one wall and two desks covering the other, filled with posters and articles. One in particular catches my eye, and I get closer for inspection. The title: '*At McCarthy Basketball Camp, teenage prodigy Tyler Hart steals the show*'. I lean in to read more, but freeze when I see the group photo, one person sticking out.

No, no, no, no…

My throat tightens, and my heart wants to burst out of my chest. I try to breathe, but there's a barrier, something preventing the air from reaching my lungs. Some would guess it's hyperventilation, but it's far from it. My lungs are begging for what they need, my heart screams, and all I can see is black. I need air; need to get out of here… I open the door and crash into a hard chest.

"What's wrong?"

"I… I… I need to go, I…"

My feet find their way, but my mind is in another dimension.

"Sweetie? What happened?" I hear Eva shout, but I can't see her since the spots are getting in the way.

"I don't know." Ty's voice cracks.

"Come here, I got you." I feel a gentle hand guiding me down the stairs, counting each one. "Ok, that's the last one. Just breathe, sweetie."

My vision clears, but my breathing is still impossible to control.

A terrified face gets front and center, and my heart breaks at the sight. His hands are shaking, maybe even more than mine.

"I'm sorry."

The last thing I want is for him to feel guilty. I falter, "No, it's not your fault; it's all me… I'm sorry."

I'm broken.

"Don't you dare apologize." He lifts his hand to touch me, but I pull back.

Panic consumes me, a scream building from within.

"I just, I need fresh air… I need to breathe."

He doesn't follow me, but he watches me as I grab my jacket, cover myself up, and, without a word, step out into the cold air. On the front porch, I inhale again and again and again.

Relief floods in when oxygen reaches my lungs. The comforting feeling is cut short by a hand touching my right shoulder, making me jump out of my skin.

"Sorry." The voice is deep, and I know it belongs to Luka before I turn over my shoulder to see his worrisome face.

"Oh God, you scared me."

I hear footsteps, then I feel him beside me.

"How old were you?"

Chills run throughout my body, so I turn to face him fully. Luka is unique, and yes, it took me way too long to find the perfect word to describe him. Tall, bulky on the outside, but soft on the inside—like a giant teddy bear. He dips his chin, allowing me a better view, so I can recognize something I often find in my own reflection. There's understanding in his honey eyes, so much of it that the number floods out with ease.

"17."

The Port is a straight-out-of-heaven place to grow up in. Children running around, their innocent laughter mixing with the fresh air; it warms my heart. Growing up in Chicago, I had no such luck with pure play on the street. In my opinion, the one good thing to come out of Chicago is the Gallaghers. Fictional people count, trust me, especially for someone obsessed with watching 'Shameless'. In the world where I reside, fiction is always better, because—fuck reality. At least, fuck mine.

Luka recommended we go for a walk, and I took the getaway without hesitation. When we arrived at the waterfront, we took a seat on a bench overlooking the water, welcoming the fresh breeze mixed with the scent of the river. Dragging the sleeves of my sweater to cover my fingers, I put my palms between my thighs and look at the horizon.

"Who?"

There's something unfathomable about a connection between two strangers. The mystery of the concept, the mere bond created with one knowing look, is beyond comprehension. My heart knows better than my mind ever could that I share something with this one person; that we can understand each other's pain. Without any sign of judgment or pity in either of us, we exchange mutual appreciation.

"My parents," he blurts, and I quiver at his admission.

"Both of them?"

His nod makes my heart crack.

"How old were you?"

"It started when I was two and ended when I was five."

"You were so young," is all I can say, tears blurring my vision.

"So were you."

"Yeah, but your parents did that to you, the same people who are supposed to protect and love you unconditionally." I take a deep, shattering breath. "I was hurt just the one time, and by a practical stranger."

"Don't ever use the word *just*; there is no diminution of trauma." His eyes are fierce but hold so much compassion.

"Did it ever get...?" I don't need to finish for him to understand my intent.

"No, it was physical and verbal. That particular line was

never crossed."

I don't know whether to sigh in relief or let out a string of curses.

With a deep breath, I focus back on the water, letting the slow current calm me.

"We had this thing in our school..." I swallow. "The seniors had one day of the year to work at the administration desk; a get-out-of-class-free card assigned to a team of two students. Except for the last semester, they switched it up; one student and a faculty member."

In the corner of my eye, I can see Luka's jaw muscles move. Rubbing my palms to warm up, I inhale.

"All we had to do was sit at the desk and log people coming in and out."

My mind returns to that dark place, and my body reacts with a strong shiver. With my nerves on edge, I try to block out the image of everything.

"I was sitting in my chair, doodling, and out of the blue, hands were on my breasts and I..." I stammer, "I-I hon, honestly d-d-didn't know what to... what to do at that moment." I take a breath and concentrate on the words. "I knew it was wrong, but I didn't move, didn't even react."

I never turned around to check who it was, but I knew. There was a history of his creepy attitude toward me, mostly just these intense stares that sent chills down my spine.

The shame I felt when I was 17 emerges, making me want to jump out of my skin. I look at Luka, trying to find something that's not present. He's listening to every word, understanding everything I'm saying, and was feeling back when I was a lost girl.

"I ran to the bathroom and stayed there for about 10 minutes trying to understand why it felt wrong. I couldn't register it."

I shrug my shoulders, shaking my head at my stupidity. My hand takes out my necklace, the pendants rubbing between my fingers.

"When I got back, the area was empty, so I went about my tasks. I was writing on the board in the small office when his breath blew in my ear. He pushed me against the wall, and I felt something hard pressing into me… I froze. I couldn't get my body to move, my mouth wouldn't scream…"

My eyes start to burn, so I close them shut.

"He got my pants down, and his hands started stretching…" I can't finish, tears piling up in the corners of my eyes. My hand drops, finding the other to hold.

Luka seethes, "Did he?"

"No," I shudder, "not all the way."

I swallow and focus on my fingers fidgeting in my lap.

"When the pain registered, I managed to kick him and run. Police came shortly after, and I spent the whole month making statements and going to therapy. All he got was a restraining order, though."

Luka takes my hand and gives it a gentle squeeze.

"The worst part of it all is what came after. The talk around the school, the name-calling, the constant reminder." I take a shaky breath. "No one believed me, and yet, I was labeled a slut and a tease." I let out a sardonic laugh. "I heard the phrase 'you were asking for it' more than I did 'Hello'." Another chuckle. "How fucked up is that?"

New tears join forces with the old and invade my cheeks.

The all-familiar salty taste hits my mouth, and I crumble.

"Did you know him?"

I nod.

"He was the guy's basketball coach." That makes his jaw clench.

He wasn't just a basketball coach; he was my best friend's coach; my ex-boyfriend's coach.

Someone I looked up to.

"Over time, his face faded, but the nightmares never stopped. And there are times I still get sick from the smell of cologne."

We sit in silence, our hands clasped, not sharing a single word or glance. Just there for each other.

Wind picks up, my ears protesting at the cold. Luka must've noticed, because he stands up. "We should get back. I don't want anyone to worry."

"Good idea." I nod in agreement before I get up, and we start walking back to the house.

"How did you deal with it?"

"It took a long time. I hid it at first because I didn't like talking about it. However, after I told my family, I felt a sense of relief. The literal scars healed, I covered most of them with tattoos, but the emotional ones are still there."

It amazes me how this man, whose facade is a literal brick wall, has so much depth and kindness. Sorrow is there; I can see it in his eyes, but I also see him refusing to let it take control.

"I was lucky enough to be fostered by a nice woman who cured me with her love of books. Our Mama made us read by bringing books from school, where she worked as a teacher.

She always said books make people smart, and she was determined to make us just that—to rise to our full potential."

A genuine smile illuminates his face, though not to its fullest.

"She created a book club for us, with weekly discussions that sometimes turn into full-blown arguments."

I can almost see it, picture them huddled up in the living room, taking turns making their point... my heart skips a beat at the image.

"We read through every genre, even romance novels written by women, to better understand them. Trauma was present in most of the books we read, and somehow, we all healed with character development. We embedded with their trauma and got through ours alongside."

"Wow, what a smart woman," I say in an appreciative tone, thinking about the story she shared with me last night.

"Oh, you have no idea," he snarks, and I chuckle.

We're crossing the street leading to their driveway when my curiosity gets the better of me.

"Where are they now, your birth parents, I mean?"

"My father is serving a life sentence for sending my mother six feet under."

I stop and turn to face him for the full, unapologetic effect.
"Good!"

We exchange a now-familiar, knowing smile.

"Can I ask you a favor?" I blurt, biting my inner cheek.

"Whatever you need."

"Would you hug me?"

He opens his arms, giving me a welcoming smile, and the moment my head rests on his chest, he wraps his arms around me the way a big brother would.

"Thank you."

"Thank *you*." I don't know what he's thanking me for, and I don't ask, taking it all in.

Safe. No better word to describe this place. Just—safe.

Chapter 35

Fifty-three minutes have passed since MJ went away with my brother. Fifty-three minutes of my feet jumping, my mind spiraling, and my heart flatlining.

When she stepped outside on the porch, I watched through the window as her whole body reacted to my brother's touch. They exchanged a few words and began to move away. With an out-of-this-world wisdom, my brother turned and nodded reassuringly, letting me know she was safe with him. Hiding behind the curtain, I sighed in relief and hoped that whatever she needed, my brother would provide it.

"I am so stupid," I gasp out in frustration, marking the fifty-fourth minute, and turn to face my mother. Her warm hand flies to my cheek, and I lean into her touch. My eyes start to fill with tears, and there's this hollow feeling in my chest, something I haven't felt happen since my parents' funeral.

"I hurt her, I…"

"No, honey, someone else did that."

The pain in my chest grows with each ticking second.

"What do I do? What can I do to fix it?"

I don't wanna lose her.

"Just be there for her, and wait until she is ready to share and face it."

I wrap my arms around my mother, resting my chin on the top of her head as she holds me tightly.

"Mama, I..." she steps in before I get to finish, "Oh, honey, I know. I could see it the moment you walked through the door."

Never in my whole life have I been so scared for another person. From the moment I met her, I saw it, felt it - the hurt. I stayed patient, hoping she would share it with me, but the day never came. As I watched her disappear from view with my brother, I found solace in the thought that she might share it with him. Luka is the most mature of us all. He's also the one who experienced the worst trauma. Right now, there's no one else better suited than he to keep her safe. And I can admit that. Still, the anxiety gets the best of me as I try to stay calm and collected. I stand up only to sit back down a dozen times; my legs are jumping, and my nerves are skyrocketing. I want to run outside and find her, but I know she needs time, air, my patience, and my support. Knowing it doesn't make it easy to sit and wait. It's agonizing, painful, and downright torturous.

"Chill, she's with Luka." Tristan comes to my side, head tilted, eyes calm.

When I don't respond, he takes another shot, "Are you worried he'll steal her away?"

I glare at him, jaw ticking - the jerk scoffs. He has that 'Mission accomplished' look, and I shake my head.

"Hey, your leg stopped shaking so..." he gloats, pointing at my still legs.

"They're back," Mama says from the window.

I spring to my feet and charge outside. My heart jumps to my throat when my eyes land on her back. A moment later, she's wrapped in my brother's arms, and I sigh in relief, knowing he worked his magic for her. I close in on them, and he gently nudges his head, telling me to switch places with him. More than happy to oblige, I get to his side as he slowly unwraps her arms from around his waist and wraps them around mine.

She doesn't protest, only sinks in, melting into my embrace. I give Luka a thankful nod before he leaves us there, in the middle of our yard. There's no place on earth I would rather be than here with her. I smell her hair, cherry dominating over something flowery. God, I never want to let her go.

"Your mother hugged me last night," she reveals.

"Oh?"

"She hugged me like a mother would."

I can hear the tear in her voice, and I squeeze her tighter, unable to come up with anything better.

"I haven't felt that kind of hug in over two years."

My heart breaks for her, but I stay silent, afraid I'll scare her confessions away.

"That's not true," she corrects herself, " I don't think I ever felt that kind of hug."

I kiss the top of her head, and an audible smile escapes her.

"This hug's not so bad either. Your family gives out great ones." She lifts her head, and the curve of her lips erases all the worries I had. My God, she is beautiful. Even with swollen, red eyes, she is still the most beautiful creature I've ever seen.

"Can we go for a walk and talk?" MJ utters, and I frame her face, wiping her tears away. Fighting the urge to kiss her, I nod, taking her hand.

Fingers locked, we find a slow pace.

"Do you remember your parents?" she murmurs.

"Not really, I was three when they died. But I dream of our mom's voice. She read to us every night before bed."

"What happened?"

"A car crash. They both died instantly. Mateo got a cut over his brow, four stitches, and I walked away without a scratch."

"You sound guilty about that."

Her cold hand squeezes mine, and I bring it to my mouth so I can warm it with my breath.

"Well, yeah, I feel it."

"Because you didn't get physically hurt?"

"Kind of."

"Tyler, you lost your parents; you didn't get out scot-free."

I let her words sink in, knowing she has a point. I grab the pendant I have around my neck.

"This is all I have left. It was my mom's."

MJ stops moving, giving her full attention to the golden circle. She examines it thoroughly, her lips curving at the details around the engraved flower.

"Her name was Jasmine?" MJ's eyes lift to mine, a twinkle in them beaming. I nod. She flips the pendant over, her thumb grazes over the heart, lingering over the letter representing me.

Reading the intent in her eyes, I answer her before she has the chance to open her mouth. "Whatever you want."

"You have to stop doing that; it's not fair, not to mention normal."

"Good thing you don't like normal."

"Well, true, but still..." She shakes her head, trying to hide the blush, but I saw it.

"Back to the favor..." I circle back, lifting her chin with the crook of my finger.

"Take me to your favorite place."

With the stupidest grin, I lower my body, giving her my back. Reading my intention, she laughs, then screams with joy. Jumping on me, she wraps her legs around my waist and her hands around my shoulders. With MJ piggybacked firmly, I stride to the only place where I can clear my head. I am sure she already knows what and where it is. She must've passed by it with Luka, and wants to share it with me. The thought makes me giddy.

Chapter 36

MJ

Okay, so the butterflies people always talk about when they describe their feelings—are they supposed to be small in size but large in number, or vice versa? Because I am currently very undecided... For example, when I jumped on Tyler's back, it felt like a rush of one gigantic butterfly that flew straight into my rib cage. Still, after he took a few steps with me as his backpack, it felt like that one giant butterfly burst into a million smaller ones that just kept on colliding, making explosions inside me. Let's not forget to mention the stupid, amazing, captivating smell that oozes from him in the middle of the freaking cold. There's something about a man who can carry you with ease that any girl would spread her legs and say, "Enjoy," and yes, I indeed just imagined that scene with a stimulating, picturesque graphic—thank you very much.

Let's talk about the state of my mind—there is none.

There's nothing, no list of possible outcomes, the what could go wrongs, no insecure thoughts, no nothing. Well, there's some previously droughted area that is now in full deluge, though it has been slowly inundating ever since one fatal October Friday, and yes, I verbalized that word—don't judge.

Maybe all previously mentioned is the reason I chose this moment to share some irrelevant information, with my cheek firmly pressing against Tyler's, rubbing on his 5 o'clock shadow. My mind takes me back to the first moment we met, when he asked me about my name.

"You know you were the first person who ever asked me what the J stands for."

The eruption of my words brings him to a halt, and for a minute, it looks like he's having a discussion with himself. He sets me down and turns to face me, like whatever I'm about to say needs his undivided attention.

"It's Joy," I reveal.

He frames my face between his cold palms and collides his mouth with mine. Well, if that's his reaction to sharing something so small, maybe I should try out this 'opening up' thing. When he parts my lips, the look on his face begs me to do just that, so what's a girl to do? Give in, I guess…

"It's stupid, but at orientation, I had that Tris and Four first interaction moment, you know, when she had that beat to choose her name…" I wave my hand through the air. "Anyway, when they asked for my name at the table for my student ID, I started thinking about how much I hated my mother calling me Maddison."

It's more the tone in which she used to say it; bitter… angry. I never had a nickname growing up, not until Damian started calling me Berta. But it wasn't mine. That's why I like Feisty so much. It's personal, my own, and that makes it special.

"So you came up with MJ," Ty concludes. I nod, stuffing

my freezing hands in my jacket pockets.

"Joy was my grandma's name, and she was the only person in this world who cared for me. She died when I was eight."

Throughout my ramble, brown eyes are firmly and intensely locked on mine, and it's a hard thing to handle; captivating, heartbreaking.

"You're the first person I shared that with." I shrug, with a silent hum.

"Thank you," is the last thing I hear before the back of my throat starts moaning at the workings of his tongue. If I thought his fingers were magical, his tongue is supernatural. He takes just as much as he gives, and when he sucks, I feel the vibration of my thighs as the ground opens up from under me. So when he suddenly stops and pulls away, I let out an exasperated breath, making his stupid, hot face grin.

He takes my hand and guides me to the river court, the one I saw on my walk with Luka. The moment we step over the outline, Tyler's face lights up. I can imagine a younger version of him shooting the hoop. The recollection of me doing the same feels different. It isn't heavy; it's just there. And for the first time since I lost it, I smile at the memory.

Drinking him in, I push away the fears, my want taking over. I feel my heart racing, begging me to let go; so I listen and jump right into Tyler's ready arms. Using my thighs for support, I lock my ankles around his back, my hands flying to the back of his head. Hungry, starving, I take the plunge. My mouth is on his, and my tongue darts inside, gripping onto his at lightning speed. Desperation is the factor of my frantic kiss, an unstoppable urge for deeper, more, everything. His one hand is firmly placed on the back of my neck while the other holds my ass. I press myself onto him, feeling his hardness while he walks us to the ping pong concrete table. He gently places my ass on the cold surface, and I unzip his jacket. My hands slide under his shirt right away. The feel of his skin, the outline of his pecs, the small, happy trail that peaks above the waistband of his pants, it's all too much, yet, not enough.

"Do you have a condom?" I ask over his mouth, not allowing him to move away. He nods, and dang has a nod ever been more fucking sexy!? His eyes are hungry just as much as mine, and the lust is so vividly present that I just lose it. My hand is inside his boxers so fast that Tyler shrieks a bit. Ok, maybe it's due to my cold hands, but they get warm as soon as I wrap my fingers around his core. I need him inside me and pronto. More so, I need to be as close to him as possible.

"I need you." My voice is hoarse, making him step away. His head turns in every direction, and I do the same. There's a tree behind him in a sort of blind spot, surrounded by bushes. I decide that's our destination. Tyler reads my mind, grabbing my hand. When we reach the somewhat secluded area, I take off my jacket, place it on the ground, and dip my head in command for him to sit.

"You'll get cold."

"I don't care if I die of pneumonia tomorrow, I need you inside of me, and I need you to fuck me breathless," I growl, knowing how needy and hungry it sounds. Like the good boy I know he is, he plants that beautiful ass on my offering, maneuvering out of his jacket. I push down my pants just enough and slowly drop down into his open arms. We stare at each other for a long beat as he wraps me in his jacket. My breath hitches at his attentiveness.

Slowly, I lean in and kiss him, gently appreciating the way he cares for me. The hungry animal from before is nowhere to be found; only the girl, desperate for love, remains. His knuckles slowly brush my cheek, the touch inviting me to look at him. There's this softness in his eyes, like they are trying to tell me something… *I see you, I want you, I'm not rushing this.*

Something in me relaxes, like a forgotten knot finally loosening. My fingers work around the waistband of his pants, sliding them down just enough to free his sculptured dick. It springs up in salute, and I salivate at the sight of pre-cum leaking from his tip. Tyler is quick, ripping the foil with his teeth, followed by latex sliding down the shaft. Gluing my mouth to his, I pull up my hips enough for him to align my center with his cock. I pull back to look at him as I slowly, so slowly, claim it.

His groaning moans send electroshocks to my senses< the firm grip on my hips makes me frantic, and the way his mouth possesses mine, there's nothing left to be tamed. My body trembles at his size, form, and when his tip gets to that inner sacred place, I combust. Should I be embarrassed that I orgasmed after merely three strikes? Probably. Am I? No, not in the slightest. I continue with the ride, catching another wave with so much ferocity. Though our movements are somewhat limited, the power is strong with this one. With me dancing around his—safe to say—python, and him launching it into orbit, nothing ever felt better.

Full disclosure, coming to this court, I did have a plan; so far, everything is going according to that plan, except it's not. Somewhere down the line, a tiny, teeny snap happened in my brain. It cut the thread connected to my common sense. This was supposed to be simple. I was to ride his massive, beautiful, magic stick, and let him fuck me stupid.

Did that happen? Yes. Is there something more? Yes, yes, there is…

Right here, on the cold ground next to a tree, two not-so-naked people are… connecting. The way his eyes captivate mine, with so much potency, I have never felt more alive. Not to mention wanted, safe, seen… My body is burning for his touch, his thrusts—*him*. And when he grabs the back of my neck, pulling me into one of those deep kisses, I explode. Catching my breath when he releases my mouth, he gives me another intense stare before he finally submerges into oblivion, breathing out my name—*mine*. There is nothing sexier than a man's fazed expression post-orgasm. With his chest rising and falling, his breath irregular, and his eyes satisfied, I stare at the man whom I am now determined to keep.

Chapter 37

Whoever said patience is a virtue hasn't been rewarded for it. My prize is worth the wait. I'm not just talking about the public display of affection. I mean, MJ is finally opening up to me.

Fully dressed, dazed in bliss, we watch the night sky while she talks about her past. Her back is on my chest, my legs wrapped around her, our hands pressed together, fingers intertwined.

She shares her experiences growing up in a bad neighborhood, feeling neglected. Even the story of her with Damian and his brother doesn't bring any pang of jealousy. The smile in her voice is so loud when she talks about her life after discovering basketball. She vividly describes her standout games, including the championship game from her junior year and the offers she received to go pro.

Everything's so clear on the surface now, displayed out for me. From the moment I met her, she's been holding back, suppressing something. So I know that this small crack is significant. When she gets to her senior year of high school, I can almost sense her reservations. Something happened to her then, and she's not ready to share it with me yet. I don't press, just hold her tighter, knowing my brother helped in some way.

This vulnerable side of MJ is the one I was desperate to see, feel, and have, and now that I have finally gotten it, all I want to do is keep it safe and protected. One thing I hope is that she feels shielded right here in my arms, by my words and actions.

When she lets out a sigh, marking the weight of her shoulders lifting, she removes herself from my grasp, takes my hand, and walks by my side back to my house in silence.

As soon as we cross the threshold, we're welcomed by two sets of concerned eyes. I help MJ free herself from her jacket, and my mother leaps onto her, wrapping her arms around her, all the while giving me daggered eyes.

"Oh, sweetie, I was so worried. Are you feeling better?"

"I am so sorry, I didn't mean to worry you." MJ bows her head and barely lets out a whisper, "I didn't think that you would be, I am sorry." It hits me how much truth those words hold. She never had anyone worrying about her. No one checked the clock for a missed curfew or lost sleep over away games.

"Oh sweetie…" My mother must've come to the same conclusion, because the look she gives MJ is the same one we've been on the receiving end of for most of our lives. I scan MJ, her eyes changing color and getting brighter. I stand there, frozen, as MJ exchanges a moment with my mother. Luka's hand lands on my shoulder, keeping me from crumbling at the sight. She's doing it; she's letting other people in, allowing them to become a part of this—us—and I can't move. My knees are so fucking weak, ready to collapse. It's when MJ speaks that some circulation returns. "Thank you for showing me what it's like."

My mother goes speechless. We all do. But we know what she means by that, and I am so happy that she has a chance to see it, feel it, and to do so here, with the most important people in my life.

"Ok, come, dinner is waiting," Luka jumps in with a calming tone, placing his arm around MJ's shoulders. With one side of her lips tilted, she takes a seat, the same one from lunch, looking at the table set out for five. Tristan comes down a minute later and takes his seat before we all say our silent prayers. My eyes crack open enough to see MJ's head down, mouth barely moving, one single tear grazing down her cheek. Never in my life have I wanted to hear someone's thoughts as much as I want to read hers now. The need to know if she's ok with everything is strong. Perhaps the question I most crave an answer to is how she feels about us after what happened under that tree.

Scared doesn't even begin to cover how I felt before, during, and after. The way she felt, the fit, the sense of belonging... her mumbled words, my name on her breath; it was ethereal.

At some point, I thought I heard her say "magic stick", which was an ego boost. Our bodies moved together so perfectly, a choreographed dance we created. But it was the depth of her stare, the way she allowed me to see her, that was truly remarkable. That look is engraved in my brain, a forever memory I will endlessly cherish.

Chapter 38

There is something in the water, or the house is cursed, or they drugged me somehow... I can't tell you what exactly, but something is definitely going on. I don't recognize myself right now.

The look on Eva's face when Tyler and I got back is one I've never seen before, at least not from a grown-up. It broke some part of me that, frankly, I never knew existed. A part that was created by years of deprivation, neglect, and self-loathing. A part that was caging all hope, dreams, and the possibility of a future. And when it broke, it freed all the belief, the desire, the faith. With that release, my heart lit up with a sense of worth. It made me think that maybe I deserve happiness... That's why, when we finished dinner and helped clean up, I came to Eva and told her exactly what she had done for me. More than anything, I needed her to know and understand the enormity of her heart. How much her simple act of kindness changed this lost girl's life.

The house is quiet, the darkness of the night at its peak. I'm curled up on the couch, deep into the chapter, when I hear quiet footsteps approaching. My whole body trembles. I know who they belong to, because only his presence can get this kind of reaction out of me. When I look at him over my shoulder, my heart stops.

"What are you doing here?"

"I'm here to hold your hand."

Can a person melt? Like, literally melt? Is that something biologically possible?

I make room so he can take the place behind me, his legs framing mine, making his chest my pillow. He grabs my shoulders and leans my back onto his chest. Taking my left hand, he intertwines our fingers and places my Kindle in my right hand. With his mouth breathing in my ear, he grazes his fingers down my arm, stroking gently before he does the same thing in the upward direction. Remember when I told you about that imaginary scene of us reading together? Well, it's safe to say my imagination has no imagination—it doesn't do reality any justice. The way this feels is nothing short of immaculate. With his chin digging into my shoulder, he reads over me, his fingers keeping up the steady rhythm.

"Are you planning on turning the page any time soon? I've already read it three times."

Fuck! I think I'm blushing.

"Well, you are an overachiever then, because I wasn't able to read a single word."

"Why is that?"

"I'm distracted."

"Distracted how?" he rasps, and my core throbs.

"Well, for starters, I feel your heart beating, your breath breathing, and your stick hardening."

"What can I say, you have that effect on me."

Breathe, MJ, breathe!

245

"And yet, you managed to read the page three times?"

At first, I thought he was messing with me, but now I have a feeling he was telling the truth.

"The only reason for that is so I wouldn't do something else."

Yup. Called it.

"Like what?"

His hand slowly slides under the covers over my pajamas and stops right between my thighs. My entire body trembles in anticipation.

"Something very, very bad," he groans, and I have to press my thighs together, trapping his hand there.

"I never pegged you for a bad boy." My breath hitches at the way he grazes that sensitive spot over the fabric.

"Yes, you did." He bites my earlobe, triggering the goosebumps.

"Fine, you're right, I did," I admit, having trouble catching a single puff of air.

His lips still at my ear, he whispers, "You know, I never had a girl in my room..."

And now my goosebumps have goosebumps.

"Oh?"

"I want to make you come in my bed," he hoarsely whispers, causing a throb down under. This seductive side of him is going to be my undoing.

"But Luka?"

"He's sleeping in his room."

I bite my inner cheek, wondering if his brother did that on purpose.

"The walls are very thick, you won't have to hold back..."

Fuck me!

His finger, I'm guessing pointer, roams around the hem of my PJs right before his hand slips under, touching my skin. He leans close, his lips brushing my ear. A finger slips inside my wet hu-ha as he whispers, "Will you let me make you come in my bed, Feisty?"

Another finger joins, his thumb pressing on my clit in circular motions, making me release a loud moan.

"Words, Feisty, I'm gonna need your words!"

"Yes, Ty, please make me come in your bed."

In a quick swoop, I am bridal-styled, and we're up. My feet dangle in the air, my fingers in his hair, tongue on his neck, while he speed-walks upstairs. Inside his room, he puts me down, taking one step back before his eyes take me in. With his fiery stare, I leisurely get rid of my clothes, trying to look sexy in the process. I can see the slight twitch happen in his pants when his hand gets to the back of his head. He bites down on his lower lip, taking the whole thing inside his mouth, and fuck if my hu-ha isn't doing cartwheels at the sight. I have never felt so desired, and I hope he feels the same way, because I want him so badly, every piece of him. Entirely bare, I back up, placing my naked ass on his bed.

"How'd you know that's my bed?"

I followed your smell…

"Lucky guess!"

"Riiight…" he drawls, a slight smirk with a side of cockiness lighting his face as he stares at me marking his bed.

With my legs spread out, knees up, feet facing down on the covers, I watch as Tyler takes off his clothes, finally gracing me with all his glory. His body is a masterpiece, every defined muscle on display, and those clenched fists. God, he was molded to perfection—for me. Pecs stretching with each deep breath, abs begging to be touched, and the V that I somehow missed, make me drool. His thighs are firm, I can see the outlines of his quadriceps, and when his boxers fall on the floor, I am blinded by the magic.

"Shit, condom," he mumbles. As much as I want to giggle, I restrain myself.

"I'm on the pill and clean," I blurt. The entire team got tested before the season started, as did the entire athletics department.

"I'm clean," he hesitates for a beat, "Are you sure?"

"When it comes to you, there's nothing I'm unsure of."

Those words somehow soften his firm gaze and bring his lips into a broad curve. He closes in on me, making it seem like he's moving in slow motion. He places his knees on the bed and slides his naked body over mine, hovering. One hand cups my face, thumb grazing my lips, before he plunges with his mouth. I open instinctively, inviting his tongue to meet mine, and God, it's so good. My hands go to his ass, his cheeks perky, muscular, begging to be squeezed by my hands and my hands alone. His mouth finds my nipple, and his tongue flicks around it, all the while his fingers play with the other. He rubs it between his middle and pointer finger, confusing my body with the sensation. When he departs my nipples with a grin, I consider murdering him on the spot. He obliterates the notion by gracing my clit with his skillful tongue. My back hurts from arching, not to mention the degree of the curvature. It surprises me how much my spine bridges out vigorously. When his fingers, three of them to be exact, slide inside, I honestly fear my back will break. The intrusion is so euphoric that it blindsides me. I imagined having him like this would be amazing, but as I mentioned before, my imagination had no imagination. This is so much better, indescribably, unimaginably better...

With his tongue torturing me, his fingers moving at a perfect pace, down to that flicking thing he does, I full on combust on his hand and mouth, and when the wave hits the last crash, he replaces his fingers with some more magic. With him inside me, it feels so right, like he was made for me. And when his eyes lock with mine, he feels just that—*mine.*

Chapter 39

If there were an accurate description of heaven, it would not be of a place; it would be of a feeling or a state... For me, it's MJ in my arms. The fact that she's in my bed, our hands wrapped around each other, is nothing short of a dream come true. Sure, I am being a stupid teenager for saying or thinking it, but in all honesty, I am glad she's the first one in this bed. None of us brothers has ever brought a girl home before; Mateo was the first. I always thought it was out of respect for Mama, so when I asked my brother why Sabrina was the exception, his argument blew me away. He said she's the one, and I didn't understand it until now.

Fuck! I just hinted that MJ is the one, didn't I? Well, sue me, lock me up, and throw away the key, but make sure MJ is on my side of the door. I am willing to go down for it and make it for life.

The happy bubble—MJ naked on my chest, hidden by the covers—gets burst by the vibrations of MJ's phone, revealing a video call request from Emma. Looking at the clock on the desk, I raise an eyebrow, but MJ turns in her defense, "It's like 9 PM in Bora Bora, and I'm usually awake at this hour."

My brow grows higher, and she immediately reacts to it. "Not like that, you idiot; I stay up late reading." Shaking her head with a huge grin, she answers the call, getting me out of the shot.

"Oh my God! Wait…" Emma shrieks, and then there's a long pause, giving MJ and me a moment to look at each other with wonder, before a familiar beat starts beaming from the phone speaker, making MJ's face go full on red. The moment that guy from SNL starts singing, the reason for her instant redness hits me… MJ bursts into laughter, and I follow, numbing the noise into my pillow, all the while 'I just had sex' by The Lonely Island echoes in my room.

"I hate you, you mind-reading bitch," MJ whisper-yells.

"Oh, no mind reading here… you have the 'I've been thoroughly fucked face'…"

Well, I can't argue with that, I was very thorough, not to toot my own horn or anything.

"You're crazy, you know that?"

"And you love it, so there's some crazy in you too, now, isn't there? Anyway, tell Ty to stop hiding and get in. I also don't mind seeing him naked, just saying."

"You're funny, thinking anyone other than me gets to see him naked."

"Possessive much?" I tease, dragging myself to MJ's side. "Hi, Red."

"Oh no, Fuck-boy; it's Emma to you!"

I give her my best soldier-like salute.

"So, how is Bora Bora?" MJ asks, rubbing her knee against mine.

"Too hot to handle and so boring," Emma whines, "I miss

251

Ben's cock!"

That one gets me choking, and MJ comes to my rescue, slapping my back while holding in her laugh.

"Oh, is someone sex-deprived?"

"No, no!" Emma waves her finger. "You don't get to tease me now that you're finally getting some."

"Sorry." MJ makes the cutest version of the puffy face.

"Bet you didn't read a single page?" Emma plays with her brows, and MJ blows out her tongue.

I watch the screen while Emma gives an expectant look, to which MJ responds by lifting her hand, her fingers spread.

"Nice," Emma gushes, this time looking right at me. Confused, I turn to face MJ, who tries hard not to laugh out loud. Obviously, I'm the punch line, but no one chooses to fill me in on the joke. All Emma says is "Don't worry, it's a good thing." I decide to believe her, not that I have any other choice.

"Anyway, I called to see how's it going, but I got my answer, so I'll just leave you lovebirds to it."

I pretend not to notice another blush forming on MJ's cheeks.

"Thanks for checking on me, and I can't wait to see you Sunday. I miss you."

"Of course you do; I am irreplaceable, you hear that, Fuck-boy?"

"No competition here, no worries."

"Oh, I'm not worried. You, on the other hand…"

"I love you," MJ interrupts with a snarl.

"I love you too," Emma beams back at her.

"I love you three," I bellow. That one earns me the combo

laugh from the two best friends, followed by a suspicious look from the naked blonde. Did I not mention she's in my bed, naked, right there next to me?! Naked.

After the call ends, she tosses the phone on the bed and scoots to the edge.

"I should probably go back to the couch."

"Yeah, you probably should, but you are not going to."

She cocks a brow. "I feel bad for what I just did with your family right on the other side of the wall, and I'm not going to push my luck by getting caught."

"And what is it that you did exactly?" I drag her back to me. Her face turns red again, and damn, how much I love to see her flustered like that. "Say it, Feisty," I roar.

"I came in your bed, hard." It's an assertive whisper, but I take it.

"Yeah, you did!"

Her hand flies to my chest, giving me a playful nudge before she stands up, picking up our discarded clothes. She tosses me my shirt first, then puts on her bra, followed by the rest of her clothes, covering herself in fluffy dolphin pajamas. As much as I want her to stay wrapped up in me, I know I have to let her go, at least for a couple of hours.

When I wake up to the light coming into my room, I check my phone for the time only to see a message from MJ waiting for me, one that shares a link to a Spotify list. Opening the playlist named 7, I find one song: 'Shower' by Becky G. I eagerly press play, having never heard the song before. I'm thankful for the lyrics displayed on the screen. Happy with the song choice to express her feelings, I stand up, with the biggest smile on my face, and get dressed. Something about adding me to her soundtrack makes me giddy, and it's a weird feeling to have, an amazing one at that.

Downstairs, everyone is already awake, drinking their coffee, and I find Mateo and Sabrina in the kitchen. They both pull me in a hug, and Sabrina hands me my warm cup with a knowing wink.

Is it a girl thing? This notion of knowing sex happened? Is that like some estrogen-induced superpower? No, scratch that, because Mateo and Luka also have the knowing look, and somehow I think my mother also knows. Tristan is oblivious, so is Mak, thank God, but still, it's 4 out of 6... we're outnumbered...

MJ is going to kill me!

I take a seat next to her, and she leans in, whispering, "They all know."

Well, that escalated quickly.

I squeeze her knee under the table, but she moves it away too quickly, adding a death glare.

"What?"

"I'm gonna kill you," she threatens through gritted teeth.

"Hey, they knew before I got here."

"Oh no, you did not just blame me!?"

"Yes. Yes, I did."

"And here I thought you were a gentleman."

"I believe I've proved to be anything but. Maybe you need a reminder..." I lift five fingers, mimicking it exactly as she showed it to Emma, indicating how many times she combusted. It only took me six hours to figure out the secret code she shared with her BFF last night.

Her jaw drops just as Sabrina clears her throat. MJ snaps

her focus to my brother's wife, who is inviting us to move to the living room.

Chapter 40

We all gather in the living room, ready for our weekly discussion. Sabrina is settled on Mateo's lap in the rocking chair, I took one of the armchairs, and the rest of my family is settled on the couch. MJ joins, her face etched with confusion, but still manages to make herself comfortable in the chair next to me.

"So, let's just go straight to the cliffhanger so we can get the frustration out." Mama's words get us all pumped up, hands flying in the air with gasping grunts as we all start speaking over each other. My eyes focus on MJ, whose head is snapping all over the place, trying to catch up with the conversation.

"I just want to point out how Sabrina should be penalized for this, because we now have to wait like two months for the next one." Tristan points his finger toward the future lawyer.

"That's why we read it so we can prepare for it," Sabrina defends.

"We could have done it in January then," Tristan bites back.

"Right, like you would be able to focus with midterms."

"Good point, no penalty for you."

"As if you could influence that." Sabrina shakes her head, and Tristan bows his head in defeat.

"Okay," Luka drags, "I think her signant is going to be mind-reading or something like that, for sure."

I rebut, "No, that would be too easy for her to have, but it's probably gonna be something that would be dangerous enough they would want to kill her."

"Good point," Mak jumps in.

"I'm sorry—" MJ wiggles in her seat "—are you talking about The Empyrean series?"

"Yeah, well, technically, Iron Flame, we discussed Forth Wing last week," Tristan answered with a smile.

I can almost see the wheels spinning in that beautiful head of hers.

"So you all read the same book?"

Everyone nods, and MJ swallows noticeably.

"The whole book?"

A chuckle escapes the male side of the family, and Sabrina answers with a dragged-out "Yeees."

"So the 'my house, my chair...' you all read that?" Her cheeks turn a new shade of red, and I think she officially holds the record for the times she blushed in my presence.

"We don't discuss those particular scenes," Sabrina quips.

"But you know what the other one read? How do boys react to those kinds of things?"

"Oh, honey, that's a good thing," Sabrina retorts, turning to Luka. "Shut your Mama's ears, please."

He obliges, Mama scoffs, rolling her eyes.

"Trust me, it's a good thing they read that stuff... Remember the bickering between Violet and Cat regarding..." she wiggles her fingers, and MJ blushes again, nodding. "Well, Mateo spent a week trying to figure out what it was, and let me tell you..." Luka coughs, followed by Tristan and Mak doing the same.

"Fine," Sabrina grunts with a sigh. "Release the ears," she orders, waving her hand through the air. Taking the place on the floor in front of Mateo, she continues explaining. "Look at it this way, think of your favorite book boyfriend," she pauses, giving MJ time to picture it. "Chances are, they read that book, learned from it, and probably act on it."

MJ takes in her words and sits there in complete silence. As if a light bulb lit up in her head, her lips tilt into a shy-like smile, melting my heart.

And there goes the blush.

She turns to face me, and I give her an intense smirk because, ladies and gentlemen, her third favorite book finally smacks me in the face.

"What?" she jerks, and my smirk just intensifies.

"Nothing." I shrug.

"Then wipe the smirk!"

"What smirk?"

"That knowing one," she says, pointing her finger at my face and circling it. "Wipe it off."

"I can't."

"Why?"

"Because I know."

She narrows her eyes for a beat, then her eyes widen when she figures out what I meant by it.

"You don't, you couldn't possibly…"

"Say you swear," I tell her with all confidence.

There's some inside jumping going on, with a side of gloating. I can't help it. She likes the mind-reading, and here I thought it was unwelcome.

"I hate you."

"Such a bad liar." I bite my lip.

"Well, don't get cocky; he's still my favorite."

I know she's referring to a character from the book, a fictional one, but it doesn't make me any less jealous. That's how crazy I am about this girl, fucking jealous of a made-up guy who in no way could even hold a torch for me, but whatever.

"Anywaaaay," Tristan cuts in, "I'm still very much in love with Mira."

"Oh, I know what you mean," MJ agrees, "She's a badass."

"Sorry, team Riorson here," Sabrina interjects.

"Pick a side, newbie!" Tristan demands, and MJ snaps quickly, "Ridock all the way."

"Approved," Sabrina stamps it.

While MJ continues to engage in the discussion, I turn to Mama. I zero in on her smile, her eyes snapping between me and MJ. The look says it all; MJ fits here. Plain and simple.

MJ is actively avoiding me, and I have no idea why. Sure, she wanted to kill me before on two separate occasions, but it's no reason to hide. It bewilders me, and quite frankly, I'm kind of into it. Knowing I have this effect on her, it might've gotten to my head a little bit. After dinner, Sabrina takes MJ to Luka's bedroom so they can get ready for a girls' night out. It was brought to my attention that Sabrina offered to take her to the only club in Boston that plays MJ's jam—Sabrina's words, not mine. It's a good thing that they are getting close, going out, and having fun, with MJ relaxing and letting loose. It's a good thing... so why am I anxious? The moment she steps out of the room, I know exactly why. Because she's sexy as hell and she's going to dance in a club full of stupid men that are gonna be all over her, and I am supposed to what? Stay at home and wait?

As she descends in what seems to be slow motion, I drink her in. Sabrina took it upon herself to emphasize MJ's best features, like her eyes, which are doing the smoky thing; her lips are flushed in matte red, and she's wearing painted-on jeans paired with a tight shirt that reveals her belly button. Somehow, all I want to do is shout 'no' and 'cover yourself up,' but I manage to bite my tongue. Her hair is down, curled up in waves, and I want to tangle my fingers as deep as possible, but I step out of the way with a stupid smile instead.

Sabrina drags her into the hall's full-length mirror, and MJ gives herself a once-over. "I barely recognize myself, but damn, you're a miracle worker."

Sabrina puffs out her chest at MJ's praise. "How do you feel?"

"Powerful?" MJ answers like she's not sure, but Sabrina

nips it in the bud, "Good answer."

Mateo appears by my side.

His wife smirks, "How do I look?"

"Like trouble."

They close in on each other, going full PDA, disregarding anyone and anything. I clear my throat, and when they pull back, I notice MJ's eyes on me.

My heart jolts, and all I can do is state the obvious, "You are beautiful."

"It's the makeup."

"Let me pull out a Kavanagh here and simply add it's the girl."

A full-on blush, the natural kind, tries its best not to show. But it's there, and I know MJ would get the reference since I saw the whole 'Boys of Tommen' series on her shelves.

"See, I told you, Eva is a genius for forcing them to read. Did I tell you I got them to read 'One Last Rainy Day', and yes, Mateo and I played out the *swish-tap-tap* scene, but I didn't last as long as Cecilia. I jumped his bone—" I cough because Sabrina has no filter—ever.

MJ's blush doesn't fade, her eyes locked on mine, and I know exactly what she's thinking about, what scene made her cheeks hot—same characters, different book.

An idea pops into my head. When she least expects it, I am going to torture her with my tongue while she reads, or better yet, tries to.

Chapter 41

After the girls left for the city, my brothers pulled out the poker set, getting us into an intense game of Hold'em. Mama went to bed early, so it's just us boys in the house, the downstairs part, that is.

I find myself unable to fully relax knowing MJ is out there without me.

"Relax, bro, she's with Sab," Mateo tries soothing from across the table. I snap him a glare, "That's what worries me."

"Don't even. You know she liked her even before she met her. She'll have her back."

I settle into my chair. "You're right."

"What was that?" O cradles his ear, acting deaf.

"Very funny. I won't repeat myself, old man; take it or leave it."

"Doesn't matter, I've got witnesses." He points his hands at the rest of the table. Tristan puts on a show with his shuffling, smirking as he lets the cards slap against each other like he works in a freakin' casino.

"You shuffling or doing foreplay?" Mak goads. Tristan raises an eyebrow, grinning. "Just making sure nobody accuses me of stacking the deck, big bro."

"What else would explain how you've won the last three hands?" Luka grunts, the sourest of losers.

"Maybe I'm just smarter than all of you," Tristan says, dealing. Two cards land in front of me. I wait while he deals the rest of them before I peek—Jack and a nine, both hearts.

Could get interesting.

Mateo gives his cards a side glance before tossing a few chips into the pot without a word. He doesn't bluff often, but when he does, he is good at it. Or maybe he just doesn't care. Luka slides in more chips. "Let's raise it."

"You do know we are playing actual money here, little bro?" Mak mutters. I call, just to see what will happen, anticipating the river. Flop comes down: ten of hearts, queen of spades, eight of hearts. Well, my hand just got a whole lot more fun. Tristan tosses in his chips without a hint of a facial expression. The turn card is the king of diamonds. I remain indifferent, not showing my inner jumping at the possibility of a straight flush. I check with my knuckles, tapping the table twice, and get the others to fill out the pile that starts to resemble the Leaning Tower of Pisa in a house of mirrors. Mateo raises, the rest of us call. Even Luka stays in, lips pursed, eyes locked on the cards. Then the river drops— queen of hearts.

"All in." I drag my chips to the center. Chairs creak; nobody says anything for a beat.

It's Mateo who leans forward, his scared brow going up. "You serious?"

"Sure am." I nod.

"Bluffing," Mak jumps in, "has to be."

Luka has his signature resting prick face, trying to get a read, tapping his fingers on the table.

"Fold," Tristan gives up, pushing back. Luka follows a second later. Mak hesitates but joins them, grumbling.

"Screw it. I call," Mateo tops my chips. I lay down the jack and nine. He stares at my cards, then looks at each of our brothers, then back at my hand.

"You little..." he mutters, laughing. "Straight flush? Seriously?"

I shrug and drag the pile toward me.

"Don't hate the player, hate your luck."

"You should play the lottery with your luck today," Tristan quips, but what he doesn't realize is that I have already won the best kind of lottery—life.

Half of lost chips later, Mateo receives a text from Sabrina saying that he should get me to the club and hurry. Blood boils with worry. We are out of the house and on his bike so fast, I don't catch a breath, speeding down the road to get to our girls as soon as possible. Fifteen minutes later, we're pulling through the crowd, desperately searching. Mateo gets another text saying they're up in the VIP area, and we tear to them. My adrenaline is pumping, and I am one move away from doing some real damage. But when I get up, everything dies down. I'm blessed by the vision of MJ, glowing. It amazes me how my body can go from worry and rage to a soft pile of mush in an instant. She's dancing near the edge of the area, her silhouette cut out by the strobe light. She moves, feeling the music, getting lost in it. Hips swaying, arms loose but graceful, hair flipping with each turn.

Sabrina comes to me and whispers, "I just thought you

should see it."

I wouldn't want to miss it.

"Besides, I have a feeling she misses you," she adds. I hug her with so much affection and gratitude that any words coming out of me would be useless. I turn all my attention back to MJ, her eyes closed, singing, yelling with the biggest smile I have ever seen on her. I studied her dance before, except this time, there's something visibly different, illuminating. In the corner of my eye, I see Sabrina jumping Mateo's bones, and I pull away from them, slowing in on the most alluring heart-shaped ass swaying in circles. The moment I get behind her, she slows down her movement, and I can feel the grin forming on her face, one reserved for me and me alone. As if the fates decided to smile upon me once more, Akon's 'Beautiful' starts playing the moment my palm touches her exposed stomach. She intertwines her fingers with mine and pushes her back to me, as if to confirm if I'm hot for her, which of course I am. Feeling the bulge, she starts moving her hips, firing up my every nerve, torturing me. I move her hair to the side over her shoulder, uncovering her neck, allowing my warm breath to mark her skin in a familiar set of goosebumps. I follow her movement, swaying my hips in sync with hers. It dawns on me that it's been like this with us from the get-go. From the very first step, we moved in tandem. The rest followed... the connection, spirits aligning, mind-reading... It all comes down to the fact that we are tailor-made for each other.

Her hands slide up around my neck, and I rest mine on her hips, trying to play it cool even though my pulse is in a full-on sprint.

The bass hits low and heavy, vibrating up through my sneakers and into my chest. A kaleidoscope of colors flashes over the crowd like a heartbeat. She turns around, leaving her fingers to play with my hair. The lights twinkle in her eyes, looking like they've been set on fire. Then she tilts her head to go along with the look, half challenge, half invitation. Not able to take it any longer, I grab the tip of her chin, slowly lifting it upward before I lean in, claiming her full lips. Pulling me close, her fingers go deeper into my hair just as her tongue plunges inside, marking its territory. We're both desperate to show each other there's no one else, just the two souls destined for collision. She parts my lips and lifts them to my ear, rasping out, "Wanna know a secret?"

"Always," I answer gruffly.

"I've never done it in a public bathroom before." Her confession gets my cock to twitch.

"We should remedy that."

"Up for the challenge?" She cocks a brow, the sight doing wonders to my hard-on. I release a loud groan before we're sprinting into action. On our way down, we pass Mateo and Sabrina, who are in the middle of their dry-humping session. Married people are so weird. I hope I'll be lucky like that one day.

"They're gonna do it right there, aren't they?"

"Pretty much."

"I love them."

I think I might love you.

The more I repeat the words in my head, the clearer they get. I fell in love with her from the moment I first saw her. Over time, with each new piece of her, I fell harder. But it's a secret I have to keep, for now.

"They love you too."

"You know what's weird? I know."

The second we get to the bathroom stall, she jumps up on me, and I plaster her to the wall. I can't get enough of her. My tongue covers every inch of her neck, collarbone, and shoulder, giving extra attention to her hard nipples. The taste of her skin is so addicting, I can't bear to part. When she turns around, lowering her jeans to reveal a lacy red thong, my breath hitches. I close in, guiding my hand over the string barely covering her core, moving it to the side before my finger plunges inside, making her knees buckle. The exposure reveals her ready for me, so I take another finger and stretch her into a loud moan. My dick is throbbing, but he, too, needs to learn some patience... this is about her. With that, I drag my other hand over her stomach and down to her clit. I press two fingers and start massaging it when she lets out a groan. I feel the pre-cum leaking from the tip of my cock, and I go feral.

"Ty..." she moans with the perfect pitch of rasp, commanding me to go harder. So I do. I curve my fingers and scrape the spot I know she likes, and she explodes on my hand. I let her ride it out, never stopping my movements. Not until her shoulders are fully relaxed.

Not able to keep away, I free my cock and guide it inside my woman, making her tremble. The feel of her, the way her pussy works around me, like an elastic band expanding and contracting, makes me lose my mind. I already know her body well enough to know she's close, so I pull my hand around her, glide it between her thighs, and press my palm on her clit. Her response is instant, rubbing on me to seal her pleasure. Yelling out my name throughout a sharp breath, she pants out her release, and I soon follow, filling her whole.

Chapter 42

Seventh heaven, cloud nine, over the moon, walking on air, top of the world… whatever you want to call it—I'm there.

After we both experienced nirvana in the middle of a public bathroom stall, we got back to the VIP, where we spent the night dancing. I met Nala, Sabrina's friend, who works here. We talked for a while, and she gave me so many book recommendations that I had to write them down in my notes app.

At some point, Sabrina dozed off, so we figured it'd be best if we call it a night. Mateo carries his wife, and Tyler and I follow, holding hands. Since Sabrina is practically comatose, Mateo takes the car we drove here in, which leaves us with his motorcycle.

"I've never been on a motorcycle before," I admit, causing that stupid smirk to appear on Tyler's face. I hate how much I love it.

"Here," he whispers, putting a helmet over my head and locking it with a click. I pout when he covers his face, but I can still feel that smirk of his. He turns around, squats a bit, and waits. It takes me a second or two, but I grin and jump on his back. With his favorite backpack—that's me—he tosses his leg over and saddles the bike.

The thing roars gruffly, and I tighten my grip around Tyler, feeling his abdomen shaking. But before I can punish him for laughing at me, his hand finds my outer thigh, letting me know I'm safe—with him—always.

The drive is slow, with Ty handling the road as the warmth of his body spreads through mine. Bliss; that's what it is, and as I sink into him, that little voice in my head creeps up.

Enjoy it while it lasts.

I barely snoozed for an hour before my alarm went off, reminding me I'm a train ride away from reality. I quickly brush my teeth, wash my face, and head to the kitchen. It's quiet, no sign of the world outside waking up just yet. I turn on the coffee machine and work on breakfast while it does its thing. I have to repay the warm welcome somehow, and figure this is as good a way as any.

Just as I'm setting the table, I hear footsteps rushing down the stairs. Tristan comes first, rubbing his eyes as he takes his seat at the table. Mak and Ty come next, followed by the rest of the family. No one says a word, and panic starts to rise.

Have I overstepped?

It's Eva who settles my nerves. "You didn't have to do this, but thank you." The others join her appreciation, and we dig in.

We eat quickly, with Mak volunteering to do the dishes so Tyler and I can get ready.

On the front porch, I hug Eva the longest, terrified I'll never feel this loved again. It's funny, really… I was 18 when I moved away from home, leaving my whole life behind, never looking back. There was no dread, no nostalgia hitting, not even a moment of hesitation. So, how is it that's what I'm feeling now, saying goodbye to these people?

From the cabin of Luka's pickup, I give them another wave. My phone's contact list has grown by six new names, with Luka telling me I can call him anytime. I seriously debate staying and never leaving this place. Alas, reality awaits me back on campus, so with a heavy heart, I watch the Hart family shrink in the rearview mirror.

The train ride is euphoric. We hold hands the entire time, listen to music while reading. At one point, our hands slide into forbidden areas, and we end up joining the track club, if such a thing exists, that is… rounding it up to three different public places I've had sex. I am officially influenced into being a bad girl and—spoiler alert—I like it!

When we arrive at the Wien Hall, he kisses me until I can't breathe any longer.

"Tell me again why I have to go?"

"Because I promised Emma we'd hang out," I remind him, smiling at his pout.

"But I don't want you to go," he whines and grabs my hands, placing them between us.

"I don't want to either, but I also don't want to get murdered."

"Well, we can't have that…"

"And why is that?"

"It'd be hard to live without you…"

Okay, I am experiencing a malfunction here.

Breathing—gone.

Common sense—forget about it.

Heartbeat—none existent.

I don't think I'm even blinking.

Did he just say that? Please tell me he did.

He frames my face between his palms and bends his knees, so we're eye to eye.

"Tell me you're mine, MJ?"

Oh, fuck.

I'm gone.

"Tyler," I say under my breath.

"Tell me, MJ. Tell me that this is real, because I can't take another second of not knowing."

There's a hint of fear in his eyes. He's stiff, his breath heavy, almost as if he's scared I will deny it. Deny him.

Warmth spreads through me, and I clasp my hands over his. "It's been real from the start."

With that, he crashes his lips to mine. "You have me; I am yours," I tell him before our tongues collide. His shoulders relax, and he closes in, wrapping his arms around me. I do the same, locking my fingers behind his lower back.

He groans when I pull us apart, pouting some more. I know how he feels, since I honestly don't want to get away from him. For the first time in a long time, I don't want to run.

"I have to go, but I'll text you later."

He kisses my forehead, and I watch him walk away. My

heart skips a beat when he does a twirl to check if I'm still there, and he smiles when he finds me staring at him.

Only when he rounds the corner do I get inside and climb the stairs until I reach my dorm. There's a note taped on our door saying 'Emma's day'. Shaking my head, I turn the knob and find my best friend on the couch, working the remote.

"You're here," she squeals and jumps to her feet before she runs right at me.

"I missed you," I tell her and wrap my arms around her. We sway from side to side, not letting go.

We spend the rest of the day glued to each other, turning it into an improvised spa day, complete with face masks, nail polish, and margaritas. I give her the rundown of my trip and everything that transpired between Tyler and me. She gives me the cliff notes of her trip while showing off her tan. We end up watching a chick flick, and when the credits roll, Ben barges in yelling, and I quote, "Your favorite dick is here!"

Like the good friend I am, I retreat to my room and cover my ears with my headset, canceling the noise I know they'll be making. My bed feels empty, and I wish Tyler were with me. As if reading my mind, my phone buzzes, and I jump; my smile is instant when I read his name on the screen.

7: *Miss me yet?*

Me: *Who dis??? New phone*
Me: *FYI, I've missed you since you left me in front of the dorm*

7: *And you have no idea how hard that was for me*

7: *I hate Emma a little bit*

Me: *Do not ever say that in front of her. She will murder you and make me help her dispose of the body.*

7: *Oh, I don't doubt that.*
7: *I hate this*

Me: *What?*

7: *Not being able to see you for a week*

Yeah, on the train ride, we tried to find a crack in our schedules, but unfortunately, there is none. We both know the week will be hectic, especially since we have to make up for missed practices from the long weekend.

Me: *I know; I can't hardly wait for Friday*

7: *Oh, really, why is that?*

Me: *You just want to hear how much I miss you and want to see you*

7: *Always*

Me: *Well, I do*

7: *I miss you more, and I am dying to see you*
7: *I hate to do this, but I am beat. I have an early class*

tomorrow

Through a yawn, I type out.

Me: *Sleep tight, don't miss me too much*

7: *Impossible… Good night Feisty*

Me: *Good night 7*

Chapter 43

Desperate for a caffeine fix, I slowly descend to the common area only to find Rebeka hovering over the coffee maker. I woke up anxious, knowing I'd be seeing Tyler later in dance class, so this is not the best follow-up.

"You look like shit!"

"Can we reschedule the back and forth after I have my cup of coffee?"

The witch with a capital B lifts the practically full coffee pot, turns it upside down, and pours the liquid magic down the drain. I hiss, hands ready for some hair tucking.

"Oopsy," she taunts, her devious smirk in place. I roll my eyes and fight the urge to bitch-slap her.

What the hell is her problem?

"You know 'Mean Girls' is turning into a musical; you should audition. You'd be a perfect Regina."

"Was that a compliment?"

I scoff, "I am tired of this shit. What is your problem?"

"You're my problem!"

Oh, she has a death wish.

"What did I ever do to you?" I thunder, sick of this high-school bullshit.

"Don't act all innocent. You have it so easy." The surprise on her face indicates she didn't want that last part to slip. But I caught it.

"You don't even know me; what gives you the right?"

"Oh, I know you, Miss Perfect."

I am far from it. Not even close.

Without another word, I forgo my coffe and storm up to my dorm.

Dance class is more relaxed than usual, with Emma on top of her mocking game, making it hard for me to focus, not to mention stay serious.

"The TA is trying to kill you with her eyes."

"Right? And it's more intense, isn't it?" I reply in a hushed tone.

Emma answers with a nod.

"It makes no sense, though. Tyler and I just got together, and she can't possibly know that."

"Oh come on, dude, she's been hating on you for two months now," she deadpans.

"Was it that obvious?"

Frankly, every time we were together dancing, it felt like we were in a bubble. So don't blame me for not realizing the world around us paid any attention.

"Oh, my God, duh." She adds a dismissive flick of her hand. "The chemistry between you two has been palpable from the get-go."

Oh.

That certainly brightens my mood. Without further comment, we both get back to our salsa steps, only one of us having a target on her back. We do the jive next, and by the time we finish, the basketball team is up in the gallery, all eyes on us.

The next song begins to open, marking the start of the cumbia section, and Emma and I share a look. It's our favorite dance. Well, I don't dare to admit to her that the cha cha is now at the top of the list, but I am excited about this one nonetheless. Without being obvious, I look up every chance I get, only to find Tyler's eyes already focused on me. Each time I catch him staring, my heart skips a beat. His broad smile is so contagious that my face goes stiff from the muscle movement. I didn't even know how much I missed him until I saw him. The song ends, and we take our break just as the boys stride inside.

"Incoming," Emma whispers, motioning behind me. I hear their footsteps approaching before they even get to us.

"Hi, Red, MJ." Ben gives us the head-nod salute. Ty pulls both Emma and me into a long hug. Feeling left out, Ben joins in.

The whistle blows, and we're off.

In our starting positions, Tyler takes his spot behind me. In a slow drag, he places his hand where his palm will forever stay imprinted, the touch sending shocks to the smallest of nerves in my biology.

"I never pegged you for a thief." He grips the hoodie I stole from his room and brings my back into his chest.

"I have no idea what you are talking about," I say, batting my lashes. Dipping lower, he comes to my ear, giving it a teasing blow. "Fuck, I thought it was hard being like this with you before, but it is so much worse now."

"Why is that?" I ask, my voice shaking.

"Because now that I've tasted you, it's impossible to keep away," he whispers so that only I can hear his confession. And there I am, annoyed because I want him to shout it from the rooftops. I want the world to know how this guy feels about me, how I feel about him... That he's off limits... And I have now officially turned into a possessive bitch.

That's new.

Possessiveness is not a part of my DNA, but he made me do it... with that magic stick of his. Naturally, I had to pick this moment to glance at the TA, her sight set on Tyler.

Yeah, his hand is around me, bitch.

What the hell is wrong with me? Who am I? And why am I ready to pull her eyes out for looking at my man?

Yup. I said it—my man.

"It's taking all of my restraint not to kiss you, touch you, fuck you," he groans hoarsely, making the inner parts of my thighs crumble. To make matters worse, he leans in my ear and releases a moaning breath, weakening the joints of my knees. My whole body blushes, every part of me burning, one breath away from combustion. But I dance through it, fire smoldering during the entire length of the song. Music fades, movement ceases, but my heart keeps on racing. He was right; it's so much harder to dance with him now.

With the approving look of Ms. Lynch, we all start packing up. Tyler hovers over me, so I take the opportunity to ask,

"Do you want to go somewhere with me?"

"I believe there's a rule regarding stupid questions."

I grin at him, wrinkling my nose.

"You never need to ask that, I will follow you anywhere and everywhere."

My heart wants to jump out of my chest, do a happy dance, and come back inside to cozy up with the notion of loving the person staring back at me.

Love?

Well, that's a new development.

"Come on," I say, grabbing his hand and dragging him outside. "It won't take long… Ben and Emma are gonna go ahead to prepare for movie night."

The confusion on his face hits me. He probably hasn't checked his phone.

"I sent you a text earlier; we thought it would be a good idea for the four of us to watch a movie tonight…" I falter, "If that's something you would want, of course?"

Ty stops moving, making me do the same. A questionable amount of worry gets the best of me at the sight of him, mute, arms crossed over his chest.

Shit, does he not want to hang out with me?

Just as I am starting to panic, he clicks his tongue. "I'm shocked you even have to ask."

"Huh?"

As seconds tick by, my heart keeps pumping louder, harder, begging for his words… when none come, I decide to jolt out, "Words, 7, use your words!"

He closes in on me, grabs my face between his hands, squeezing my cheeks hard enough to make fish lips, before he crisps, "Let me put it this way. There will never be something that I won't want to do with you. Am I making myself clear?"

With my whole body on fire, I nod, desperate for him to tame the flames, whichever way he wants!

Chapter 44

Girls basketball practice... MJ dragged me into the basketball gym to check out the girls' team.

"I did some stalking. Their second-string point guard has transferred to UCLA, creating an opening. I talked to the board for a chance to try out..." She takes a deep breath, keeping me in suspense. "They gave me a month to prepare."

Is it weird to feel proud about it? Fuck it! I'll own it—I am proud!

"How do you feel about it?"

Shit, I sound like a therapist.

"I don't know... Weird, I guess, scary..." She shrugs. "But I want to try."

"Good. Now, spill; what do you have on the team?"

While I wait for her answer, I do some scanning of my own. The energy is good. The point guard has good technique, but I can say with confidence that MJ has a better handle on the ball.

"They're third in the division, and they have the teamwork portion down. I know most of the players; the only problem is Rebeka." She says her name with spite, nudging her chin, then adds, "Number 6."

I nod.

"She lives in my dorm, on my floor, and hates my guts, not that I know why!"

I make a note of that and file it away. How dare she hate my MJ? But I digress...

"That one girl aside, would you want to be part of this team?"

Her eyes, glued to the ball bouncing in the hands of the playmaker, well up. It's weird, but unlike the last time I saw her with a basketball, there's not a shred of pain, only longing. By the looks of it, she's ready to welcome the game back into her life, and I want to be a part of it.

She nods.

"I meant it, you know? If you need someone to practice with, hell, if you want me to pass you the ball, know that I'm your guy."

Emphasis on your.

"Thanks, I'll keep that in mind. Now let's get through this movie so we can christen my bed."

She smacks her mouth shut, which gets a reaction out of me. I probably wouldn't read much into what she said, but now... color me intrigued.

"What?"

She comes to a stop, her face turning red, all the while her eyes turn to the floor. I grab her chin gently between my fingers and pull it up, demanding her ocean attention.

"Feisty, use your words for me, please." My voice is barely above a whisper, but I am too eager for the answer.

"Oh, God... don't laugh, but I never had a guy in my room

before you…" She bites her lip, eyes averting, the action itself giving me what I need.

"Why would I laugh at that?"

She shrugs.

"Let's just say that the only fireworks that happened were thanks to a toy I had, which broke, and I haven't replaced it in over a year."

As much as I'd like to gloat here, this is a serious topic that I want to explore.

"And before?"

"I was in a long-term relationship…"

"How long?"

"Three years!"

Fuck.

"What happened?"

"It doesn't matter."

Yeah, I don't buy it.

"It does to me. I want to know everything about you, even if it will make me cringe."

"He left for college without a word, and that was it."

I can see, from the way her whole body just tensed up, that it is not, in fact, it. But I don't want to push. Honestly, it doesn't feel like she has any lingering feelings toward the guy, but it could just be my wishful thinking.

Going into our usual post-dance routine, she hands me one earbud, and we start our walk to her place, hand in hand.

I bite out a laugh when Jason Derulo's 'In My Head' starts beating in my ear. She shakes her head, but doesn't blush this time, just gives my hand a tight squeeze.

"I think your playlist algorithm likes me," I gloat.

"Yeah, I kind of hate it."

"I figured," I chuckle, "The red cheeks are a dead giveaway."

She smiles, but it doesn't reach her eyes, reserved. She appears to be debating whether or not to say something. She takes a breath, a decision made before she clears her throat.

"Can I ask you something?"

"Always."

"On the train, you got angry after I showed you my playlist…"

I slow the pace, turning to face her.

"What did I do?" There's vulnerability in her voice, and for the first time, I hate it because I'm the one who put it there.

"I'm sorry, you didn't deserve that," I falter. "You amazed me, and then you said that it was unintentional; so I reflected, getting into my head that because you weren't deliberately trying to impress me, you didn't actually like me."

There's a beat of silence—a long beat.

Then her whole body starts shaking, barely able to contain her laughter. I see her trying so hard not to let it out, mouth pressed tight, shoulder trembling. A high-pitched snort escapes her nose before she clamps her hand over her face.

"What's that all about?"

"I was on a train to meet your family, and you thought I didn't like you?"

"Well, you bring out the insecurity in me."

She snorts again. Beneath the embarrassment, I feel the tension in me ease. Her chuckle is warm, teasing—the kind of laugh shared with someone you like.

"That's funny, 'cause you bring out the confidence in me."

She pulls my hand, making me stumble into her. Rising on her tiptoes, she presses her lips to mine. The quick peck still manages to cause small puckers on my flesh.

Her favorite song starts to play, and her face lights up in sync with mine.

"So how did you get into music before you were born?"

"A lot of it I got from Tree Hill and an assortment of books; the rest came with the smart shuffle." Her hand grips tighter, sending bolts straight down my spine.

"And you?"

"Mostly Luke's doing. He had the remote monopoly, and VH1 was always playing old hits, so we were all brainwashed into it."

"Looks like you had a good influence."

All I do is nod, and we spend the rest of our walk focused on the music, the feel of her hand keeping me afloat.

When we get to her dorm, Ben and Emma are in a lip lock on the couch.

"Get a room," MJ sneers. I drop my bag and take a seat on the far end, where MJ joins my side.

I have no idea what movie we're watching. There's a girl, a guy, some cars, one red (I think)... that's it. All my attention is on MJ. She's in my arms, my hand playing with her hair, while her fingers draw something on my thigh. Her cherry scent invades my senses, and as if it's connected to a memory of the first time I touched her, it takes me back to that exact moment.

The couple next to us is sharing the same state of mind, neither watching the screen, their gazes locked on each other.

Before the first credit roll, doors slam shut.

Clothes discarded, I hover above MJ spread across her bed. I take in her exposed skin, mapping out every freckle, every mark, and tracing kisses down her body, giving special treatment to the spots that cause extra moans. My fingers graze up the length of her inner thigh, slowing down before reaching El Dorado. Pulling on my hair, she lifts her hips, begging for attention. I oblige, with my face between her legs, letting out a soft, cold blow over her clit. She buckles, and I drag out my tongue, sliding it up the line of her arousal. The wailing sound grows more distinctive as my fingers slip inside. They dig deep, on a mission. If this bed has never had a chance to feel her fall apart, I am going to break every spring, ensuring that every fiber of the mattress remembers the feeling. Adding another finger before curving it the way she likes it, I take a moment to look up at her—scattered, shattered, but put together.

She's a walking contradiction, pained and happy, distraught and collected—just *perfect*! For me, meant to be, made for.

She comes apart on my fingers, riding the wave till the very end. Breath shallow, chest pounding, I get on top of her, our gazes locked in a haze. I grab the hardest part of me, paint it with her cum, and slowly slide inside, feeling her stretch. The movement starts slowly, our eyes unblinking, souls crashing. Her deep blues are like the ocean, begging me to drown in it. And it's precisely how I feel. Unable to breathe, to exist if not for her—with her.

And I see the exact resolution in her eyes, almost tangible.

I want to hold on to it, knowing the weight of it, the mere worth.

Needing her closer, I pull her up on top of me. Her legs close around me as she starts her dance. Three little words linger at the tip of my tongue. But I don't set them free.

Right here, in his lap, him inside of me, our eyes in an intense, deep session, something breaks inside of me—again. But it isn't so much of a breakage as it is a collecting of pieces kind of thing. For the first time in forever, I feel whole, right there in his arms, as he fills me up in every way possible. All I want to do is scream out, tell him what he does to me, how he makes me feel, how much I need him. Scared to do so, to let him all the way in, I mute the words, but my mind yells them out as loud as it can allow it. The moment we both explode, those three words are an echo in my head, and I hope with every ounce of my being that he can see them, feel them, know them.

I love you.

Chapter 45

Excitement overwhelms me as I enter the basketball gym, Emma under my arm. The whole walk, she kept repeating the 'you got this' spiel, and it worked. I needed the boost. We take our seats in the second row, right behind the Lions' bench, taking in the wild atmosphere. The 'Anderson' gymnasium is filled with people wearing Blue Devils colors, yet it doesn't overpower the Lion fans. Fun fact: The Devils and the Lions share the same colors and are the biggest rivals in men's college basketball. This game is the one I chose to attend due to the bet I made with Tyler about a month ago.

Duke was once my dream, and I find it poetic that this is the first game I attend. The teams are already doing their warm-ups, and Emma immediately locks eyes with number 5. The warm and fuzzy Emma is at play whenever close to Ben, and it's by far the best version of her. That is, until they get into an argument, when all bets are off and the claws are fully extended.

The noise of the crowd dulls around me, like someone has stuffed cotton in my ears. One second, I am laughing with Emma, and the next, my eyes land on the number 7—the navy blue number 7.

My stomach drops, and I freeze. The only move I can make is to clutch Emma's forearm.

"What the fuck, dude?" she yelps.

Nothing, no words escape me, just my nonexistent nails digging into her skin and eyes focused on the one person I couldn't blink away.

"Maddie, are you ok?" Emma's voice is distant, muffled.

NO!

Inside, I am full-on screaming, but nothing gets out. Not a single sound.

"Shit, Maddie, breathe, dude!"

I can't; there's no air, nothing coming in or out.

Searching the line of my sight, Emma gasps, "Shit, is that?"

I nod, at least I think I do, I'm not really sure.

"What do you want to do?"

He hasn't seen me yet, but it's only a matter of time.

Shaking my head, I finally turn away, facing her. My vision is blurry, and I can't see her; I can only discern her outline. She grabs my hand and holds it tightly, waiting for a decision. After what seems like an eternity of standing in one place, my name is being yelled out, and the sound of Tyler's voice jolts me, prompting me to turn and face him. Suddenly, my vision is clear because I can see the worry all over his face.

"I need to go." My gasp turns into a shouted "NOW!"

I bolt. Running blindly, feet slipping on the steps, knees bumping into legs. I hear groans as I clumsily shove past people. Someone calls my name, but I don't care. My breath gets caught in my throat like I got punched in the chest. All I know is that I have to get out. The gym lights blur as I push through the doors. My heartbeat thuds in my ears, fast and messy. My feet don't stop running until I find myself on the floor of a bathroom. I drag my knees to my chest, the smell and the sight of the five urinals telling me I have inhabited the boys' bathroom.

Well, fuck me.

Mumbled voices have a discussion right behind the door I am pressed against with my back, my ass on the dirty floor, and my face buried in my palms.

"I need to talk to her!"

Jamie?

What the hell is he doing here? And why does the sound of his voice feel like it's ripping me apart? Where the hell is Emma? I need her.

"You lost that privilege a long time ago!"

There she is, defending me, protecting, and keeping me safe because she knows I am not ready for this.

Jamie starts fighting back, "You don't know me," but Emma doesn't allow it. "And you don't know her. She developed a hell of a right hook, and it would look so good on your left smug eye!"

Dang, Emma is on fire.

"Emma, where is she?" Is that Tyler?

"What happened?" That's Ben.

I think.

"Who the hell are you?" Tyler roars, and Jamie repeats the same question.

"We're MJ's friends, now do us a favor and step away

from the door and introduce yourself." That is Ben's demanding voice.

"MJ?" I hear the confusion in Jamie's voice at the mention of my name. There's a pause before he continues, "I'm James, I'm Maddison's.."

Emma jumps in with a shout, "He's the *jerk* who left Maddie when she needed someone the most. Full disclosure, that is the only title you are allowed to use, you got me?" I know she has pulled out the hands-on-her-hips stance.

You go, girl.

There's a long, muzzled beat. I can only imagine some intense stares being crossed, but I can't confirm it. I can't face any of them.

Why now?

Why the hell is this happening now?

"I just want to talk to her." Jamie's voice finally breaks the silence.

"If she doesn't want you to, then you should leave," Tyler commands right before the crowd goes wild, reminding all of us of why we were here in the first place.

"Please, all of you leave, you have a game." That shouting sound comes out of my mouth.

"Feisty, please, come out." God, the effect Tyler's soft rasp has on my body - instant goosebumps.

"Please, just go, play, I will be there, I just need a minute - or ten," I beg, my voice cracking with desperation.

"She's right, guys, you have a game to play. I will take care of her." Emma must've given them a pointed look because no one dares to retort.

Footsteps fade out, followed by a gentle knock

accompanying Emma's whisper, "It's clear."

I step away from the door, and Emma rushes inside.

"Oh, honey," she gasped, "look at you." She pulls me in a hug, and I collapse.

"How is this happening to me right now?" I weep on her shoulder.

"I think that's just how life works."

"Everything was perfect. Until about ten minutes ago, my life was as perfect as it could be, and now..." I wipe my face, sobbing, "Now it's all fucked up again!"

"Talk to me, give me the detailed walk-through!"

A flashback of my life before Columbia plays through my mind. Memories of a lost girl meeting a boy. Memories of a friendship that turned into a relationship. My first kiss, my first time, my first heartbreak, my first everything was with Jamie. The same person who cemented the bricks together, closing me on the inside.

"Don't hate me," I clear my throat, "But I'm still not ready to share the whole story."

I am broken.

She glares at me, full of worry. Emma takes my hand, giving me a lifeline when she asks, "Do you still love him?"

"A part of me will always love him in a way. We grew up together; he was my friend first. It took a long while, but I got over it, so why does it hurt so much?"

"Because he hurt you, and you haven't allowed yourself to heal properly."

"How do I do that?"

"By opening yourself fully, I suppose."

"What do I do?"

"I can't answer that for you, but whatever you do, you have my full support."

The buzzing sound makes me jump out of my skin.

"Shit, the game."

"We don't have to go there."

"We do; I promised Tyler," I shudder.

"He'll understand."

I have no doubt about it. He's been doing it thus far.

"I know, but… " I shake my head, and she nods in understanding.

The look on her face tells me as much, even if I myself can't fully process what I am thinking. Everything is fucked up, but despite it all, one thing is irrefutable: Tyler deserves me being there. He's earned it.

Chapter 46

My concentration is at its lowest point. Nothing except MJ comes to mind; she's all I think about. I can still hear the sound of her mumbled cries.

We are halfway through the first half, tied on the scoreboard. The black mamba, known as Jamie, is the center of the Blue Devils. He's one of the best centers in the league, and he also happens to be the person who broke Maddie's heart, making him enemy number one. Somehow, our team picked up on the tension between the Devils' center, Ben, and me. There's a sense of comfort knowing I have their support if push comes to shove, even if they don't know the whole story. Lucky for the SOB wearing the same number jersey as yours truly, he's been keeping his mouth shut so far.

The ball hits the hardwood with a sharp thump as Ben dribbles past half court, sweat sliding down his temple. Every muscle in my body is wired tight. The gym is packed, wall-to-wall noise, but all I can hear is my heartbeat hammering in my ears.

And *him*.

Camped out under the rim like a damn statue. Six-foot-five, arrogant as hell, and apparently not over her.

Coach barks something from the sidelines, but I don't catch it. My eyes snap to the bleachers. She's back. Perched in the third row, hands folded, eyes locked on the game. On me or maybe on him? I can't tell, and I hate that I even have to wonder. Ben passes left, cutting hard around the arc. I catch the ball, my defense sticks with me, but I am already thinking two moves ahead. It has to end at the rim. I want the score, but more than that, I have to put it in his face, let him know she's moved on, and not just with anyone—with me.

We run the pick and roll. Taking advantage of the screen, I slip into the open lane. Then he's there. Stupid Jamie. A damn wall of muscle and attitude. I fly up anyway. The ball bounces off the rim, and I ricochet off him, hitting the floor with a grunt. He doesn't even flinch, only stands over me with cold eyes.

"You sure you're built for this?" he mutters, loud enough for everyone to hear.

I want to swing... God, how I want to.

But I won't

But I won't - for her.

So I get up, without saying a word, and jog back down the court with my fists clenched, one thought burning through my skull—*she's mine.*

Coach calls a timeout, and we huddle up. The team needs this win, and I need it more. Adrenaline rushes through whatever part of me it needs to, and I go back in the game with charged power. Ben joins the hype, and everything shifts. We play a whole different kind of game, one that involves some intense mind-reading. The ball gets passed between us without a millimeter of deviation. The home team's shots go through the hoop, increasing the numbers on the scoreboard to our advantage.

The rebound ball flies straight to Ben, who calls out our next play. Finding the opening, I sprint to the key. Midair, the ball finds my waiting palms, Jamie's hand coming up too late, the rim just above my outstretched fingers. I slam it hard. The backboard rattles, and the crowd erupts. With a soft landing, I turn before the cheers even hit. I don't even register the shove before the ref blows a whistle. He's unraveling, marking his second foul.

As they line me up for free throw, I dribble once, twice—the ball light in my hands. I glance at her, on her feet, not for him - for *me*. I sink the shot with a swoosh.

"Stop looking at her," the Black Mamba growls, pushing out his chest, forcing his face to mine. For a center, he's under the height norm, and for a shooting guard, I am above it, making us mere inches apart.

I sneer, "Make me!"

Before his hand is up in the air, someone pulls me away. Snapping my head around, my face turns red at the sight of Ben and Colt.

"Don't do it, man, you'll just make it worse for her," Ben whispers in my ear, and the mention of MJ gets me to look at the bleachers. The place she was sitting before is empty. Gone, nowhere in sight, and I want to punch the asshole more now than ever. The sound of a whistle, with the intervention of the referee, calms us enough to get separated. We have 15 seconds left in the first half, and I tell the coach to substitute me. His loud curses follow me up the stairs as I sprint in hopes of catching up.

"I need to go back and see if he's ok." I hear MJ's voice coming from around the corner. I round it, speaking abruptly, "Who do you need to see?" She jumps, snapping a hand on her chest, then sighs with relief, and it's all the answer I need. Pulling her into a hug, she wraps her arms around me and buries her face in my chest.

"I'm so sorry," she murmurs, and continues her babble, "They wouldn't allow us to get to the court from the stands, so we tried to go around, but it's locked."

She was coming for me, not running away... My breath hitches.

When she pulls back, my eyes drop on the pendant dangling right above her heart. A jolting pain goes right through my heart at the sight of the number 3 next to the number 7. This entire time, I've been thinking it's kismet that she has my number around her neck. Taking a step back, I shake my head in disbelief, not wanting any of it to be true.

"Is he the reason you don't play anymore?"

"What? NO!" She shrieks, taking a step toward. I step away.

She grabs the back of her neck, and her face drops.

"He left me for a game we both loved, and I never looked at it the same. Love lost all meaning; the game lost all meaning," she rambles.

"Is that true? You don't play anymore?" Jamie's voice makes my blood boil. I don't have to look back to know he's behind me, but I do see her eyes jump to his.

MJ goes silent, and my heart cracks.

"So that's why I couldn't find you on any roster?"

Pointing at the Lions' trophy case, I choke, "This is her roster now."

I watch him look at MJ's accomplishments, watch him fall apart with realization.

"I can't believe you don't play anymore. Damian never said anything."

Everything falls into place. This is the brother she vaguely mentioned, never revealing his importance.

I glare at MJ, who has her guilt written all over her, a knife straight to the chest. Eyes firmly locked on her, demanding the answers that are already breaking me, I ready myself for the twist of the knife to follow.

"What was your number when you played?"

"7."

Strike one.

"Damian's?" my voice cracks, begging it to be 3.

"4."

Strike two.

"His?" I point at the guy, whom I've realized is honoring her with his jersey, all the while looking at the girl who's honoring him. Her eyes fill with tears, and one escapes down her cheek.

"3." It comes out as barely a whisper, but my heart hears it loud and clear. Oh, how wide of the mark I have been. The story I wrote out in my mind about her pain, her loss, past and future, was penciled in all wrong, and I misread it all.

Come on, Feisty, say something. Fight for me.

My heart cracks. It's my first time experiencing heartbreak, and MJ's silence adds to the anguish.

Strike three.

Chapter 47

If there is one thing that will surely haunt me for the rest of my life, it's the look on Tyler's face. So much hurt, and I'm the culprit. I hurt him, the last thing I ever wanted to do…

He's walking away, and he has every right to.

"It's not like that, Tyler, please," I wail, my vision blurred.

I'm broken.

I love you.

But nothing comes out. He stops without turning, like maybe he has heard my thoughts, and a hint of hope lights up. It's extinguished when he steps out of sight, but not out of mind.

"Please, Maddison, can we talk?"

It's all wrong; the name coming out of his mouth is all wrong.

"Go back to the game, Jamie."

"The game is not what's important now."

I laugh with a side of exaggeration.

"Could've fooled me." I wrap my arms around my chest, trying my best to keep my heart at bay.

"Look, I am sorry for how it went down…"

That statement earns him a scoff. So many emotions stir

up inside of me. There's a fight somewhere deep in my gut, with no winner in sight, no inclination whatsoever of the one to overpower them all.

"I tried tracking you down, but no one from Chicago knew where you went, you're not on social media, and I couldn't find you on any basketball teams."

He scratches the back of his neck, flexing his muscles, something that used to take my breath away.

I take my time, soaking him in. He has changed so much. His shoulders are broader, his arms bigger, and his muscles are more defined. His hair is shorter than ever, missing his coiled curls. It makes him more serious, and I'm not sure if it's a good thing or a bad one. His facial form is also more defined, with a triangular jaw transitioning into a more oval shape, hidden behind an inch-long, thick beard. His hazel eyes still have a slight redness in them, and the outline still appears as if he had put on eyeliner around the frame. So much has changed, but he's still that little boy I wanted to eat up, thinking his skin was made of chocolate. He's the same kid who kicked Jack's ass after he put gum in my hair during recess. The same guy who taught me how to drive, gave me my first drink, and stayed with me through my first hangover. The same person who told the world we would be together forever.

"We'll go to Duke, graduate, we'll play in the same city, and then we'll buy a house, get married, and we'll have three kids, two boys and a girl. Oh, and a golden retriever in the backyard."

His words rush by like a gust of wind, but come out with a different tone, a mocking one. None of it is right; it's the nostalgia playing tricks on me. My heart is beating strongly, each beat sounding like the syllables forming the name of the person who walked out on me mere minutes ago.

"You seriously haven't played since..." Jamie gets me out of my deep thoughts.

"Haven't touched a ball or looked at one." I don't disclose that short game with Tyler at the half-court, a memory I will forever cherish. The pressure on my chest intensifies at the recollection.

"I guess you found a new love," he says, lifting his chin to the team picture next to last year's trophy.

Studying the golden plaque, he marvels, "Player of the year, damn. How did that happen?"

"The short version is, I tried out for volleyball and made the team. Turns out I am good at it."

"Clearly," he chuckles, "then again, you always were good at sports. Remember Little League baseball."

The memory of swinging the bat that was way too big for me makes my lips curve into a smile.

"So, Duke, huh?"

"Yeah," he breathes it out.

"When did you transfer?"

"Last semester."

I nod. After we broke up, he chose UCLA. In the course of the two years, I was miraculously sick when we had to play the Bruins. I would also hide in my room whenever the guys played against them.

"What's it like?"

"Empty..."

His words sure are, because even though he's saying all

the right things, it's a little too late. Desperate for redirection, I reveal, "The national team gave me an official invite."

"The fuck, Maddison? Seriously?"

It's MJ! I want to yell, but press my lips together. He doesn't know this version of me.

"Duke keeps on calling every month. They are getting on Coach's last nerve."

"To transfer?"

I nod.

"You're not taking it?

I shake my head.

"But, Duke has always been your dream."

"It was," I correct, "it's not anymore."

My heart is weeping in the direction where Tyler disappeared, and my eyes follow.

"You love him?"

"I don't know what love is," I croak, letting that sink in a minute. The other night I thought I felt it, that I was ready for it, thought I had it...

Before I lost it!

"Don't say that. We loved each other."

Somehow, those words don't get the desired effect, because I feel nothing. He takes a step closer, and I take two back.

"I never stopped loving you; you've been on my mind 24/7. I tried to track you down, but you became a ghost. I still love you, always have, always will."

And there it is. The big revelation, the words I have been desperate for, finally spoken. Except, they come out of the wrong person.

"I thought you did. I honestly believed that with every fiber of my being. But it was not the case," I seethe. "If you truly loved me, you would've believed me."

"I did," he counters, and I ignore the pain in his eyes.

People chatter somewhere around the corner, taking advantage of the halftime.

"You left me when I needed you the most, and not only that, you did so without a single word, not even a stinking goodbye."

I'm broken.

"I never got over you. Fuck Maddison, I am wearing your number for God's sake, and you, you're wearing mine." He points at the picture of me holding the plaque in the center of the glass case.

"No!" I shake my head in scorn. "And funny that another person had to put that one in your head. Shows how much you pay attention to details. Besides, the number on my back has nothing to do with you and everything to do with me."

It's a reminder... not to trust, not to fall. A token of the past I buried and rose above. All on my own.

"Look, I'm glad you are doing great, and Duke—wow, I am so proud of you, but other than our history, there is nothing left between us," I lament.

He sighs at my words, and I know they're weighing on him.

"My life fell apart, and I had no one." I notice him flinch, showing me he's only human. I can't stop now; I have to put it all out there and get everything I never got a chance to off my chest.

"You watched while the whole school degraded me, and

then you left." He looks away, and I know I struck a nerve. I'm not proud of it, but it needs to be done to set myself free.

"So, no offense, but there is no excuse for your behavior, and you can lie to yourself all you want, but that sure as hell didn't feel like love to me."

"I'm so sorry, I will never forgive myself for how I acted, but..." Tears fill his eyes, and the sight does nothing to me. For someone who is a full-blown empath, it's odd.

"Feel however you want, do whatever you want, but know that I am good here, without you."

We stare at each other for a long beat, our wheels spinning. I see the exact moment when it sinks in.

"For what it's worth, I am proud of you."

And never have words held so much weight. Because once upon a time, this person was my everything. He was the first person to notice my passion for sports. So for him to say it, even under these circumstances, is everything.

"Thank you, I mean that."

"Can I hug you?"

That makes me freeze. Dropping my head with a nod, I step closer.

The moment his arms wrap around me, I know what it is—closure. One chapter is now finished, and I am ready to fill out the next blank page, even if it is with hurt.

Chapter 48

Unanswered texts, unreturned calls, and complete avoidance are all I've gotten from Tyler for the past week. I am all up in that can't eat, can't sleep state.

Hollow.

I understand why he is angry; I agree with him a hundred percent. And all because I went silent. It was like the words were there, at the tip of my tongue, but something held them back while I just stood there like the coward I am.

The look he gave me, not to mention the pain in his eyes, when he came to the wrong conclusion, one I didn't even rebut, still guts me. I think my body wanted to spare him.

He deserves someone better, someone who isn't so broken.

Rubbing the pendants between my fingers, I recall the time I got them, a birthday present from Emma. It was some time after I made the first string and got to choose my jersey number. She was by my side when Coach offered me the lucky number 7. Emma held my hand when I shook my head, deciding to retire the past. She listened when I told her why I wanted to separate volleyball from basketball, and she understood that it wasn't the same kind of love. So she gave me a piece of both to keep with me always.

Emma is the only reason I've been spending every night on the half-court. She disrupted my plan for staying in my room, dwelling, and got my ass moving by cashing in her—or better yet, my IOU. Every night when I finish catching up on basketball, I hope I'll run into Tyler. No such luck, though.

Music in my ears, my old Iverson ball in my hands, I did my best to regain the game I once loved most. It's an unexplainable feeling, the way my body knows what to do, how every breath I take is a relaxing one. My chest is full and empty at the same time. Full for regaining an old love and empty at the loss of another. He's the reason I got it back, the feeling I never knew I could experience again. Freedom, the sense of belonging... Tyler did all that without even trying... He gave me back the future I had erased, only for me to hurt him in return.

Every night, I dream of his brown eyes, and every morning, I wake up with more guilt piling up.

When Saturday finally rolled around, my nerves got the best of me. I barely got through my morning shift.

With all life drained out of me, I slump on my bed, spent. It's the day of the Christmas benefit, so I have to regain my energy.

My heavy eyelids swing open at the sound of Emma's loud shriek.

Heart racing, I jump to my feet and bolt toward the sound. As soon as I get out of my room, I have plenty to see. Sabrina—unfazed; Emma—screaming in disbelief, pointing at her idol. Shaking my head, I grab Emma by her shoulders and move her out of the way, allowing Sabrina to come in.

"What are you doing here?" I gape at her.

"I promised I would help you get ready?" She steps inside like she owns the place, wearing high heels and a tight, creamy-peach dress that traces her curves.

"Yeah, but I thought…" I stop myself, unsure if Tyler has told her anything. The look on her face indicates she knows.

"I love that boy, but I am not a person who breaks her promises, not even for my brother-in-law."

And then I get pushed. Yup, my ass hits the ground—hard.

"The hell, dude?"

"Excuse me for reacting." Emma's hands wave through the air. "Oh, and what in the actual bananas? You know her? And what do you mean by brother-in-law?"

"Is this the friend who has a me shrine in her room?" Sabrina asks, amusement in her voice.

I nod.

"And you haven't told her about me?"

Bad friend!

My conscience scolds.

I drop my head with a slight shake. When I lift it a second later, Emma's eyes are sending lasers at me, and that's how I know I messed up.

"Wait. You told The Queen about me? And the wall? Ok, someone pinch me, because this can't be real."

Sabrina obliges quickly, choosing Emma's upper arm to tweak. She screams, but promptly starts apologizing, "I am so sorry, my Queen. You can do that as much as you like." And then she bows. She actually freakin' bows. I pinch the bridge of my nose, shaking my head frantically.

"I like this one." Sabrina points her thumb at my best friend.

I gasp, giving Emma my full attention. "I'm so sorry, I forgot."

"You forgot?"

"Well, can you blame me?"

"Just because you orgasmed after a long drought doesn't excuse you from mentioning you met Sabrina freaking Furst."

"It's Hart," Sabrina corrects.

"What?"

"Yeah, she's married to Tyler's brother."

Emma's jaw hits the floor. Okay, not exactly, but I'm sure it does in her head.

Knowing the error of my ways, I just went straight to the penalty. "How many IOUs is it gonna take?"

"If I could just intervene for a sec," Sabrina lifts a finger, "we don't have much time, and I believe I was booked to beautify the two of you."

"You did that for me?" Emma covers her chest with both hands, tilting her head. "Even though you hate makeovers?"

"I'd do anything for you, and you know it."

"Aaaaaaaa," Sabrina mock-whines. "She also gave me your measurements, so I brought some choices." She opens the door and drags a rack on wheels inside, around a dozen dresses in various prints filling it. I join Emma in her jaw drop.

"Ok, you're off the hook," my best friend yields, her fingers roaming the fabrics before us. I sigh in relief, mouthing a 'thank you' to Sabrina.

In the blink of an eye, our room is transformed into a

beauty studio.

Sabrina worked on Emma first, curling her hair while I showered.

I am in charge of the music, so I quickly mix all the pop songs to complement the theme.

'I wanna be bad' by Willa Ford plays while Sabrina does Emma's makeup like a total pro. I eye the dress she chose for me, patiently waiting on my door frame. Satin blue, to match my eyes—Sabrina's words.

I try my best not to let dread overlap my excitement. Yesterday, Tyler didn't show up for the final rehearsal, something I had predicted, much to my dismay. Miss Lynch said we already had it down and that we would do fine.

It's a benefit to help raise money for the athletic department, and friends and family are invited.

By the time Sabrina is done with me, I can barely recognize myself. Both Emma and I stare at our reflections in the mirror, feeling like fucking princesses. My BFF can't stop tracing the intricate red lace of her killer dress.

I look at Sabrina's expression in the mirror, admiring her work.

"How are you doing?" she asks, hands crossed on her chest, a genuine care in her tone. Her hair is styled in a side braid, and her lips are a devilish red, matching the shade she has chosen for Emma.

"I'll be fine." I wave it off.

"Look, I didn't know you before, but I saw you grow in a span of two days, right there in front of my eyes. I saw how reserved you were from the start, how you pulled away from the emotions swirling around. Two blinks later, you were a different person, more open, more relaxed, free."

She places her polished hands on my shoulders, turning me to face her. With her high heels, she's towering over me, my feet still bare. "You know that I was the one refusing to accept my feelings for Mateo?"

I shake my head.

"He was the one who never gave up, pursued the hell out of me, knowing that it was the only way I would see it."

She pauses for what I can only presume is for dramatic effect.

"Same as how Tyler saw that all you needed was time to figure it out on your own. I think you need to do the same for him now."

"He deserves better."

"Why do you say that?"

"Because..." I hesitate, "I'm broken beyond repair. I couldn't even tell him the truth. It's too late now anyway."

Emma comes to Sabrina's side and gives me her soft expression, one reserved just for me.

"No, honey, it's not too late, and you know it. Even a blind person can see that the boy is crazy about you. But, you need to tell him everything," my girl soul mate jumps in with her wisdom.

There's nothing I want more than for him to let me back in... Back in the place I belong... but if I tell him the truth, would he look at me the same?

Excusing myself, I bolt to my room and do the only thing I can think of—make a playlist for him.

Chapter 49

OUR Soundtrack

Timeline of US

Honest - Song house
Bad Liar - Imagine Dragons
Happy - NF
Silence that remains - The Horrors
Someone to you - Banners
Let you love me - Rita Ora
Takeaway - Chainsmokers
If you want love - NF
By your side - Jonas Blue
Here with me - Marchmello
Kiss me - Dermot Keneddy
Shower - Becky G
Fall into me - Forest Blakk
Don't let me let go - Illenium
Daylight - Maroon 5
Wasted love - Ofenbach
Say nothing - Flume
That could've been us - Tyron Hapi
Last Song - Alan Walker
There till the end - JERUB
With you - Dean Lewis
Don't give up on me - Andy Grammer
Hold on - Chord Overstreet

You & Me - James TW
Locksmith - Sadie Jean
Halo - Haley James Scott

Chapter 50

The basketball gym has been transformed into a prom-like ballroom. Tables are spread out, white cloths tied with a blue bow, a live band playing, and people moving on the made-up dance floor. My brothers are all here, looking dapper in their suits, Sabrina tucked under Mateo's arm, beautiful per usual. Mama is especially glowing in a dark green suit, a look that suits her well, considering she's not much of a dress-up person. She looks fantastic with little makeup, and her hair pulled up in a tight bun, letting the world see her beauty. We all took our turns dancing with both her and Sabrina, with my heart pumping the entire time, knowing I would soon have to face MJ.

I spent the week in a state of agony. I couldn't get that asshole's face out of my head. I wanted to push past it, forget it, but couldn't condemn myself to. She is my biggest weakness, everything I ever wanted, and so much more.

I miss her. There, I said it.

Earlier, while Ben and I were getting ready, I got a ping on my phone, a notification stating that a playlist had been updated. I skimmed through it at first, but then I zeroed in on the title, and my heart sank. Most of the songs I knew, but those I didn't, I listened to carefully, devotedly. The more I drank it all in, the more my heart ached. A raging war broke out; one side wanted to run to her, the other fought back. Alas, the anger mixed with hurt won in the battle of my ticker. So I plastered on my best smile and tried my best to get through today.

My palms are getting sweatier by the minute while I dance with my sister-in-law.

The moment MJ walks through the double door, my heart does what it has always done at the sight of her—it jolts to my throat, taking away my breath. Beautiful is not enough of a word to describe this girl, a dream come true, mesmerizing.

I lost so much when I was too young to understand it, got lucky, and found a new family who made me their own. I spent most of my life scared that I would lose them as well, losing the comfort and safety. Falling for MJ only multiplied that same fear, knowing the loss would be that much worse. And then I found out she was still in love with someone else. As much as it killed me, I had to let her go, despite my heart's protests.

And now she's here, like a freaking mirage, taunting me... Killing me.

"You ok?" Sabrina's voice snaps me out of the spiral, noticing the line of my sight.

"Yeah. Thanks for helping her." I called her last night to explain where she could find MJ's dorm. Sabrina is a woman of her word, so no matter how wrapped up about it all I was, I couldn't allow any of them to pick a side, not that Sabrina ever would. They formed a strong connection, so who am I to break it? Sabrina rooted for us from the start, the first to acknowledge my feelings. After Thanksgiving weekend, she sent me a photo from the club, one she took of the two of us dancing, a moment in time caught with a snap. I didn't have it in me to change it as my phone background.

"I love the girl, and I made her a promise so…" She lifts her shoulders, giving me a frown.

"I don't want her to lose what she got with any of them, you know?"

I twirl her around and pull her right back, making her braid slap my chin on the return.

"And I don't want her to lose what she got from you."

"Emma told me she's been practicing basketball, so I think it's safe."

"Oh, honey, I don't mean the game," she clarifies, her features softening.

I figured as much.

"She couldn't even look at me, Sab."

And it's not just that, it's that she didn't even try to fight for me, for us.

"Why can't you just consider that maybe the whole thing has nothing to do with her ex?"

"You didn't see the way he looked at her," I counter.

"Why are you focused on him? All I see is a girl hurting, and it's all for you. But Ty," she hesitates, "I think there's more to the story, and I think it's bad."

"What do you mean?"

The racing beat of my heart overpowers the bass from the speakers, and I try to contain the fire trying to spread inside me.

"I can't explain it. It's a feeling, something I can see in her eyes. She thinks she doesn't deserve you. She said that you deserve better."

"What?"

But she's perfect.

That's what I want to say, but I decide it's best if I drop my head instead.

The song ends, and we get back to the table where our family sits. My eyes roam the room, searching for the girl in blue. The whole table has the same expression on their faces, pointed at me, and I can't take it, so I choose not to. A hand squeezes my shoulder, and without turning, I know the grip belongs to Ben, a friend I don't think I deserve. He has been by my side the entire time, trying to cheer me up.

"Hey, isn't that Coach Jackson?" He points at the far end of the gym. I narrow my eyes to get a better look.

"Shit, it is. That guy fell off the face of the Earth."

He was one of the best high school coaches in the entire country. I met him once at a basketball camp, and though he was a fantastic coach, he didn't click right as a person.

'I like me better' starts playing, and my eyes flip to the dance floor. Instant relief flows through me when I see Emma dragging MJ to the center. With a fake smile, she indulges her best friend and yells out the words, their song, their story. They dance their choreography with Emma trying to animate MJ, failing until she pulls her in a hug, and a genuine laugh escapes MJ's mouth, leading up to her closing her eyes and letting go. My heart reacts to her swaying hips, her lips curved upward, a freeing sight. Her hair is half put up, half down, curled in spiral locks, and her dress... It does something to me. I'm sure Sabrina picked it up, knowing it's my favorite color—the color of MJ's eyes.

When the song fades, Miss Lynch takes the stage and announces the first act, which is a ballet of some sort. Five girls start twirling around a couple in the middle, who face each other without moving. Suddenly, the woman is airborne, and the guy catches her safely. Not being a ballet guy, I have to admit, it's somewhat amazing to watch. Miss Lynch stands behind a microphone once again, and the anxiety rises at her announcement of the basketball team.

MJ is on the opposite side of the dance floor, sharing a table with her best friend and whom I assume are Emma's parents. She walks toward me, head down, pace slow, fingers playing in front of her. She takes her spot before me, never looking back. Those goosebumps appear at the collision of my palm and her stomach. She doesn't cover my hand with hers like she normally would, making my hand feel incomplete.

The music starts, and we move, like we've been for the past two months, emotions lingering around us. Her presence sends me into oblivion, but I manage to keep my feet firmly on the ground. She glides across the floor, and I follow in perfect sync. Turning around on cue, our hands touch, sending a familiar surge of impulses through my entire body. Her darkened lashes pull up, slowly lifting her gaze to mine. In a soul-crushing lock, we move sideways, never breaking the connection. It hurts how beautiful she looks. Distant, fragile, yet so strong. The song slows down, and she turns her back to me, my hand sliding to the place it belongs. This time, she brings her fingers over mine, hovering—not touching. Our feet sweep to the sides with each step forward, repeating the action in reverse. Just as I gather the courage to speak out, the chorus begins, making her pull away. This time, we're not face-to-face; not really, since MJ's eyes are glued to the floor, and they stay there until the song ends.

I want to tell her that not a minute has passed without me missing her, without wanting her, but words fail me. The gym explodes with cheers, and only when the noise settles does she mumble a silent 'I'm sorry' and beelines to her table. I do the same, my heart sinking lower with each step that takes me farther away from her.

Closing in, I get a standing ovation from the table, each brother slapping me on my shoulder. Mama is crying, with Sabrina next to her on the verge. I take my seat, and Sabrina gets to my side. "I mean, the song choice is spot-on; it reminds me of the two of you."

"Wait, you understood it?"

She nods with a beaming smile. I know Sabrina speaks Croatian, so that must be the song's language.

"What's it about?"

"Love, belonging... The guy sings about how everything before her was meaningless... as I said, spot on."

She has no idea how right she is, because even though I couldn't understand a single word, I knew that the song was made for the two of us. A loud crash of a chair to the floor interrupts the dwelling process. Someone rushes past me, and then I notice Luka darting over the dance floor in the direction where MJ is standing, petrified. Emma is by her side, nudging her, but MJ is frozen still. I get up and bolt in their direction, the rest of my family following, not understanding a thing.

Chapter 51

I forgot how to breathe.

My chest keeps tightening up, and my eyes can't blink.

I don't move. I can't.

My nightmare caught up to me. It's right there, across the dance floor, laughing.

I pinch myself—not a nightmare.

This is real. He is real.

No! No! No!

Someone's shaking me, voices around me are yelling, but I don't react, don't shut my eyes. I don't function. All I can see is his face, and everything comes back to me.

So tight

You were asking for it

Slut

Whore

You're lying

I don't believe you

"Is it him?" I know that voice. Luka? Luka is here; I know it; I feel it.

A breath, thank God, I am breathing.

"Maddison, is that him?"

"What's happening? What are you talking about?" That voice belongs to Tyler. He sounds so worried. Does he still care? God, I wish my vision weren't blurry so I could see him.

Why is that monster's face all I can see?

"Maddison, look at me!" Luka tries to be firm, but it's impossible; he's a marshmallow.

"Sweetie, are you ok?" Eva? She is here... They all are; I knew that. I saw them the second I stepped inside. All I wanted to do in that moment was to run to them, but I couldn't. I hurt Tyler, and I didn't deserve them, none of them.

Are they here for me? Would they believe me?

"Maddison, is that him?"

Him. It can't be, though? He was erased; I made sure of it.

"Maddison," he screams out, de-trancing me.

"I. I. I..." I turn to face Luka, my vision clearing up at the sight of him, crunched down to my eye level, the softy that he is.

Shit! Shit! Shit!

What do I do? I wanna die right now, can I do that?

"Call 911," Luka says, taking out his phone and handing it to Sabrina.

"What? No!" That's me, full-on panicked.

"Do it!" Luka demands.

"What do I say?" Sabrina's confusion is evident.

"Say there's a sex offender here who violated a restraining order."

"What?" A mixture of voices yells out.

Shame eats me up so much that I can't get rid of the lump in my throat. My chest is heavy, and all I want is to crawl into a hole.

"Just do it, I'll explain later," Luka barks, dragging me away from everybody.

No! No! No!

Not now.

The palpitations of my heart turn into loud pounding; sweat emerges, and then my fingers start to shake first, followed by my knees.

I'm going to be sick.

On cue, numbness sets in, accompanied by light-headedness.

I really don't want to faint in front of everyone.

We're moving now. I think. My feet are dragging behind me. Is someone holding me? I guess I feel a hand around my waist.

Focus.

In for four.

Hold for four.

Exhale for four.

"Luka, wait. She's having a panic attack. Get me some water," Mak shouts. Or at least I think that's his voice. It sounds pretentious, like him.

"Maddison, focus. Tell me something you can smell."

Confusingly, I start sniffing.

"My sweat."

I hear a mumbled chuckle.

"Good. Now tell me something you can feel."

I take in a breath, swallowing. "Um, Luka's arm."

"You're doing great. Now tell me something you can see."

I shake my head. All I see is him. I don't want to see him.

I try to pry my eyes open, but my lids are heavy. I do it again, and this time, they open.

Black spots are mixing with the moisture in my eyes, disturbing my vision. I rub my eyes, open them, and spots are still there. I take another breath, repeat the rubbing, and slowly lift my lids.

"Your glasses."

It's the first thing I see when my eyesight focuses.

"You did so well. Keep breathing. Steady."

Mak's hands are rubbing the sides of my arms. And then I feel it. My lungs are coming to life with the fresh air. We're outside.

"Don't worry, we will take care of everything." Luka stands in front of me, his hands on my shoulder, reassuring me in every way possible that he has me.

"I don't understand what's happening," I sob, holding his shirt for dear life so hard that I don't think he'll ever get rid of the wrinkles I caused.

"Leave it to me; trust me."

"I do." It's the only truth I know at the moment.

My knees are so weak I can barely stand.

"I know you do, now breathe; I am here, and I'm not going anywhere."

"How did you know?"

Now that I see him clearly, his sadness eats at me.

"The look on your face mimicked how I felt the first time I saw my father after he was arrested."

"I'm sorry," I choke out, guilt all-consuming.

"What for?"

"For making you remember the feeling."

"Oh, Maddison.." His voice cracks. "Can I hold you?"

"Please," I mutter before he wraps me up.

"Luka?" Tyler's voice sounds pleading. I feel Luka's head shake, but I can't see anything, my face buried in his protective embrace.

Sirens illuminate the night, red overpowering the blue, and Luka waves at the two police officers who step out of the car. As I try and fail to focus on the exchange, I hold in the scream that begs to erupt out of me. I want to disappear, not exist. A strong arm holds me while the whole parking lot turns into a spectator show. Every set of eyes is pointed toward the two officers dragging a man in handcuffs to the car. A woman runs right behind them, screaming, "What's going on? Where are you taking him?" Then I notice Rebeka pulling the woman back.

What the hell is happening?

"Let's go!" Luka takes my hand and drags me to his truck. He sets me on the passenger seat, and Emma takes the place next to me, replacing Luka's hand with hers. Luka slams the door shut and goes to speak to one of the officers. I watch their exchange, the vein in Luka's neck sticking out. He looks so angry. I check the rearview; Tyler's staring at the truck, confused. All because I couldn't tell him, couldn't share the worst parts of me. And it's killing me.

I avert my gaze to my shaking hands, and then everything goes black.

Chapter 52

Emma

It takes two slaps to wake MJ up. I hated doing it, but Luka made me.

My best friend is lost and scared, and the complete opposite of the girl I grew to love. The MJ I know is a strong-ass bitch, fearless to the core with an unstoppable right hook. But she is not swinging; she's drowning. Nothing I do works, nothing I say helps, and I am terrified seeing her like this. The grip she has on my hand matches my own. All I know is that I can't let her go. Her gaze is empty, pointless, that of a zombie. There is a pulse, a heartbeat, unsteady but still there.

Luka is driving us to the police station, where MJ is supposed to give a statement. I don't know if she'll be able to do it in this state. We are following the police car that has taken a man from inside the gym. They handcuffed him and dragged him through the crowd before they practically shoved him into the back seat. I try and fail to connect the dots.

MJ stays silent the entire drive. She wears the same blank expression that suddenly showed up during our rant at the table.

Luka parks his pickup and gets out to help me guide MJ to the police station, where we are told to take a seat and wait to be called out. Not long after, Ben barges in, followed by

Tyler and other people who, I guess, are his family. And Sabrina fucking Furst in tow—correction, Sabrina fucking Hart. I still haven't comprehended the fact that I spent the majority of the afternoon being pampered by the Queen of Boston.

Tyler looks a mess, confused and scared. Seeing all these people worried about MJ makes my heart warm for her. She finally had it, and now this is happening, whatever it is. I am officially mad at the universe for not giving her a break, one she undeniably deserves. Tyler takes a knee in front of MJ, and as if a touch of his hand were magic, she takes a breath of life.

"Why is this happening?" she gasps out, and I see Tyler's mouth twitch.

"I'm sorry. I know it's hard to face after all this time, but you need to give them a statement. I know you can do it. I can go in there with you." Luka squats down next to his brother, and for a huge guy, he surprises me with all the softness toward her.

"I want Emma to come with me." She turns to face me, muttering, "If that's ok with you?" Her eyes are begging, and there's no way I would ever refuse her. "Of course, I'm here every step of the way."

"I'm sorry." Her apology is pointed at Tyler, and his jaw ticks. "Don't you dare apologize to me, or anyone for that matter. We're here for you. I'm here."

Those words trigger a new wave of emotion, and there is little that can be done about her ruined makeup. She shares a look with Luka, who nods to confirm whatever her eyes are conveying.

"Miss Stevens, we're ready for you." A woman in a suit waves toward a door. At that moment, my parents enter the station, and I nod, signaling to them that I am going with MJ. They understand what I put out and take their seats next to the others.

I stand up with MJ next to me, shaking. We both take our time walking toward the open office, closing in on the woman who called for her. She lets us go inside first, motioning toward the two empty seats with her hand. Holding MJ's hand, we both sit down, watching the woman round the table and sit across from us.

"I am Captain Teressa Montgomery. First, I want you to know that this is a safe space, where there is no judgment, only my full attention and sympathy. With that said, I want to inform you that Mr. Jackson will be facing felony charges," the woman says, and MJ's eyes widen. The Captain continues, "When we ran his fingerprints, we found your case. Since he is a registered sex offender, he was supposed to inform his caseworker that he had moved, and he failed to do so. He also violated his job restriction and the restraining order that is still valid."

MJ goes rigid. She starts shaking her head frantically.

"No," she gasps. "That was the only thing they promised me, that he won't work around kids; they promised," she sobs, lifting her knees to her chest, placing her bare feet on the edge of the stool.

"They promised. They promised…" she repeats, rocking back and forth. I watch my friend fall apart, completely losing it. I recall a venting session where she shared a scene from her book about a guy singing to calm his friend down.

Rampaging through my mind, I try my hardest to remember what song it was, but come up blank. Then it hits me. I lean in close to her ear and softly hum the melody of our song.

Her breath slowly steadies, her blue eyes lifting to mine. "And that is why you are the world's best friend." I pull her into a hug, her body relaxing into mine.

"Maddison," the Captain calls out, "Can I call you Maddison?" she asks. MJ nods, slowly letting me go.

"I need you to tell me, in your own words, what happened on the 13th of January 2021."

I sit there, listening to my best friend take a trip down the worst part of memory lane. My heart breaks as she cries over a man who tried to invade an innocent girl. About a man who took a part of that innocence, who took away trust, freedom, and safety. All I want is to hug that seventeen-year-old girl, and in a way, I am, because the person I'm hugging, as she recoils, is that girl. When the captain goes outside to give us a minute, I reflect on all the times she jumped when I came behind her back, all the times she closed herself off, all the times she refused to accept love. And all because that girl never healed, and right now, here in this place, with all these people, I know a part of her is working on it.

"The entire school turned against me after, calling me a whore, a slut. No one believed me because the coach was well-loved. Each time I opened my locker, it was stuffed with hate notes. Boys started picking on me, cornering me to put out since I was asking for it."

This is killing me, knowing she was alone.

"Oh, MJ. Why didn't you say something sooner? It all makes sense now, how you react to sexist comments, why your body goes stiff when someone comes out of nowhere."

Her head drops, and I watch her fidget with the necklace I gave her for her birthday.

"One day, I got ambushed in the locker room by the entire basketball team. They were angry because they'd missed two games after the coach got fired, so they forfeited the championship."

"Was Jamie one of them?"

She nods, and I'll be lying if I say it's not my first time contemplating his murder.

"He begged me to retrieve my statement, that he had scouts coming..." she trails off, and I clench my teeth.

Ok, that guy doesn't deserve murder. It would be too merciful, and I am not a merciful person.

So torture it is.

"Can you call Sabrina in here?" MJ asks, and I stand up, nodding. I walk to the door, and when I open it, the first thing I see is Tyler snapping in my direction. When he sees me, his eyes are asking so many questions; questions I don't know how to answer. So I turn to Sabrina and motion for her to come. She sprints, the sound of her heels clanking over the tiled floor echoing through the precinct.

"What happens now?" The bad-ass lawyer side of the model comes to light the moment the Captain comes back into the room. Sabrina is standing behind MJ, her hands holding my friend by the shoulders. She looks so tall, owning the room, and I know it's all an act for MJ's benefit because I can see the worry in her eyes; she cares.

"We will take over the case; he will be prosecuted for violating the conditions of his restrictions."

"Will there be a trial? Maddison doesn't want to face him."

"If it gets to a trial, her written statement will be more than enough; she will never have to face him again."

A loud grunt comes from outside the door, followed by a scream, and all the women in the room jolt to their feet, eyes wide in shock.

MJ yells out Tyler's name almost as if she has a feeling, and we all rush outside the door, finding Tyler restrained by one officer and two of his brothers. On the opposite side, the devil is still handcuffed, being picked up by two male officers on each side. The man, in his early fifties, has the smuggest of faces and now sports a split lip, thanks to Tyler's hard knuckle. MJ's eyes are locked on Tyler, but her body is still shaking. The moment the asshole turns to face her, I feel nauseous.

"Maddison," he growls, revealing the creepiest of smiles. "Turn around, let me see that ass, I had dreams of that ass."

POW!

This time it's Luka's fist leaving a mark on the smug's face. The officers take the guy out back, and MJ falls to the floor with a scream filled with so much pain that every single person in her surrounding area feels it. Tyler drops to his knees. "He's the reason you freaked out on Thanksgiving, isn't he? You saw him in the picture in my room?"

MJ doesn't speak. I watch Tyler closely, and I know he is doing his best to hold it together. The guilt on his face is more than obvious.

"Fuck Feisty, I am so sorry. I hate myself for everything."

Her head wants to shake, but he doesn't allow it, framing her face between his large palms, imploring her to look at him.

"Please," he begs. But she's not there. Her walls are back up.

A guy resembling Tyler pulls him up to his feet and drags him outside. Luka swoops MJ up and carries her out to his truck, me in tow. I stop to give my parents a hug and tell them I'll go with MJ to our dorm. They nod in agreement and say we'll meet up for breakfast.

The drive is quiet; MJ is not blinking, barely breathing, while I hold her hand, sharing a couple of worried looks with the driver. When we finally get on campus, MJ is half asleep. I navigate the way while Luka carries MJ to her bed. I slide inside next to her and watch him tuck her in with a gentle peck on her forehead. He scribbles something on a piece of paper and lifts it to me. "Call me. For whatever, whenever. Understand?" I nod, and he leaves, though hesitantly.

Beside me, MJ hasn't stopped shaking, not even when Ben snuggles next to her.

The three of us sit there in silence, holding hands.

Loud pounding on the door breaks the silence, and Ben offers to check. An angry Rebeka, our 'neighbor', storms in yelling nonsense, "Why would you do that? Why would you say that? What is wrong with you?"

I stand up, getting in her face. "What the hell are you talking about?"

"He's in prison because of what you said," she shouts over my shoulder, pointing a finger at MJ.

"Why do you care?" I push her, making her crash into the wall.

Good.

"He's my stepdad."

"What?" I turn to find MJ on her feet, even more frightened.

"You heard me. So tell me, why did you lie?"

I am all about ready to cut a bitch, but MJ's soft voice stops me. "Can you leave us?"

That question is pointed at Ben and me. We both protest, "What?"

"Please," she asserts, her voice and her eyes synchronized with the plea level, and all I can do is cave.

"We'll be outside." I grab Ben, and on our way out, I point a death stare at Rebeka.

Chapter 53

Fearful eyes stare back at me, an expression I saw many times reflected in my mirror. He hurt her too, no doubt about it.

"You're such a liar," she snaps, face red, nostrils flaring. And I swear there's steam coming out of her ears.

"Rebeka…"

The rise and fall of her chest is all I can focus on.

No words can fix it, help it… There's nothing to be done, so I pull a Hart, spreading my arms to lock her in.

"What do you think you're doing?"

I answer by tightening my squeeze and waiting.

"Let go of me, you freak," she yelps, but doesn't try to push me away. I squeeze even tighter.

"I can't breathe." Her voice cracks.

Not loosening my grip, I feel the moment her shoulders sink, followed by a soft sob.

"You weren't lying, were you?" She trembles. Or maybe that's me.

I shake my head.

"When?"

"Four years ago. You?"

"Summer break."

I slowly bring my hands to my sides and take a step back, allowing her to see me.

"Did he ever?"

She backs away, fidgeting before she makes a slow head shake. Sighing in half-relief, I sit on my bed, tapping the space next to me. She contemplates for a beat, but eventually takes me up on it.

"No, it started with playful flirting, a couple of grazing hands around my back."

My core, my fists, everything in me clenches. The guilt. I can't shake it; it's too much. If only I were stronger, maybe...

Rebeka's shaky voice interrupts the inner spiral. "He got more graphic, saying stuff about my body and what he wanted to do..." She swallows, and I watch the motion of her throat. "One day, he barged into my room and pinned me to the wall after I got out of the shower. I managed to push him away and escape."

"Did you tell anyone?"

"My mom, but she didn't believe me." She tries to laugh, but fails. "Figures, she's not my biggest fan."

"I know the feeling," I admit. "What happened next?"

"That's it; I got here and didn't see him until tonight."

"I hate him."

"Me too. I hate my mother."

"I hate mine too."

"She didn't believe you?"

"Honestly, her not believing me hurt the least. It was her telling me that I had to go back to school and face the kids who were calling me a slut. It was her correcting me after the first time I spoke to the cops."

"What do you mean?"

"Since I was a minor, there needed to be a guardian present. So when I told the police officer what had happened, she asked me, saying it was protocol, if there was anything I did to provoke him?"

"The fuck?"

Both of us cringe.

"I know. And I said that I had my period and that maybe I rearranged my pad here and there." My stomach crumples. "When we got outside, you know what my mother told me?"

"What?"

"This is a direct quote: 'You can't say period; the correct word is menstruation'."

"Shit!"

"Messed up, right?"

"My mother told me that I was being jealous because she had a good-looking man, and I didn't want her to be happy." She lowers her head, looking at her clasped hands between her thighs.

"We should introduce them, make them join the world's best moms club," I scoff, and we both chuckle. It turns into a manic laugh, which ends in tears.

"I'm sorry," I mumble.

"*I'm* sorry."

"What are you sorry about?"

"For the way I acted," she falters. "Confession?"

"Please." I bob my head.

"I was jealous," she uncovers with a shrug.

"What? Why?"

"How easy you had it, the friends you made, the volleyball, the fact that you trained for three months and got to be the Player of the Year. I'm so sorry."

"And here I was thinking I had done something." I try to lighten the mood, my voice playful.

"I was so stupid, especially thinking you had it easy. You worked so hard, and I diminished it."

"Look, it's not like I didn't hate you in return, so let's call it quits and start over."

"I would like that. Friends?" She extends her hand for a shake. I glare at her.

"Friends hug." I open my arms, and I know she tries to tame the eye roll, but she leans in anyway.

"I can't believe you stopped playing." I don't know how, but I hear disappointment in her tone.

"I'm actually going to try out for basketball," I confess.

"What, seriously?"

"Yeah, I've been practicing, but I still have a long way to go!"

"I doubt that."

"Does that mean you'll welcome me to the team?"

"With open arms…"

Funny how a tragedy brought light out of a situation. Knowing I'm not alone anymore, and that the asshole is behind bars, my shoulders feel lighter.

"You want something to drink?"

"Rain check? I have to deal with my mother."

I nod. "If you need anything, you know where to find me," I offer, and she smiles. We walk to the door together, and when I swing it open, my breath hitches.

There he is, on the floor, leaning on the outside wall of my room, looking devastated.

"Tyler?" It's barely a whisper, but his eyes shoot to mine, and he's on his feet so fast my head starts to spin.

Emma informs from the couch, "He refused to leave."

I smile, and Rebeka stealthily moves past me, muttering, "See you around."

I don't respond, too busy looking right into my favorite shade of brown.

"What are you doing here?"

"I am so sorry, MJ. God, I can't even..." I drink him in. The rise and fall of his chest, the tremble in his voice, his fidgety hands at his sides. He's nervous.

"No, Ty. I'm sorry. For letting you believe... For not..." I slam my eyes shut, shaking my head so fast I almost faint. "You were so good to me and I..."

God, what do I say? How do I fix this?

"No, Feisty. I jumped to conclusions. I couldn't see. I am sorry."

"For fuck's sake, stop apologizing and kiss already," Ben shouts from the sidelines. I give him a pointed, deadly stare before I grab Tyler's shirt and backtrack to my room, pulling him with me. He slams the door behind him and does something I'd never expect. He drops to his knees, presses his forehead to my stomach, and unleashes a pained, wordless sob.

Chapter 54

"I'm sorry. I am so fucking sorry," I bawl, sunken on my knees, but even that isn't enough to express my regret.

"Can you please get up? I'm not strong enough to pull you."

"Debatable."

She's the strongest person I know. And after what happened to her, I am sure she's an actual superhuman. To go through all that and still find a new purpose, I am in awe of her. When Luka revealed everything in the police station, I was ready to kill the monster that hurt my MJ. It took everything in me to stop after one punch. My family grounded me, kept me from causing more damage; though the blood that dripped from his split lip gave me some satisfaction.

Slowly, I stand on wobbling feet, but before we can lock our gaze, she bends her head down.

"I am not good at this stuff."

Referring to the playlist, I disclose, "I know, and I appreciate you trying to tell me in your own way."

"I'm sorry I didn't fight. I just..." she trails off, "you were so patient with me, and I was ready; I was so ready."

She tangles her fingers, fidgeting with them.

"Then I saw Jamie, and all the flashbacks took over, making me realize I'm still so messed up."

"Feisty, don't you get it?"

Her eyes lift to mine.

I step closer, my hands covering each side of her puffy face. "You're perfect."

"Tyler, I am broken."

"Maybe so, but you're perfectly broken for me."

The trembling of her lips is my undoing, so I cover them with mine. An explosion erupts, one for the books. She falls into me, arms going around my neck for the sole purpose of getting us closer. I oblige, wrapping her in mine, slowly dragging them down so I can lift her. It takes two steps to reach the bed before we meet the mattress. Our kiss never breaks, not while I wiggle her out of her dress, not while she unbuttons my shirt, not the entire time we work around discarding all the barriers between us. When we are all but flesh and bone, I sit on my knees to admire what's in front of me; bare, exposed, and vulnerable. With each kiss pressed down the length of her body, I imprint my words into her skin.

You're perfect.

And then three soft words I've never thought I'd hear come out of her in a whisper. "I love you."

I stop my movement, get to her eye level, and pierce to the deepest part of her soul.

"Say that again."

"I love you, Tyler. I am so in love with you; I can barely breathe."

Wow. Just... wow.

"God, Feisty. You have no idea…" I slam my mouth to hers, taking the declaration, sucking it so that it can reach the center of my chest.

"For the record, I fell in love with you the moment I laid eyes on you. And it was not a gentle fall. It was a crash of mass proportions."

That causes her to chuckle.

"Did it hurt?"

"In the most beautiful way."

"Yeah?"

I claim her mouth again, our tongues doing all the talking. Something in my soul ignites, and I close my eyes, enjoying all the feels spreading through my entity. She spreads her legs, allowing me to invade the space between them. She locks me in with her ankles, her way of telling me she is never letting go. And I am right there with her. It's her hand that slips between us, aligning me to guide me into my rightful place. It's her heart beating for me. It's her movement that makes me feral. And it's her words that make us both explode with pleasure before we both dive into a peaceful sleep.

A shrieking alarm wakes me up, but I don't budge. MJ is using me as her pillow, and nothing has ever felt better. Her hand grazes my chest, and she drags her head, one eye popped open, as if to check if it's real.

It is.

A beam illuminates her face, and it's not the sun; it's a smile so broad that it has the power to send my heart into tachycardia, seeing that it reaches her eyes.

We take a shower together, taking every chance to grope each other. I stay in the shower a bit longer while MJ gets ready for her shift at the diner. I begged her to take me with her before we got up, and it turned into a cute little argument. I said I'm never leaving her side, and she told me I'm crazy. We settled on me waiting for her in her bed—naked. That was her only request, and I am more than happy to oblige.

"Can I use your toothbrush?" I ask her as she steps back into the bathroom, wearing her work attire: jeans and a plain white shirt.

"What's mine is yours," she says and gives me a smooch.

My phone is filled with unread texts and unanswered calls, so after I brush my teeth using MJ's toothbrush, I type out a group text to my family.

Me: *I'm ok. She's ok. We're working on it.*

I add MJ to the chat. Her text is immediate.

Feisty: *Does this mean that I am now a full-fledged member of the Hart book club*

SIL: *Hell yeah, it does!*

Mak: Y*ou have to earn your right to be able to recommend, just saying*

Feisty: *Wouldn't want any special treatment.*

Tristan: *You already got it the moment Ty gave you the best piece of bacon*

Luka: *Still hung up on that?*

Tristan: *Don't expect me to ever get over it*

Mak: *Don't be such a baby, there are ladies here*

SIL: *I don't see any ladies; do you, MJ?*

Feisty: *Nope, no ladies here; only bad-asses*

O: *Damn straight.*

A separate thread pops up.

Luka: *You're a good one, you know that.*

Me: *Thank you*

Luka: *It was all her.*

Like I knew he would, my brother picked up what I was putting down. And as much as I thought I wanted to be the one she'd opened up to, I know now that it was supposed to be Luka all along. He gave her what she needed: his understanding and compassion. I would've probably freaked out, gotten angry, and turned on the pity, which would've brought her to pull away. Luka helped her open up, made her feel safe, which in turn brought her closer to me.

Me: *I love you, and I appreciate you*

Luka: *I love you too, and I love her.*

Me: *It's impossible not to*

Luka: *Happy for you*

Me: *Thanks*

With that, I plug my phone into MJ's charger and slump onto her bed, patiently waiting for her to return to me.

Chapter 55

As soon as I step foot in the diner, Tessa beams at me, "Why are you all smiley?"

I shrug, humming my way to my locker. A quick change later, I dive into the morning rush. For the first time in what feels like an eternity, I am truly happy.

Sleeping next to the boy of my dreams will do that.

The doorbell jingles, but I don't even bother glancing up. My hands are full, one with a pot of coffee, the other balancing a tray loaded with two plates of pancakes drowning in butter.

"Table five is still waiting for their toast," Derek barks at our boss. Ian's head pops out of the passage window, hairnet slipping over one brow.

"Tell 'em to take it up with the toaster," he mutters just as I mouth the exact words. It's his go-to retort. Setting down the plates with a practiced smile, I ask the couple, "Anything else I can grab for you?"

I wipe my hand over my apron, covered in syrup. The place smells like a mix of bacon grease and burnt coffee. The brew is weak, but the regulars never notice, probably cuz I kept their cups full like it was a religion.

By 11:30, the crowd has thinned, the booths littered with the aftermath of the breakfast rush. It takes me half an hour to clean my section to a state of spotlessness.

I untie my apron, stuff it in my locker, and swap my clogs for a pair of beat-up Converse. Derek jiggles the tip jar in my face, and I take my share before waving everyone goodbye. The cold winter air bites at my neck as I step outside and start walking to the bus stop. Time is of the essence here; I have someone waiting for me. Someone who is very, very naked. I press my thighs together at the thought.

Last night, after all the emotions died down, Tyler and I fell asleep in each other's arms. We never finished clearing the air, and I know a conversation is imminent.

Being back in his arms... God...

When I step on the bus, I take out my phone and open the playlist, ready to listen to the songs that marked a journey, at least my side of it. One double-take, some hardcore eye rubbing, and intensive blinking later, I gawk at the screen. Staring back at me is an altered playlist, lacking twenty-three songs, only three remaining—none added by me.

Little bit better - Caleb Hearn
Got it in you - Banners
Moja Malena - Sasa Kovacevic

I stare at the last song, confused. I tap for it to play, and get instant shivers at the opening melody. The song from class, the one I've been dancing wrapped in Tyler's arms for over two months. I notice a link attached to the song, and with a quick tap, it redirects me to a Dropbox file. The screen buffers for a couple of seconds before the image clears. A photo of scribbled paper is staring right at me, and I have to enlarge the image to make out the words. Right there, in a woman's handwriting, is the translation of the song, our song. The title gets me chuckling.

Sabrina's rough interpretation
I watch you get prettier every day
Just yesterday, you were more beautiful than any
A character from old Russian novels wakes in me
Crazy for you, more than anyone

Now I know everything was meaningless before you
I loved and drank, but I was all alone
Life was nothing special, baby

If I say I love you from here to the sky,
Just close your eyes and give me those honey lips
For everything you wish for, I will agree to
Just tell me yes

Dance this dance with me.
While the moon shines for us
A soft tune that feels so good to us
Just know that I will always be by your side

I see you get prettier every single day
Your beauty takes my breath away
When we walk, happiness always follows us

You don't know tears, I don't know fear
Everything was meaningless before you, and now I know

The first time I listened to the song, I focused solely on the melody, since I couldn't understand the words. After I danced with Tyler, the music took on a whole new meaning, my mind marking it as a love song. There was a brief moment I wanted to ask Miss Lynch the name of it, but chickened out. Google wasn't helpful either, and now there it is, in black and white, attesting to my assumption. Each lyric hits like a needle puncturing my lungs. The memory of Tyler's touch, his smile… My fingers trace his imprinted outline on my stomach, tears flowing of their own accord.

The song plays on a loop until I reach my room, tears running down with each step I take. Stretching my arm, I reach for the doorknob, swing the door open, and my heart flatlines.

"What's wrong?"

The worried expression on his face, the intensity of his care for me; I can't get enough of it…

"I love you."

"So why are you crying?"

"Because I am happy."

He peers at me, tears breaking the barrier I know he's been holding up. His hand reaches mine, electricity powering my nervous system, and before I can blink, I am on his lap, cocooned.

Pulling back enough so we can lock eyes, I take a breath and let it all out.

"Jamie is not the only reason I quit basketball, and yes,

he was one of them, but not in the way you think."

I swallow a lump, feeling my shoulder sag.

"Everything about the game reminded me of the pain, and I got all those feelings back. The hurt, the betrayal, it was all there, and I couldn't handle it. I never looked at it the same. Jamie was my best friend first, and he chose the stupid game over me. They all did. The entire school..." I choke on air, trailing off.

"No one believed me. My own team hated me. All practices and games were canceled after I reported what the coach did."

We are both a sobbing mess, and something about him being so open with his emotions gets the best of me.

"I picked the number 3 so I would never forget it."

And there it is, all out in the open.

"I am sorry I took it the wrong way."

"Jamie hurt me, but you need to know that I don't love him; I never really did. Not like I do..." I bite my tongue.

"Like you do what?"

"Like I love you."

His eyes flash, and I revel in how the words light up something in him. Expressing them has the same effect on my beating heart.

"Thank you for sharing it all with me."

"Thank you for listening, and for giving me back the game I lost."

And there it is, the pride in his captivating brown eyes, all for me.

"All this time, I thought that you were my missing piece, but you turned out to be the very thing that glued all my pieces together. You made me whole," I declare, my heart out in the open. He sweeps it away with a kiss so intense, taking away all the weight. Every part of me lights up, flames spreading like wildfire. Nothing feels as good as his lips on mine, and I never want that to change.

"I love you," he whispers, "God, how I love you." And then he pulls me into his arms, locking me like I'm the most precious thing to him.

"Don't let go," I mumble into his chest.

"Never."

I believe him. I trust him.

Chapter 56

TWO MONTHS LATER

Friday night is different nowadays. After my practice, I run to the dance studio and watch the last minutes of MJ's dance class. Then I kiss her for five minutes before she has to run off to her basketball practice.

Juggling between volleyball and basketball took a toll on her, but she pushed through and persevered. There's a whole committee working around the game timetable so that she can do both. She has both teams behind her, the entire freakin' school cheering her on, and me beside her every step of the way.

She declined the offer from the volleyball national team, listening to her heart. I am proud of her, knowing how hard that decision must've been.

Every practice, I watch her kick ass, set new records on both courts, and thrive. Her journey, her story, is one for the books. Despite her frantic schedule, she never missed any of my games, with my number and name on the back—one I plan to give her in the near future.

Right now, I am staring at the two best friends dancing, their faces twisted into mocking laughter, as they focus on nothing but each other. Their friendship grew stronger, and MJ's glow got brighter. Every few seconds, her eyes drift to mine, pulling me in. She either winks or licks her lips, teasing even from afar. She has that effect on me, always.

And when I think my heart can't beat any faster, she locks her eyes on mine, giving me the whole of her with one honest glance. After she fully opened up to me, I only loved her more, and that love grew every day. I know we have a long way ahead of us, and I am aware of all the obstacles we will surely face. Still, I know that our love will be strong enough to face anything, just as it has been all this time.

"Tyyyy," I barely hear the scream before MJ plasters her whole body onto mine, like a fucking koala bear. Yeah, I am the tree in this scenario.

"I missed you," she mumbles, pressing her soft lips to mine.

"I missed you more." I hug her tighter, her ankles locking around my waist.

"Impossible," she retorts, nose wrinkled, grazing over mine.

She's wearing my Christmas present, a hoodie I had made. 'My real boyfriend is better than my book boyfriend' is written in bold; beneath it says 'Fuck Noah Riley'. She laughed when she opened it and teased me for being jealous.

I was; I admitted as much. I'm not so much these days.

We spent Christmas apart. I was at home with my family while she visited her mother to work on their relationship. Not to toot my own horn, but I'm the one who encouraged her, knowing she needed it to heal fully.

We talked every second of every day and met up before New Year's. We spent it in bed, like an old couple; it was perfect. I was inside of her while the ball dropped on the screen behind us. We entered 2025 with her screaming out my name—no better way to start the year off.

Her smartwatch beeps.

"Dang it," she groans, bouncing down; my arms instantly feel empty.

"I have to go," she frowns, and I kiss it away.

"I know. I'll wait."

My hands find her cheeks, lingering.

"Every time I tell you to go home and wait for me, and every time you stay and watch." She rises onto her tiptoes, claiming my lips.

"You're crazy, you know that?" she marvels, "But you're my crazy, and I love you."

"I love it when you claim me."

"I'll do some more claiming in bed later." She wiggles her eyebrows with a wide smirk before she runs in the direction of the girls' locker room. I take my seat in the nosebleeds, earbuds in, and my book in hand. The book is a front; I get too distracted by the blonde wonder to read any words in front of me. I love watching her play, every second of it. I hope to be there in the future, cheering her on, whether she chooses basketball or volleyball. Her number one fan. Always and Forever.

Back in her room, where I practically moved in, we're lying on the bed - her back on my chest, my legs wrapped around her. She is now part of the family book club, and we're two-thirds into the week's read. We do this every night, alternating reading aloud to one another. I can picture us, five years from now, doing the same thing, maybe with a baby monitor on the nightstand. About a month ago, we had a conversation about kids. We both want a bunch of them after we make our marks in the world of sports. She surprised me when she told me she wanted to adopt or foster as well.

"I want to do for someone what Eva did for you," was what she said, cracking my heart wide open. We envisioned our entire future then, creating the perfect picture.

The personalized ringtone reserved for Emma snaps me out of my gaze. MJ wiggles to the edge of the bed and answers with a low, "Everything ok?"

There's a beat of silence, then she jumps to her feet, turning to face me with the biggest smile, gasping, "No."

She covers the speaker with her palm and whispers, beaming at me. "Check your email."

I stretch over to the nightstand and grab my phone. My jaw drops when I read the sender - Amateur Athletic Union. I read the body content multiple times. My name next to the words: Most outstanding athlete at the collegiate level in the U.S., who demonstrated qualities of leadership, citizenship, character, and sportsmanship on and off the field.

MJ tosses her phone on the bed and jumps on my lap.

"I think we'll have to buy a big old house to hold all our awards." Then she kisses me, hungrily. Her clothes are off before I get a chance to inhale fully. She works mine just as fast.

"I am so proud of you," she says, planting kisses on my chest.

"How did Emma know?"

"Coach called her; she thought I was still at basketball practice."

"Why would your coach call?"

"Oh, right... I'm also a recipient." She shrugs, like it wasn't that big of a deal. Spoiler alert: it is.

"Feisty, you held out on me."

"I wanted you to have your moment."

This woman.

"I like sharing my moments with you," I tell her, biting on her earlobe, causing her to whimper.

"I know you do, and I love you for it."

"I love you."

"Now, how bout you put all that love to use..."

"Yes, ma'am."

And then I flip us over, crashing her back on the mattress, my lips pressing on her skin. Starting at her neck, slowly, I cover every inch on the way down. Her hips buckle, back arching at each contact. Those delicate fingers find my hair, undecided between pulling and pushing. Mine slip between her thighs, finding her ready. I look up only to find her eyes already on me.

Needy, she's so needy, and she's going to beg any

second now—I am sure of it. I am a greedy bastard when it comes to her; that's the only reason my fingers circle her entrance, teasing gently. Her hips nudge, so I pull away, causing an exasperated groan. She tugs on my hair, giving me her glare, stubborn to beg. My tongue slips out, dragging over her length, and she buckles, adding a loud moan.

"Read to me, Feisty," I say, my voice hoarse, giving her clit a mere peck.

"Now? You want to do that now?"

I cock a brow in challenge.

Protesting, she takes her Kindle and starts reading the first sentence aloud. The second is barely a whisper, me sucking and flicking my tongue around her most sensitive spot. Her eyes close shut, and I stop my movement.

"I am going to kill you."

"And I'll help you bury my body; now read!" I demand.

She obliges, her voice shaking as my fingers probe as deep as they can go.

"If it doesn't, she may need IV antibiotics, and… and… Oh, God.*"*

"I'm pretty sure God is not mentioned in the book."

She releases a loud, displeased growl; I smirk.

"That is going to be a much bigger pain in the neck."

I twist my fingers on the way in, curving them before I reach the spot.

"I… I…."

Her breathing is all over the place; shallow, quick.

"I'm not sure what I'm going to do if that happens, but I'll cross that bridge when we come to it."

I suck on her clit, adding another finger. She tosses the

Kindle, causing it to crash to the floor. "Fuck this!" She pushes my head down, squeezing me between her thighs. I chuckle, and she squeezes on tighter, barely leaving any breathing room. Then she caves. "Please, Ty."

"Please, what?"

"Finish me. Undue me. Love me the way only you know how."

And like the good boy I am—I get down to it.

Epilogue

THREE YEARS LATER

Holding her hand, I squeeze it tight, enough to let her know I am here, knowing she's seconds from bawling her eyes out. As a simple piece of fabric rises, I stare at her, unable to hide the state of awe. This woman had my heart from the first breath I took when my eyes landed on her.

As the announcer's voice reverberates around the gym, listing all her achievements, I lock eyes with Luka, wiping a tear, proud like a brother, his wife by his side. He finally found his person; well, actually, he got two. She came with a kid, and he loves him as his own. Mama is by their side, eyes glossy, and the biggest smile on her face. Sabrina is next to her, holding her mini replica over her hip, while Mateo has the other one on his shoulders. Tristan and Mak are in the row below with their girlfriends, hooting and clapping, while Clair, MJ's mother, tries to keep her sobs at bay.

It took them a long time to resolve their issues and reach a point where they could start anew. Since then, their relationship has only blossomed. Clair has been there, front row, at every Lions game, and later, at every game MJ played for the Connecticut Sun after she was drafted. She also came to every game of mine that didn't overlap with MJ's. I was the first pick for the Celtics. MJ and I got ourselves a house halfway between our arenas.

The last three years were challenging, stressful, and adventurous. Our love grew with every hiccup we faced down the road, and we got through it together. She found her way back to me, to basketball, and her mother. She welcomed a new future for herself and chose to share it with me, thereby completing me.

Can you keep a secret? There's a reason why MJ can't keep her tears from falling.

This morning she surprised me with breakfast. The memory comes out like a flash.

She pulled out the big guns in the form of pancakes. When I noticed the third place setting, I narrowed my eyes at her. "Are we expecting someone?"

"Yeah, in about eight and a half months—give or take…"

I must admit, it took me a minute, but when it hit me, everything on the table crashed when I jumped to my feet.

"What?"

I looked at MJ, glowing, a waterfall covering her cheeks, nodding like one of those bobbing toys. I swept her up in my arms, and she locked them like it was programmed into her. We twirled around the kitchen till she told me she was going to be sick.

I turned into a protective helicopter parent in a heartbeat. She love-hates it, but I can't help it. She's going to give me the best gift; she's going to make me a father. Spoiling her comes with the territory, and the life growing inside her.

The loud cheers of the crowd pull me out. So many people are here to share this big moment. The announcer continues…

🏀 NCAA Women's D1 single-season points record
🏀 NCAA Women's D1 Career 3-points leader
🏀 NCAA Tournament records: points, assists in a game in NCAA tournament history
🏀 3× NCAA season assists leader
🏀 AAU Sullivan Award Recipient
🏀 2x AP Player of the Year
🏀 2x Naismith College Player of the Year
🏀 John R. Wooden Award
🏀 2x USBWA National Player of the Year
🏀 2x Wade Trophy Winner
🏀 3x Nancy Lieberman Award
🏀 3x Big Ten Player of the Year
🏀 3x Dawn Staley Award
🏀 3x Big Ten tournament MOP
🏀 3x First-team All-Big Ten

Ladies and gentlemen
The reigning WNBA rookie of the year
and the greatest of all time…
Number 37—Maddison Joy Hart

The end

Chapter 1

Luka

The transition from spring to summer is the worst part of the year for me. Work is in full bloom, overloading my already heavy shoulders, and the mixture of heat and humidity is a whole different kind of hell.

Sweating through every inch of my workwear, I take off my hard hat with the sole purpose of taking a breather. Two guys called in sick today, so I had to step up to keep the timeline on track. Naturally, they picked today to get sick, leaving me to do all the heavy lifting on this damned heat.

Superstition wasn't part of my upbringing. I usually don't pay it much mind. But today feels like it's working against me. A black cat must have crossed my path, or maybe a mirror shattered nearby. That's the only explanation for all the bad luck I've had so far.

Aside from the two guys on my payroll who called in sick, my truck broke down, leaving me at the mercy of public transportation. I stepped in some stinky dog shit, which got me barefoot, while I furiously scrubbed my boots, cursing under my breath. So, to sum it all up, today was not one of the good ones.

As I chug my practically boiling water, I glance at the workers, panic in their eyes, shearing around the site. I've come a long way... Started out as a boy doing odd jobs for my neighbor for some extra allowance. Now, I run my own business. Over the last few years, I worked hard, learning everything I could about the craft. Over time, my skills and knowledge grew, so I felt ready to bet on myself.

Unlike my brothers, I was not much of a bookworm. I enjoyed spending my free time with my nose between the pages, but I wasn't one to study. There was no lack of intelligence; I just never craved or needed to prove it with a piece of paper. I am more of a hands-on guy, something that the rough skin and blisters around my fingers can prove. The fact that I was profusely called '*The Hulk*' came in handy during my specific kind of education. I could carry a load in my weight well before I learned to jerk myself off, so there's that.

The constant nickname is not hated as much as begrudged. People see my exterior and think I'm an impenetrable shell without feelings. Much to their dismay, I am far from it. I also bleed, have a steady heartbeat, and am the opposite of the tank everyone around me labels me to be. Everyone, that is, outside of my family. My mother and my brothers know me better than that.

The last clang of metal echoes across the site as the crew packs up for the day. Tools are being tossed into bins, boots scrape clean. The sun is sinking low behind the crane, reflecting over the windows we put in today. I wipe the sweat from my brow with a gloved hand and lean on a stack of wooden beams. This part of the day is my favorite, when the noise dies down, and everything stills... when I can just breathe.

Some of the guys are still laughing near the gate, making plans. We share a nod in passing as I head to the container. My phone buzzes, and I know who the message is from before I bring the screen to life. I smile when Mak's name appears, asking if I need him to pick me up. I quickly reply to my older brother that I will take the company truck and lock the screen.

This place, my life, is everything I once wanted. I am successful, healthy, don't owe anybody anything... by every external measure - content. On paper, it's all solid. No one from the outside looking in would think I was missing a damn thing. But at the end of the day, the empty space in my bed tells a different story.

I am lonely.

I run a hand through my hair, leaning back to stare at the sky like it might have an answer.

It doesn't.

It never did.

I tried dating, swiping, flings, but none of it stuck. They all wanted something shinier than what I am, more polished, less worn out. Someone without calloused hands or stories that lack happy endings. I look at the empty frame of the rising building. Someday, people will live here. Laugh here... Love here.

I wonder how it would feel to come home to someone who notices when you walk through the door... who cares how your day went, not just out of politeness but because they need to know.

Knowing I have an overwhelming number of agonizing emails to go through, I decide to bail, too drained. Who knew that emails would turn out to be the most frustrating part of my job? Mateo, brother two out of four, keeps saying I should hire an assistant. But honestly, I can't bear to put anyone through that kind of torture.

As I lock the container, my eyes trace a single beam of light to a vision in yellow.

A few steps reveal another figure - a much smaller one. It's the cutest little boy, his eyes fixed on the spinning barrel. Without a blink in sight, he focuses on the truck, eyes locked, mouth hanging open. One hand swings while the other grips something delicate.

He's wearing a blue shirt and matching shorts, his feet hidden inside rain boots. A hat on top of his head, a couple of stray light brown locks escaping from the sides. Slowly, my eyes roam to the person the other hand belongs to. From her red sneakers, bare legs, a sundress reaching her knees, up to the chest, exposed neckline, right to the most beautiful face I've ever seen. Oval-shaped, set of full peach lips, hazel eyes by the looks of it, and wavy hair falling down her side, light brown, like honey.

"Oh, sorry. We didn't expect anyone here. He's obsessed with that mixer." She gives me a shy smile, but the fear in her eyes is impossible not to catch. It wasn't so much her being scared of me as it was the expression a kid would have when caught red-handed, fingers in the cookie jar.

"It's no problem, the site is closed down for the day," I deadpan.

I soak in more of her details, unable to unglue my eyes

from her, too mesmerized. Curiosity gets the best of me, so I indulge it. There's not a single shred of imperfection there, apart from the pain that seems to penetrate the kind smile she puts on. Freckles cover her face, even her forehead, but mostly around her nose and cheeks. They play around her skin with every sun ray that illuminates all of her glory. Ready to get myself out of this weird, creepy state she pulled me into, I kneel in front of the boy who is still all into the mixer behind me.

"What's your name, little fella?"

Fella?

Where did that come from?

"It's Declan," she cuts in, and I look up at her. "He doesn't speak much." A genuine smile lights up her face as she adds, "He has autism." The way she's expressed it, with pride, strikes me right in the chest. I turn my focus to Declan, understanding his hand movement and the lack of interest in me. Kids are often the only humans who see beyond my exterior, but this guy appears indifferent to my presence.

I stay on my knees and hold out my hand. He meets my gaze, then gives me a strong high five. A zing of pride rushes through me, and I stand up, buzzing from the contact I've been gifted.

"He is verbal, mostly when he needs something," she chuckles, "but he doesn't fully get communication. For example, he didn't understand your question, though he does know his name."

I nod, standing up, not able to look away. She's breathtaking.

"TMI, I'm sorry, I don't have a filter, it's a character flaw, and usually someone needs to gag me."

She smacks her hand over her mouth so hard that the sound echoes around the site.

"That came out wrong, sorry again. Just tell me to shut up and I will, otherwise a whole lot of word vomit will come, and by the sound of it so far, it won't come out good."

One thing's for sure: this one is a fast talker. That whole sentence lasted a second.

She takes a deep breath and shakes her head, making me straight out laugh, head tossed back and all.

I take in their similarities. They share the same mouth and the exact shape of their eyes, though hers have more green in them. He also has freckles, but not to the same extent, more as if they are just starting to manifest. Desperate for more information, I extend my hand. "My name is Luka."

"Do you live on the second floor?"

I cock a brow.

"It's a song." She shakes her head again, smiling, right hand holding Declan, her expression apologetic as she offers me her left hand. "I'm Nora."

I grab it tight, feeling the piece of metal on her finger, one that shatters whatever I was starting to envelop.

Sabrina

Kesha's voice shouted as my alarm woke me up, the lyrics of 'Tik Tok' reverberating. With eyes wide open, I leaped out of bed, threw on my clothes, and brushed my teeth. I descended the marble stairs of my prison to sneak out the back door before Rea, our maid, made her dusting rounds. I ran through the literal maze that was our backyard and shimmied myself through a small crack in the hedge until I was touching concrete. The moon was still at its peak as dawn began to fade. I got in my hidden Jeep and started the engine, setting the checklist on the passenger seat.

Our garage had over a dozen cars at my disposal, but every single one of them was unique and easy to spot. And for my task at hand, I had to be incognito.

This Jeep was mine, not theirs - my version of a getaway car. With the first address entered in my Google Maps app, I drove off into the literal sunrise coming up before me. Passing by the iron gate surrounding my prison, I cringed at the family crest in the center of it, and yes, we had one of those - a symbol that used to represent power. Now, all I could see were the lies associated with the name plastered above it.

The name itself - a deception. My parents were clever. Well, my father was.

When they emigrated from Dubrovnik during the Croatian War of Independence, my father, being the respected man we all thought he was, used his connections and fled to the US, taking his newly wedded wife with him. They made a new life here with high expectations. Our original family name was Knezovic, meaning something akin to a title of a monarch's son, similar to a prince. My father wanted to keep the meaning, and he chose the German translation to mark the new beginning.

Drum roll, please...

The Family Furst was born, making it our new history.

By the time I was born, they had already established their empire, hiding behind fake smiles to maintain the well-respected, rich, and famous act. The name meant something in this city. I was born into it, the title it came with, a silver spoon, and all.

Now, my billionaire parents owned more houses than they could count, as well as cars, boats, and planes... They practically owned the air we breathed, and once upon a time, I admired them for everything they have accomplished. My ignorant self didn't know better.

As I cranked up the stereo, one I had installed myself in this beat-up, sorry excuse of a car, a smile spread across my face. It was no ordinary smile, oh no. This one was special, one that I didn't have the luxury of producing much often. This particular smile had only one mission, one definition, and one meaning.

Vengeance!

The path I have chosen was not an easy one. Especially for a 20-year-old, soon to be 21, who still lived with her parents in the castle they made to flaunt her away in. The Barbie doll who's heard the saying 'smile for the camera' more than any other. The same girl who was her mommy and daddy's perfect little princess. So, why was I sneaking out of this so-called castle and driving a rust-infested Jeep, you ask? Well, it's a long story, and lucky for you, I like 'em long.

This one started a year ago when I uncovered some disturbing facts regarding my father. It opened a can of worms, and my curiosity got the best of me, so I kept on digging. Behind my parents' backs, I did a complete 180 and switched my concentration to law. At the time, I was a 'proud' student of Harvard Business and economics, while I took online courses at the Harvard Graduate School of Design. I had to keep it secret for two reasons. Reason nr. One: my mother. For her, the notion itself would be unacceptable, because God forbid her daughter did something meaningful. Nooooo. I had to be the mirror of society; our family name was at stake here. And reason number two, my father. To uncover all the dirt on him, I had to obtain a lot of legal files, and what better way to do it than to infiltrate myself in the circle. What I didn't realize at that time was how much I would love all the legal bullshit. Now, I could even picture myself in a courtroom defending the innocent. And on some weird level, I had my father to thank for that. Because it wasn't for his secrets, I would still live in the bubble, happy to do as I was told, and I would never have discovered myself.

The anchor keepsake dangled from the rearview mirror,

the memory of the only place that shielded me from the flashes that my eyes had grown accustomed to by the age of one. I came out of my mother's womb a model, and I mean that literally. Two minutes old, that's how old I was when I got on the cover of Boston Common, cradled in the Amelie scarf. And yes, you guessed it - the empire was Fashion. I was born into that world and lived in the spotlight, where I learned how to do my makeup before I could walk. I never resented it or hated it much; it was simply all I knew. Thankfully, I wasn't world-renowned. My so-called fame stayed inside the city limits. I didn't do any modeling for anything other than promoting my family brand.

With the sight of a red light, I hit the brake and turned up the stereo, bobbing my head and letting Little Mix's 'Power' transform me into a tone-deaf siren.

Acknowledgements

First, I want to thank my only support system - my husband. Without you, I never would've taken this step. Thank you for believing in me and being my rock.

To my kids who made my dreams of becoming a mother come true… Mommy loves you the mostes.

I want to thank each person who took the time to read my words.

To Sunny, the first person who read my stories and gave me the push I needed to continue my journey.

To my beta readers and editors for helping me make the story better

And last but not least, I want to thank the Holy Trinity of BookTok for getting me back into reading, which eventually turned into me writing…

Lena

Also by Lena Knight

Brick-ed series
Averted
(Sabrina & Mateo)
Anticipated
(Aria & Cillian)

Fostered H(e)arts series
Nothing's fair in Love & Basketball
(Ty & MJ)
Nothing's fair in Love & Marriage (coming soon)
(Luka & Norah)

About the Author

Lena is a wife, a mother of two, and somewhere along the way, she lost herself in her roles. She has a master's degree in Physical Education, but after her son was diagnosed with autism, she proudly pulled on her stay-at-home-mom shoes. She rediscovered herself through books and the new worlds they opened up. Reading turned into writing, and a new passion was born. Lena grew up never believing in herself, but thankfully, there are people in her life who gave her the necessary push to try... so this is her... trying.

You can find her on:
Tik Tok - authorlenaknight
Instagram - authorlenak